The Prince and the Scribe

by

Logan Kelly

The Prince and the Scribe

Cover Art by *The Wild Rose Press, Inc.*

The Wild Rose Press, Inc.
PO Box 708
Adams Basin, NY 14410-0708
Visit us at www.thewildrosepress.com

Publishing History
First Edition, 2025
Trade Paperback ISBN 978-1-5092-6033-1
Digital ISBN 978-1-5092-6034-8

Published in the United States of America

Dedication

For Tyler, who has brought my words to life through art, and who has waited way too long for this one.

For Josh, who told me to keep writing.

Preface

Fort Lauderdale, Florida, is a far cry from the typical fairy tale setting; at least, that's what I thought when I started on this bizarre task. I soon realized that it's not so different after all. Thick forests, bogs, creatures that make your stomach turn, and a mixture of great people, terrible people, and weirdos. It is also the place where I first discovered *The Scribe's Collection of Fairy Tales and Nursery Rhymes*.

I never would have guessed that—five years after that discovery—it would play such a massive part in my life. In fact, I'd forgotten about my first encounter with the book for the longest time. It was the summer after my senior year of high school, six months after I'd come out. Fort Lauderdale was weird in the best possible way for a young gay kid, a sort of South Florida Haven for the queers. Just a few weeks before school ended, a gay thrift shop called Out of the Closet opened on the beach. It was in this very place on a hot Saturday afternoon that the wheels were set in motion.

My best friend Sarah asked if we could go. Still freshly out—I hadn't even gone on a date with a boy yet—it seemed like the perfect place for my "being gay in public" inauguration. I sipped my Big Gulp as Sarah searched through the racks. Her digging seemed as though it was going to be endless, and I was already getting bored. I left her to meander.

It was then that I saw it amidst the generic collection of raunchy paperbacks. The small, faded book packaged in green paper stood out due to its lack of male tits and impossible abs. In yellow Baskerville Old Face were the words *The Scribe's Collection of Fairy Tales and Nursery Rhymes.*

I picked it up. I read the description on the back, flipped through the pages, and found myself puzzled. It was filled with fairy tales, all right, but ones I hadn't heard of, like: "The Boy in the Tower with the Long Hair," "The Devine Lady's Husband," "The Prince and the Pirate"—that last one might have belonged had it had more spice, but after reading a few lines, it was clearly nothing that would make Mother Goose blush.

Sarah soon appeared with a handful of clothes she wanted to try on for Pride. I agreed to suffer through her cringy fashion show, placed the book down, and followed her to the bench outside the dressing room. Sometimes, I worried she thought this was some sort of *Will & Grace* friendship, but I knew I had way too much nuance to be the gay best friend. As I sat through her makeshift fashion show, I completely forgot about the book.

I wouldn't come across it again until the week before Christmas break, my senior year of college. I was attending the University of Hartford in Connecticut. Going against the wishes of literally everyone, I was a film major because no matter what anyone said, I was going to buck the system, graduate with an internship at Warner Brothers, Universal, or something, get a movie deal, and make my big *Jaws*-esque breakout, before marrying either Troye Sivan or Colton Haynes—cause why wouldn't I?

But then came my final in my Advanced Screenwriting class. I'd worked all semester on an action-adventure script that had a gay flair. Because if there's one thing that would make the genre more interesting, it would be sexual tension between two brawny guys. I was sure Professor Sherman would love it so much that she would have no choice but to call in any favors she had to get it produced. Obviously, it would have to be indie, but I was okay with that. *Brokeback Mountain* was, and everyone loved it.

She read the submissions at her desk and when I knew she was on mine, I watched her like a hawk. She closed it and looked up at me. I didn't bother to pretend like I hadn't been watching. But after her lips formed a pitiful smile, accompanied by a nod, I not only wished I had looked away; I wished it was my time to go to the big gay suburb of Heaven.

Sadly, however, I survived. The next day was feedback in front of the class. I found myself in the front row, with my knee doing the gay, anxious bounce. For a second, I tried to convince myself that I had misunderstood her look, that there was still a chance it would be a triumph.

That hope lasted about as long as a reality show marriage. I still remember how cold my core felt, how my teeth chattered, how my privates felt like they were in my stomach, my stomach felt like it was in my throat, and my throat was—somewhere it shouldn't be.

"Wordy, unfocused, unfilmable."

It didn't matter what else she said; she made me a "has been" before I was a "here and now."

After the mutilation of my future was done, I sat there stewing. I don't remember whose script was destroyed next, and I didn't care. There was no way it mattered as much as *my* destruction. Destruction I knew

I didn't deserve. Then, inspiration struck. I decided I wasn't going to stand for having my dreams gutted and screwed like "Defying Gravity" being belted by a high school drama student. After class, I waited, ready to give my professor the whole drag queen read treatment. That's what I thought, at least. When the last student left the room, I remembered who I was and that I actually wasn't a brave, snarky gay but a shy, nerdy one.

Her back was to me at first. "It wasn't bad, you know," she said.

I sat stunned. The moment of reckoning was upon us, and I didn't have a reckoning bone in my body. "What?" I asked.

"Your script. It wasn't bad." She turned to face me. "The basic idea is fine. It wasn't your best work."

"I—with all due respect professor... I don't think I agree?"

"Is that a question?"

She was good. "No," I corrected, still unsure. I cleared my throat. "No, I don't agree."

"And that's fine. But you have to understand, this was your final. You've done great work all semester, but this just didn't live up to the standard. It's too preachy. You have to *show,* not *tell,* in a script."

Immediately, I was annoyed. I knew *that.* It is the most basic of rules. She listed several other screen sins I'd committed, and—to be fair—they were valid to an extent. After a while, I realized that all of her critiques had nothing to do with my story. It was all technical and structural. It was at this moment that my favorite unwilling pastime, overthinking, decided it was time to take the stage and do a tap.

Maybe she doesn't like the story at all. Maybe this

is her way of being kind. Maybe the story is so bad that the only thing she can do is focus on the structural elements. In that moment, I knew my career was over. I couldn't stand listening to how I overused parentheticals anymore, how I relied far too much on dialogue and not enough on action blocks. I felt my anxiety boiling over until finally it burst from my mouth like a belch from an acid reflux suffering Santa Claus.

"Professor! I get it. But what about the *story*?"

She stared at me for a moment, her green eyes wide behind her glasses. I'd been silent as a monk secretly banging a nun all semester, so it's safe to say I surprised her. But, soon, her signature calm returned. "It was a *very* good story," she said. "But it wasn't told correctly. I can tell by your unhinged jaw that I said that wrong. Let me rephrase that: It's a very good story, but hon, it's hard enough to get a movie about *our* community made to begin with. If you were, in theory, to try to sell this, it would be impossible."

"Okay, I get there's the technical stuff, but really, there was no way to tell this story and keep it in the confines of perfect three-act structure," I defended. Then I realized: "*Our* community."

She pulled her chair to my desk and joined me at my level. "Yes, dear. You didn't think you were school's token gay, did you?" she joked.

"Kind of," I said, resting my head against a palm.

"Let me ask you something...This script in particular, it's very personal to you, isn't it?"

If there was one thing I didn't want to do, it was to reveal to my professor that I had been so wrapped up in my plans since I was a freshman that I didn't go out and meet any boys and that I was a twenty-one-year-old dork who still hadn't kissed anyone since leaving home. Naturally, that's just what I did. After a lengthy confession, most of which I don't remember, I finished with: "I'm just thinking this story…it's my chance to make my mark. This story—I want it to be something that our people see themselves in. And, maybe, just maybe, be the one that opens the doors for them that have never been open before.

Painful, agonizing silence. I thought about making some half-baked joke and fleeing like the clown from *It* was chasing my ass. But finally, she smiled. "Come with me, hon. There's something I want to show you."

****

It wasn't long before I realized we were heading to the campus library. I spent most of my free time there, ironically, this semester writing my final. If I wasn't there, I was in the Student Union, also writing and staring at the straights, indulging in embarrassing PDA. She took me up to the second floor, around the promenade, and to a set of glass doors all the way toward the back. There was an older librarian on guard at his small desk. Though I spent most of my time here, I'd never seen these doors nor the old man in big quirky glasses that guarded them.

"Hey, Arthur," she greeted.

"Going in?" asked Arthur in a voice so cheery, it's a wonder he didn't soar out of his chair.

"Yes, please."

He turned slowly and stood, giving his ass a scratch that I'm sure he thought no one would notice. He pulled a ring of keys off a hook on the back wall, unlocked the doors, and held one open.

"Thanks," Professor Sherman said.

"Be careful what you touch," Arthur told me with less warmth than Professor Sherman had received.

"I could say the same," I replied. He just stared at me blankly. It didn't matter. I'd always have the dirt on his hygiene.

"What is this?" I asked Professor Sherman.

"It's our rare reading room. These are books that the school has acquired but are such hard finds, they have to be read in this room, and some that can't be read at all."

"A book that can't be read, sounds like my Italian grandmother staring at a bowl of Olive Garden pasta."

Professor Sherman chuckled respectfully. "There's one book in particular that I'd like to show you."

I followed her down to a far, dusty row of shelves. She slowed down at one section in particular, so I knew we were close. Running her finger up and down, until she pulled a book from the shelf with a satisfied "Here it is."

I didn't recognize it at first. And why would I? It was nearing a half decade since I spotted the book I never read in that thrift shop, but once I saw the title, the memory was unlocked.

"This is one of my favorites," said Professor Sherman. It's been out of print for—I'm not even sure how long. And it probably won't ever go back to print again. It's never been a success. Do you know why?"

I shook my head.

"Because the people in power feared what was inside."

I looked it over again. "Isn't it just a book of fairy tales?

"To the naked eye."

Gross, I didn't like to think of my professors or

parents even knowing the word "naked."

"But it's so much more," she continued. "Take a look through it."

I flipped through the pages just as I had a few years before and was again met with the unfamiliar collection. "Yup, that sure looks like a bunch of fairy tales."

"Ever heard of any of them?"

"Not one, honestly. I guess that's why it's 'rare reading.' "

"What if I told you that they weren't written that way? That they weren't a collection of fairy tales, but one large story?"

"I'd say that's not what the cover says."

She smirked, reached into her jacket pocket, and produced a small notebook. She jotted something down on a page and handed it to me. "Do me a favor. Look up that name. You may have to go to the second or third search page."

"Oh, I can't do that. Everyone knows that going there leads to a void from which you never return."

"I'm serious. Look him up. You might be surprised with what you find."

****

I didn't want to admit it, but surprised I was.

"Eric Allard was a late nineteenth-century author. Known for penning the unsuccessful collection of fairy tales..." Blah, blah, blah... *"He used his own experiences and name for the character of the Scribe...*

Allard famously said on his deathbed that his stories were never released in the way he'd written them. He claimed that the stories were torn apart by publishers to hide the queer nature of what he'd written."

Wait, what? My jaw dropped like a rusty carnival

ride finally giving out.

"Whilst many refute his claims as that of a dying, unsuccessful writer, some indeed support them and have deeded him with having written the world's first gay fairy tale. It is unlikely that we will ever know the truth, as all early editions of his manuscript are lost…"

I sat back in my chair. The late nineteenth century. That means he would have written them only a couple of decades after the Brothers Grimm did their famous collections, and they certainly didn't write anything queer…Well, unless you count Rumpelstiltskin. Something about him never seemed hetero to me. As I went to bed that night, I kept thinking about Eric, about how his queer stories were allegedly changed. If Professor Sherman was to be believed, they weren't even stories but one large book. One large gay fairy tale, the world's first.

My curiosity shifted into thoughtfulness. If only I'd had something like that growing up, I thought. If only I had been able to see myself in something so formative as a fairy tale. Maybe, just maybe, growing up wouldn't have been so difficult. Maybe writing a good script with gay characters wouldn't be so hard. Maybe my dream future wouldn't seem so impossible. Then, my mind shifted again. A line from the article I'd read popped back into my head: *It is unlikely that we will ever know the truth.* But why did it have to be that way? Because there weren't any known copies of his original manuscript left? In this day and age, that answer didn't seem good enough. So that night, while lying wide awake in my dorm room, a new dream was born…

****

I gave myself a three-month deadline, which turned

into another three months and then another two for clout or something. But I'll never forget the day I finished it. I'll never forget the nightmare it was to secure rights or to even think about publication, but I was able to reconstruct what I think is the most accurate retelling of Eric's original story, featuring a fancy new subtitle, one I would have appreciated back when I first discovered it.

Before you proceed, here's some literary housekeeping: I'll be popping in from time to time with context and commentary, specifically from which stories each chapter was rebuilt from. My commentary text will be italicized, but if that's not what you're looking for, feel free to ignore little, talkative me. I should warn you that I found the work way lewder at some points than what you might think for a fairy tale, so reader discretion is advised. Finally, despite some changes, despite some things that may seem out of place for its time, despite how outlandish some of it may seem, please remember that, at its heart, this is a story of love, a story about fighting for the people that matter most, and a story of magic…

Enjoy *The Prince and The Scribe: A Reconstruction of the World's First Gay Fairy Tale*…

Part One

Chapter One

"The Long Walk Home"
Published in The Scribe's Collection *as "A Pauper on the Road."*

There once was a young man known as Eric Allard. He was charming of face, thin of body, curly of hair and modest of means. He had arrived back in the Kingdom of Belle Terre from his long, worldly voyage only the day before this, and yet he still faced many miles on the path along the sea before he would arrive at the home of his mother. The many hours he'd face upon his feet did not weary him, however, for he was happy to be home and finally back in the same kingdom as Prince Ti'Louien. Now, twenty, he'd not seen the prince since he was seventeen years of age, but it did not matter. It was not a challenge to recall the prince's hazel eyes, blond-brown hair, or sad mouth. It was said the prince never smiled, but on that long ago day, Eric swore he saw a flicker of intrigue on Ti'Louien's famously distraught face.

Eric had been a composer of sonnets since he was three, though he never fancied the idea that his work might one day be something of anything. That was until he saw the prince. It was a sunny Sunday afternoon. He sat upon the grassy hill behind his family home, overlooking the sea that would turn cool with the approaching Autumn. He composed a story that he deemed epic, filled with mermaids and pirates and even the cheating of gruesome death. Lost in the story for hours, his concentration was only broken when he heard the approaching brigade of horses. Young Eric looked up to see the white mares that drew forward a golden coach. They galloped proudly on the path below the small hill where Eric sat perched. Though he'd never know such riches, he always enjoyed the pomp and circumstance and arrogance of royal affairs, for they brought him both delight and chuckled amusement.

However, no such amusement at the expense of the frivolity passed from his lips this day, not after he laid eyes on the precious being inside the carriage. Prince Ti'Louien's eyes were focused down at first. Eric had heard tales of the young prince's uncheery disposition. His temper was the stuff of legend. Based on what Eric had heard, he'd always imagined the prince to be something of a pompous brat. But that was far from the boy he saw now. This young man was simply the most beautiful sight that Eric had ever encountered. The only displeasure he found was the sadness that dared to lurk on such a wonderful face. Eric refused to take his eyes off the prince, for he knew not if he would see him again, and it proved to be wise that his glance remained locked…

As the carriage pumped over the stony seaside road, Prince Ti'Louien felt a pair of eyes upon him, distant and unfamiliar eyes. When he looked through the gold-plated window of his carriage, he found the poor young man who would not look away. The prince knew not how to feel at first glance. The entire royal family was used to stares and gawking. However, Prince Ti'Louien was never a popular royal, always seen as the family's sad, scandalous heir. Thus, the looks he received were never of the kindest sort. This look, however, was not of the normal sort. This look was simple, kind, and fascinated. And still, there was something more behind it. Something Ti'Louien had never experienced when another person cast their eyes upon him. At first, it intrigued the prince, but then fear overtook him, the fear of a connection he did not understand. Thus, he removed his eyes from the young man.

As the young Eric watched the prince take his glance back downward, he continued to smile and watch the carriage. Though the prince may not yet know it, in the youthful, hopeful heart of Eric, he knew that he'd just seen the most beautiful soul that had ever roamed the world between the Heavens and the Underworld. When the carriage was out of sight, he returned to his writing, still listening as the horses hooves and turning golden wheels grew faint, knowing something beautiful had just begun. Something he was anxious to pursue.

However, pursuit of the prince would be a dream that was forced to wait. Just three weeks later, Eric would set out on the worldly travels he'd promised his mother, Ruth, in which he'd partake. He joined a crew of merchants and would sail the seas around the enchanted kingdoms and beyond in order to educate himself, for, as Ruth once put it "It was the only way to know what to write about." Indeed, she was right. Whilst at sea, his writing became more wonderful and insightful. After years of effort, the night before his ship docked back in the Kingdom of Belle Terre, he finally completed his epic poem. Since seeing Prince Ti'Louien years earlier, his goal to write something of the myths with which he'd grown shifted. Instead of an epic about dragons and merfolk, the story he'd written was that of a great love, one he hoped would catch the prince's eye, somehow, someway. He had great thrill upon completing his final page, but just moments after the victory, a concern set in.

Eric flipped back through the pages he'd written. He read sections he once thought were poetic, and others he'd previously found groundbreaking. As he pored over his words, he began to wonder if they were indeed worthy of one such as his prince. It had wonderful imagination but was it anything that would stand out amidst the literature Prince Ti'Louien had surely read? Even now, along the path where first he saw the prince, Eric wondered. But despite his worry, he reminded himself frequently to hope for the best, for the story may have been written, but it was still a long road to get it to the prince.

****

If you've made it this far into my reconstructed work, I assume you're intrigued enough to keep reading, so the midpoint of the chapter seemed like a good time to break in. While parts of this chapter were among the easiest to recover—it only got harder from here—I still had to take a hefty amount of license, based on what was known *about unlocatable pages. I hope the text I wrote blended well enough. But I guess if you're with me so far, let's keep going. On TV, they say you need to give a show three episodes before you decide if you're going to stay with it or not, so why not give this a three-chapter test? It might be the closest I ever get to writing a series anyway.*

****

His feet were sore, and his eyes were tired, but a delighted smile pulled at the corners of Eric's lips as he came upon his childhood home, a small, welcoming hovel. Its windows caught sight of the sea in a way that was both comforting and beautiful. He may not have been rich, he may not yet have his prince, but he knew himself to be lucky whenever he saw his home.

Eric came to the door and took a deep breath, excited to see his mother. Before his hand met the knob, the door creaked open to reveal a man so burley, the sight would have made the Pope tremble in his Holy trousers.

"She's well worth the price," said the beast before pulling his belt over his chubby belly and sauntering off.

Eric watched him go with an embarrassed grin and a shake of his head. He wondered what the man would think if he knew the hooker he'd just paid well was Eric's mother. He waited a moment before re-entering for his mother to…get her affairs in order. Ten minutes seemed as though it would be enough time. After all, she was a professional. He walked into his childhood home, the smell of familiar fairy moss soaring up his nostrils as he inhaled. His mother had kept fairy trinkets around their home his entire life, not just for the décor, as many in the kingdom did, but because she truly believed in their powers.

Eric's admiration of the scent was cut short. "Shop's closed up for the day, and so am I," called his mother from the only other room they had. "My son's coming home, and he does not need such traumas." Ruth appeared from around the corner, her jaw dropped with embarrassment, but the urge to laugh in her eyes.

"Nothing like a warm welcome home from your mother." Eric grinned.

"Business is booming! You must be prepared."

The two shared a laugh before they embraced. "You

look good, my son."

"Thank you, Mother. How is it you look exactly the same as you did when I left?"

"Oils from the fairy rivers, of course! One must keep a supple face and a big old bosom if one wants to remain a professional."

Eric smiled. After seeing the world, he knew not if he shared his mother's superstitions, but he happily allowed her to keep her beliefs. He looked around his home, thrilled to be back and ready to truly begin his quest.

"What do you want to eat?" asked his mother. "I can get you some muttonless mutton, or unsalted cabbage soup."

"Still on your fad diets, I see."

"Don't make fun of your mother. If I'm to remain the most triumphant tart in town, I need to keep slender."

"I'll try the muttonless mutton, I suppose."

"Coming right up. You won't even taste the difference."

Ruth stepped outside and made way for the firepit. Eric knew not what supper would bring, but whatever stomach cramps awaited, it mattered not. He had greater matters on his mind. His thoughtfulness was not missed by his mother. She watched as her son lingered in the doorway, while she stoked the fire.

"What's going on in my son's imagination?" Ruth asked.

"Oh, nothing, Mother."

She dropped her ladle into the pot of boiling nonsense, placed her hands on her hips and thrust her breasts forward with a vigor that frightened Eric. She only did so when she was preparing to scold him or trying to entice a customer. Seeing as the latter was unlikely, he thought he should prepare himself.

"Don't lie to your mother," she ordered. "It's a sin!"

"All right," Eric replied, stepping forward. "There's something I've been keeping for some time now. Do you remember when I was younger, before I left to see the world, the day the royal carriage rolled by?"

"Of course I do! I was servicing the village friar at the time and was worried they'd come to arrest me and hang him up by his—satchel."

"Anyway, that was a special day for me. I was writing on that rock just over there when I heard the approaching horses. The glimmering gold of the carriage caught my eye—"

"Darling, I know you have a way with words, but be on with it."

"It's only that I remember that day so poetically."

"Oh, for the love of the gods, we're going to be here for hours, aren't we?"

"All right, all right. Well, the carriage was carrying Prince Ti'Louien. I'd heard of him and the legends of how he looked."

"Yes, they say he looks as sad as a whore's dog. I wouldn't know, though. I've never had a dog."

"Well, he did look sad. But he wasn't ugly or unpleasant like they say. I thought he was beautiful. And that day…he stole my heart as he rode away in his carriage."

Eric had never shared anything about his romantic desires with anyone, not even his beloved mother. Thus, his nerves were wracked. His mother stood in silence with a hand wrapped around her brazen hip.

"Well," she began, "bugger me, I was *waiting* for

you to finally tell me you like what I like. It's grand!"

"Mother, you don't need to make such a deal out of it."

"Let me have my moment!" Suddenly her excitement became realization. "The prince! You're infatuated with the prince."

"I would say it's more than infatuation."

"Don't be daft. It's an infatuation—for now. But it can become love."

"Well, while I was away, I *did* complete my collection for him."

"Wonderful, wonderful! You must use that."

"I hope to, but I admit I don't know how, and as I've thought of it more, I don't know that it's indeed good enough."

A smile composed of thrilled knowledge stretched across Ruth's lips. "I know who can help us."

"Who, Mother?"

"We shall visit the Violet Sprite."

****

Congratulations. You've made it the whole way through my first reconstruction. Let me promise you right now that this is not a coming out story. Eric's reveal to Ruth is it for the book. Thank God too, because they're not in style anymore and, frankly, I don't think this book would have been published if it was. Now we can get to the real *story. It gets better—if not weirder—from here.*

Chapter Two

"The Deplorable Prince"
Published in The Scribe's Collection *under the same name.*

Before you start this chapter, you'll need a little context. It's one of the rare chapters that shared a name with the fairy tale which it was published. However, the publisher took liberties. The story follows a stuck-up prince that would make Kris Jenner look like Dolly Parton. The arrogant prince struts through Belle Terre like a drag queen at brunch, upsetting his subjects with his attitude toward them. In the end, it turns into this sort of "The Emperor's New Clothes" thing, minus the old man nudity. Sadly, the censors really ripped the heart out of this segment. While much of the original text was hard to find, I did my best to reconstruct it after spending hours on Gmail with professors who at least knew the storyline of the missing parts.

****

Prince Ti'Louien never did like his name. He had all of his friends call him Louis…or he would have if he *had* friends. Creating companionships never came particularly easy for him. His father, the Good King Joshua, passed after succumbing to what the doctor/barber/butcher/matchmaker called Peasant Flu. The event was traumatic for the boy and even more so for his mother, the Good Queen Krystal. She grieved, she

9

ate, she spiraled in grief, till, one day, when the prince was ten, his mother emerged from her chambers in respectable dress to announce she had decided to remarry. The news came as a shock to all, especially the prince. What's more, she'd decided in no uncertain terms to marry the Royal Blacksmith, Richard Desmos.

Concern and disbelief would not sway her majesty, not even from her son, despite how close they'd always been. The prince had only ever seen the Blacksmith in passing. Thus, the decision made little sense to him. When it came time to meet him formally, Louis could not help distrusting the man, despite the kindness he showed at first. This was the beginning of Louis' sadness. Once the marriage was official, the sadness turned to depression, and the now King Desmos showed his true colors. He was a tyrant to his new son and controlling of his still sorrowful wife. Though they were now married, and no monarch of Belle Terre had ever been disgraced with a divorce, Louis hoped every day that his mother would come to her senses and announce the marriage was over. However, such a day never came. Instead, a far worse one did...

It was an otherwise balmy and bright day when Louis and Queen Krystal readied to travel to the seaside villages of the kingdom, a trip that the queen and her son had always participated in each month to ensure the fisher folk had all the need. Louis readied in attire that was respectable for his position in life, but not too arrogant, for his mother instilled in him at a young age that there was more to life than flaunting their wealth. He was particularly excited about the venture, as it remained the one tradition that he had with his mother in which his stepfather did not participate.

He finished tying himself into his garments when, from behind, King Desmos stood in the doorway, reflected in the prince's mirror. It was hard to believe that this man had been but a humble blacksmith not so very long before, for he stood with a fearsome poise and dressed in dark wear that suited him well. Though still only a teenager, that day, the boy looked at his menacing stepfather without fear.

"What is it, Stepfather?" asked Louis, casually fixing his cuffs.

"If I've told you once, I've told you a thousand times." King Desmos began his reply with his usual, deep husk, "You may call me either Your Majesty…or Father."

"If it's all the same, Stepfather suits you just fine."

"Spoiled little—" The king grunted under his breath, before composing himself back to his usual iciness. "I have some news and it's not the most pleasant. You must maintain your temper for the sake of the crown."

"For the sake of my lunch that I'd like to keep down, I will try," Louis mumbled.

"Your mother has been taken unwell," King Desmos coldly explained. "Her grasp on reality has faltered. It seems the loss of your father finally got to her, and she has been taken to the asylum. You'll have to make the trip alone. Be careful and try not to be taken by any bandits. The poor out that way are *so* vile."

The king left his stepson stunned. Louis could not believe the horrors he'd just been told. His beloved mother locked away after apparently going mad? He did not believe it, not even for a moment. He'd never trusted his stepfather and now, he trusted him even less. He would not stand for his scheming. Louis marched himself to the royal planning chambers, the room in which the king was often held up with the queen, releasing noises that made Louis' stomach churn.

When Louis arrived at the door, there were no squeals of pleasure or paternal ecstasy. Instead, he was greeted by the sight of two palace guards.

"Nicholas, Evers," the prince addressed the guards, as he moved to the doors with purpose. The guards moved in closer to one another, blocking the golden door handles. The prince looked up at the brutes. "What's the meaning of this?"

"Sorry, Your Highness," said Nicholas first. "King gave us strict orders that you weren't allowed to pass here through this way."

"Don't be ridiculous, Nicholas. Let me in, please."

"Sorry, but we can't do that now, or we'd be put in the stocks," Evers chimed in.

"He's right," Nicholas continued, the two still standing close.

Louis eyed the two cunningly. "At least you would go together. How many prisoners can say that they're stocked next to their bumbuddy."

"Your *Highness*!" Evers dramatically bellowed.

"I would *never* sin with a bloke!" agreed Nicholas.

"Oh, come now," the prince casually continued. "Everyone experiments in guard and executioner school."

"Never once!" Nicholas proclaimed.

"Well—only once for me," added Evers.

The prince dropped his glance with embarrassment as Nicholas gave his fellow guard a stunned look.

"Your Majesty." Evers tried to change the subject. "I have faithfully served the kingdom for seven years now and have never once said anything out of line."

"Not even how poorly the kingdom handled the scarlet plague." Nicholas nodded.

"Yet, now, I cannot remain silent. Why would you ever think such a thought about us?"

"I think you know why," Louis replied knowingly.

It was an insinuation that was enough to inspire the guards to double-check their close stance.

"You *are* a little close," Nicholas noted.

"Why, you bastard! I'm only guarding the door."

"See that that's all you guard," Nicholas quipped.

The two began a brash and petty argument, allowing Louis to slip through unnoticed. He found his stepfather talking of hushed business with two wrinkled members of the court. "Stepfather," the prince called bravely.

King Desmos' shoulders tensed. He looked upon his court members and dismissed them. With a huff of his nostrils, he turned to the prince. "What are you doing in here, Ti'Louien?" he asked coldly.

"It's Louis," said the prince with the intention of both defending himself and in hopes of getting under his stepfather's skin. "You owe me *several* explanations."

"Once again, we disagree, *Ti'Louien*. I've told you everything you need to know."

"I very disrespectfully disagree," quipped Louis. "What have you done to my mother?"

It became clear to King Desmos that his stepson was not going to cower the way he hoped. "She's gone for now," the king said flatly. "And, now, *you* have to go."

"You insane bastard. You truly think I would do such a thing?"

"You have a royal duty."

"And you must have a royal jewel stuck up your flat

arse! I'm not going!"

Silence hung between them once more. "Guards!" called the king.

The doors opened, and in came the still bickering Evers and Nicholas.

"Oh, bollocks," said Evers upon seeing the prince.

"Guess this is our fault," Nicholas added.

"What can we do Your Highness?"

"You can take the prince from my sight and to his carriage you two flittering fools."

"Oh, they do think we're fairies," Nicholas whispered to Evers.

"Shut up, you idiot!" Evers ordered.

Nicholas took one side of Louis and Evers the other.

"Come along, Your Highness," Evers ordered the prince.

Louis stared down the king, a glare which the monarch by marriage matched. "Enjoy your trip, Ti'Louien."

"This isn't over," the prince warned. He shook free from the guards, and he led himself from the room. Though he appeared strong, his heart was heavy. He approached the carriage he was to take with nothing more than forced duty carrying his feet. Making the journey without his mother was a challenge he never thought he'd have to face. His once bright eyes were dull and listless, his dimples were faded to obscurity.

The sea, which Louis had always enjoyed to seeing when such a venture was made, appeared now as a horrendous reminder of his tragedy. Its crashing waves were no longer beautiful, but a violent messy void. The countryside now appeared as a wasteland, filled with nothing but grass and insects. Indeed, nothing he saw could alter his harrowed mind. Not until he caught sight of the young peasant boy on the rock above the road. The boy stared at Louis with a glimmer in his eye and a charming smile upon his lips. The young man was clearly not noble, and Louis wondered how he afforded the parchment he held in his hands, but indeed, he was the most beautiful person the prince had ever seen. And for a moment, he was not so alone in the world…

****

In the years that followed, Louis had only *one* goal on his mind: getting his mother back from the asylum. However, his efforts were continually blocked. Frustrated, but not discouraged, he finally managed an audience with the queen. He expected to find her in despair and disheveled, a shell of her former self, vying to be freed to return to her kingdom and her child. What he found was far worse than he could have imagined. Gone was his mother's regal dress and jewels, but worse, she seemed content with her confinement.

"You can't seriously be happy here," said the prince.

"Oh darling, it's very much all right," Queen Krystal reassured. "I'll be better before you know it."

Louis could not believe what he'd heard. It was that day that he knew his happiness was completely gone and he vowed he would not smile until his mother was free. His upset reputation grew more and more with each drab appearance. It was not long before the kingdom decided upon a nickname for him: The Deplorable Prince.

****

It was a wonderful afternoon in the Kingdom of Belle Terre for many, but not for the prince. He was now nineteen, and in the eyes of the kingdom, more deplorable than ever. When he walked through the village, he often went in disguise and this day was no different. He cared not what the denizens thought of him, but to walk through unnoticed, ungawked upon was the only true escape he'd had from his horrible life over the last few years. His cloak was bland and not crested with frivolity. He roamed the cobblestoned road, watching families and lovers, greeting each with a hidden disgust on his lips. With the approaching anniversary of his mother's capture, another year of failure, he found no joy in even this outing. Thus, he decided it was time to return to the palace. As his stroll began to end, commotion broke out down the road. Max Day's Fresh Sausage & Buns cart broke free of its brakes and soon the buns and sausages within them wildly rampaged cobbled Castro Street.

Citizens fled and screamed from the attacking meats, however, in the chaos Louis spotted a lost little boy in the middle of the crowd. The cart sped toward him with bumping madness. Without a second thought for his own safety, Louis made haste for the boy and launched him out of the way. The cart crashed against a nearby wall, sending the slounged meats sky bound. While it made a mess, thankfully, no one was hurt.

"Are you all right, boy?" Louis asked as he caught his breath.

"Yes," said the boy. "Thank you for saving me, old man."

"I'm not a—Oh, you're welcome, son," the prince replied, trying to keep his irritation at bay.

"It's the prince," he heard an unseen woman proclaim. Louis realized that his hood had fallen from his head, exposing the features with which everyone in the kingdom had come to despise, despite their being beautiful.

"The Deplorable Prince, you mean," Max Day added. "Look what he let happen to my cart! My buns will never recover."

"I saved a child from your careless setup," quipped Louis.

"*My* child!" exclaimed a portly man as he busted through the crowd toward them.

Initially, Louis expected some sort of thanks from the distressed father, but with one look upon the man's face, it was clear to Louis that this was not what the denizen had in mind.

"Take your hands off my boy," ordered the man. "I don't want him learning any *nasty* habits from the likes of *you*!" The man violently ripped his son away from Louis, causing the boy to wince with pain. "What are you doing in our village? Are you trying to bring the *rest* of the kingdom down with your deplorableness?"

"They say your glare is so cold and is cursed to bring misery to anyone who sees it!" cried a woman in the crowd.

"They say the reason you can't find a princess is that you're a miserable wretch!" called another stranger.

"Go back to the palace and live your miserable life," said the boy's father.

Louis had endured enough and would not allow such sullied words to be thrust upon him without defense.

"You know what?" he began, rising from his still fallen position. "You're all so quick to speak up with the rumors that *you've* created. You have nothing but wicked thoughts about me and, yet not one of you knows me."

"We don't *care* to," proclaimed the man.

"Then why bother me with such attention?"

The man could not respond to the prince's wise return. Instead, he decided to go for the prince's weakness. "King Desmos should've locked you up with your looney mother!"

"Well, I still think you should thank me. Not only for saving your son, but for allowing the cart to be destroyed. Maybe without all the sausage and buns, you can finally work on seeing your feet!"

The portly man shook red with offended rage while the rest of the crowd spoke up with a chorus of disgusted noises and boos.

"That's right!" called out Louis. "I'm the Deplorable Prince! Why hide it anymore? You can all tell the world how much I upset you and how ashamed you are of me. I shall never conform to your simple mindedness, and I shall sing it proudly forever! May you all fall victim to the curse of my gaze!" He spun around madly with wide eyes, glaring at each citizen. The superstitious folk ran from him.

However, there was one who refused to flee. One who watched the prince from a distance. To see how terrible the rumors about the prince had grown over the years made Eric's heart weep.

"You sure it's him you want?" asked Ruth, as she joined him at his side. The two had begun their journey to find the Violet Sprite.

"Yes, Mother," Eric stated without a hint of waiver.

His mother nodded and placed a hand on his shoulder. "Then let's continue our journey."

Chapter Three

"The Violet Sprite"
Published in The Scribe's Collection *as "The Honest Boy and the Sprite."*

Eric and his mother trekked for the better part of an hour. By now, his feet were tired having taken two long journeys in a day, and he was more than a bit skeptical of the superstition, but after what he saw in the village, he was willing to try anything if it meant winning the prince's heart. Finally, they arrived at the foot of the famous Cliffs of Mary.

The path to the top was steep and treacherous, but Ruth assured it would be worth the journey. By the time they reached the peak, sunset had become dusk, which had become twilight. A thousand stars shined overhead, though Eric did not notice them at first. He was focused on catching his breath.

"We should have brought water," Ruth said.

Eric looked up from his hunched position. "How is it that you are perfectly fine?" he asked between his huffs.

"Professionalism. Now, get it together my boy. It's almost time to call him."

Eric stood, released one last cough. "All right, you're the expert. How do we do it?"

"It's very simple. Look up to the center star in Orion's Belt."

"…And?"

"And what?"

"I just look up at the center star and he'll appear without any effort?"

"Well, not with that attitude."

"I'm sorry, Mother. It just seems to me that in the stories, it takes a little more than staring at the sky to summon an all-powerful, ancient being."

"Who are you calling ancient?" called a voice with an accent from the North of Ireland.

Eric was startled, while Ruth was thrilled. They both turned toward the direction of the light, lovely voice.

The Violet Sprite floated above the cliff's edge, his feet pointed daintily above the rocks. His size could not have been more than three inches, and thus it was difficult to make out most of his details. The little figure waived his wand, releasing a rush of starry sparkles around him. When the magic cleared, his size matched that of Eric and Ruth. He wore a violet gown and no shoes. His skin was clear, his long hair blond. Finely arched eyebrows hovered perfectly above his blue and purple eyes. On his sparkling, crystal-like lips, he wore an impatient stance.

"Are you—are you him?" Eric asked.

"The ancient one you spoke about?" quipped the sprite.

"Forgive him, your enchantedness," Ruth knowledgably said. "He didn't mean anything disrespectful by it. Right, son?" Ruth turned to Eric and shot him an intense look of suggestion.

"Oh, yes," Eric agreed by the force of his mother.

"You see," Ruth said to the sprite, "My boy, bright as he is on the page, he's a bit simple when it comes to addressing powerful and wonderful beings such as you fare folk. Isn't that right, darling?"

"Oh, yes. *Horribly* simple," Eric agreed, trying his best to be convincing.

"And *clueless* about magicology," continued Ruth. "Isn't that right, boy?"

"…Yes. Clueless…" Eric continued to oblige with a frigid tone.

"And *no* sense of sensual fashion."

"Oh, that I can see." The sprite giggled.

"All right, enough!" shouted Eric.

"Oh, so he does have some spunk," the Violet Sprite acknowledged "I like him. He's cute too, despite it all."

"He's my pride and joy," agreed Ruth.

"What a sweet mother." The sprite nodded. "And nice tits too."

Eric's head was spinning, and he was beginning to think he'd slipped into some uncultivated dream. Still, he was willing to endure the hallucination if it meant winning the heart of his prince. The sprite approached him, his feet nearly floating with each step.

"Tell me, my boy," the Violet Sprite began. "Why is it you've sought me tonight? It's not money, like most young people, it's not looks like most old. Is it for a sensual time? No, that's not it. But feel free to seek me again if it ever is." The creature looked him over, reading the scribe like one of his stories. "Ah, there it is," he said with epiphany. "It's *love*. Well, my loss then. You're in love with someone, someone out of reach."

"It's true…" agreed Eric.

"I wonder who it is that captured the heart of such a beautiful young man."

"You can't tell?" Eric asked.

"I'm knowing, not nosy. Heavens, child. I have *some* class."

Eric chuckled, beginning to like this dream made creature. "It's someone I've yet to really meet. Someone who I've only seen in passing. And who I fear that, no matter how hard I try, will always be out of my reach. Prince Ti'Louien."

"Oh, feck," said the sprite. "Indeed, that is a challenge. But what are fairies for if not granting wishes and all that nonsense."

"You really think you can do it?" Eric asked hopefully.

"I don't."

Eric's gleaming grin dropped, and his eyes filled with confused heartbreak.

"But I think *you* can—with a little *help* from your favorite spritely icon." He waved his wand with flair and suddenly, at Eric's feet, there lay a parchment and quill.

He picked up the dull items. They did not *feel* magical in any sort of way. "What are these for?"

"I thought you were of the creative sort. Don't tell me I'm wrong."

"No, you're not. It's only, how will these help me win the prince?"

"I can sense your talent, ambition, and love are all one. You'll need to do the work."

"You mean I must compose *more*? But I just finished a huge collection of tales. And I'm proud of it."

"But not completely?"

Eric became silent. His eyes fell to the dirt road below his feet.

"Oh, don't get all blue on me. I know the Blue Sprite and they're far too much for me. I can't *stand* another. If you want to be the Royal Scribe, you'll always have to write more."

"*The Royal Scribe?*"

"Of course. Now, you go home and write the next one. Pour your heart, soul, and testosterone into it. Then, when it's done, you go to the palace. Work hard enough, it may be the best thing you've ever written. If not, make it as good as you can, and if your heart is in it, you'll become the scribe indeed, and be one step closer to your prince."

Eric nodded. His heart filled with a mix of emotions. When his mother convinced him to come out to the cliffs, he hoped the magical solution would be immediate. But now, here he was, having to begin work that he loved but also dreaded, for it was work without a certain end, and that terrified him. It shifted his goal from being the "here and now" to being "the someday, maybe, should nothing get in the way before he finished." Still, it was the work he knew he could do, the task he was *willing* to do if it meant saving his prince from sadness.

The sprite returned to Orion's center loop and was gone, leaving Eric and his mother alone.

Ruth smiled at her son with great glee.

He looked to her, as he took in all that had transpired. Then, a grin stretched his small, pink lips. "I suppose I should get to work."

****

This was maybe my favorite chapter to translate in Part One of the book. Most of the Sprite's dialogue was lifted directly *from what Eric had written. However, his description was…of its time. I took inspiration from one of my favorite drag queens. I'll let you decide who that is. I don't know if we'll get their clearance by the time this is published. If the day ever comes that I can reveal it, I expect them to play the role in the movie version that will almost certainly never happen.*

Chapter Four

"The Queen's Return"
Published in The Scribe's Collection *as "The Mad Queen Returns."*

This was a chapter I dreaded. The story it became was the stereotype of a fairy tale. Queen Krystal and her struggles were relegated to the "Evil Queen" troupe. Luckily, Professor Tyler Harney of Oxford—a wonderful source in general when it came to research—was able to help me track down all *of the original chapter. Anyway, enjoy the first completed and barely edited original version of this reconstruction.*

****

When it was announced that Queen Krystal was returning, there was much jargon throughout the kingdom. Some were *thrilled* that their beloved queen was healthy and back in the palace. Others discussed her apparent madness as though it were some sinful disease. But no matter what the denizens of Belle Terre felt, they were all hopeful that her return to the kingdom would set her miserable son on the straight and narrow.

It was three weeks after the runaway cart incident that the queen's carriage rolled through the cobbled and finally repaired village street. Citizens lined the road for miles to see their queen. Some were excited to see her glamour, others were eager to see if she looked ghastly and insane. Both hopefuls would claim they saw what they'd lined up for, as she waved from the windows of her golden carriage. It traveled to the end of its route on the palace drawbridge where Louis stood on ceremony with King Desmos. The two had not spoken since the king brutally scolded the boy after the mess in town. It was all they could do to stomach the sight of each other for the queen's return.

Louis watched intently, both nervous and excited to see his mother. His stepfather's abrupt decision to bring her back so out of the blue made him suspicious. Yet, the prospect of his mother returning and life going back to the way it was meant to be allowed the prince to indulge in the last bit of hope that he held within.

The carriage rolled up the bridge and into the courtyard where Louis and King Desmos waited. Queen Krystal smiled widely and waved with even more gusto than before at the sight of her son and husband. The coach man came around and opened her door. "My darling boys," she cheered with arms wide, making way to her son and her husband.

"Mother," greeted Louis, who began the steps to meet her halfway, only to be cut off by King Desmos.

"Welcome home, wife," King Desmos greeted with forced warmth.

The queen held out her hand for a kiss. The king took it, but once he noticed Louis' longing eyes focused on his mother, Desmos took Krystal in his arms and kissed her madly without much dignity in front of all. When their lips finally parted with a rude, wet smack, the king squeezed the queen's royal buttocks.

"My son," Queen Krystal greeted. "It's so wonderful to see you."

"Mother." Louis smiled, approaching his mother for

a hug, a hug that wasn't met. "Is everything all right?"

"Of course, my boy," Krystal reassured unconvincingly. "But this is no such place for affection. What will the commoners think? Now, come along. I'm starved." Queen Krystal and King Desmos walked into the palace, standing uncomfortably close.

Louis watched with disgust. No sense of the situation could be made by him. She was never one to deny a hug from her son and the hypocrisy she spoke was far from her ways. Whoever this was that returned from the madhouse, this was not the mother he knew.

****

The next few days were filled with even more peculiarity. Queen Krystal was swift to make unfathomable changes. A focus on fashion and circumstance became her focus, vanities that had never been her concern before. Policies meant to help the people were literally thrown out the window, the scrolls on which they were written cascading down and piling on the head of the village flasher, David. The heirloom decorations that Krystal had so treasured were removed at the apparent order of the queen.

"But, Mother, you *love* these old belongings," Louis argued at the sight.

"Don't be so sentimental," Queen Krystal responded. "One shouldn't hold on to things with no worth."

To replace her priceless collection, Queen Krystal brought in decorations of gold and marble. Possessions that made their once cozy castle gaudy and excessive to the point of embarrassment.

Family dinners became affairs of pomp and circumstance, quiet parliament meetings filled with shouts and vile language. But the worst of it all came at night, when sounds so loud and so vile came heaving from the room of the queen and king and poured down the hall to Louis's bedchamber. He got into the routine of having an extra pillow to pull over his ears, but even that wasn't enough to drown out the middle-aged huffing.

Indeed, none of what was occurring in the palace felt right to the prince, and he wondered what had truly happened to the woman he'd known and loved while she was locked away…

****

Yeah, I know; it's gross. Straight sex is weird. But I promise this all fits into the plot in its way.

Chapter Five

"The Brave Little Scribe"

All right, this was an interesting case—for me anyway—because this chapter, while mostly obtainable for me, was not *included in any way in* The Scribe's Collection. *None of the experts I talked to knew why. Some thought that it was maybe lost at the time of publication. I guess that can sort of make sense, but there was no evidence that this chapter was ever missing. Another theory I heard was that it* was *included in the collection but had been so severely changed that it was unrecognizable. But, after a hefty amount of research that kept me from binging the final season of* The Marvelous Mrs. Maisel, *this theory was also shut down.*

After a few more weeks of research, I got an email from a Dara Young. As it turned out, she is a direct descendant of the author *Eric. She confirmed that, much to the anger of her Great-Great-Grandfather, the story was never adapted or published. While I had my answer, I still didn't know* why *it was excluded. The publisher was long out of business. Which meant I had to do my own theorizing.*

I was frustrated by that. I like definitive answers. Fan theories drive me crazy and are often very wrong, yet here I was, creating one. But as I read the chapter and added the few little fill-ins that I had to add, I realized something: It was an act of censorship.

SPOILER ALERT: This is the chapter where Eric and Louis finally meet. It's one of my favorite chapters. It reminded me of those butterflies I always felt when I met an interesting boy. One that was tall, curly topped, and probably in gray sweatpants; you know, the romance that the stiff shirts find inappropriate. The romance that they all also experience but like to pretend isn't okay when it's...yah know—hand flip. Never mind the fact that straight fairy tale couples usually tongue at the end of their stories. Anyway, you get the idea. Enjoy the not so lost chapter. It's kind of great.

****

Eight weeks had passed since Eric and his mother called upon the Violet Sprite. He wrote day and night, and night and day. He only stopped to eat and drink when Ruth forced him. His scribblings were so passionately loud that they would disturb Ruth's clients mid thrust. Likewise, the sounds of his mother at work irritated his creativity. However, both soldiered on and, finally, on a starry midnight, Eric wrote the final words of his new collection.

Beaming with excitement, he could not wait to share the stories with his mother in the morning. Impatient, he began to read them himself. His grin soon dropped, however, replaced by an uncertain frown. While his stories were indeed well composed, and perhaps, his most thoughtful yet. However, now he found his words insufficient, and he worried that they were not the touchstone the sprite had predicted it to be. Such worry would keep him up all night, he was sure. Still, there was nothing he could do now but lie in bed with his reservations.

With reluctance, Eric retired to his loft, removed his

tunic, and rolled over in his small bed. As he lay on his back with his eyes shut, a peculiar, ringing sound approached from the distance. Closer and closer it drew. Suddenly, his window opened and the jingling began to dance around his ear. When he opened his eyes, he found the Violet Sprite sitting at the foot of his bed, legs crossed, chin resting upon the same hand in which he wielded his wand.

"My, my," said the sprite. "Who knew we'd end up in bed together?"

Eric sat up, the blanket falling from his bare torso.

"Oh, and would you look at that," the little fare folk continued. "I get quite a show at that. I always did like them skinny."

"What are you doing here?" asked Eric.

"Oh, so not excited to see me? That's a kick in my rather cute arse. Well, I could sense you needed me. I'm not normally one for house calls, but I suppose I'm fond of you."

"That's very kind."

"And you're very thin. Now that we've got the obvious out of the way, why don't you tell me what's troubling you?"

"Don't you know already?"

The Violet Sprite gave Eric an irritated glance.

"Right, I forgot how this works. Well, you see, I finished my new collection."

"Sláinte!"

"But, I have some concerns."

"Concerns? Such as? You used the quill and the parchment I gave you, didn't you?"

"Of course."

"And you worked as hard as I told you to, did you

not?"

"I did. But, I'm worried that it's not that good…"

"Your collection?"

"…Indeed," Eric admitted with sorrow.

"It seems to me you've done all you could."

"Yes, but what if it's not enough? What if no matter what I do, it's not enough to win the prince?"

The Violet Sprite sighed. He was never good at the warmth and guidance part that people expected of fairy godmothers, but he was fond of Eric and didn't want to disappoint him.

"Perhaps I can put it another way for you: The closer you get to following your dream, the scarier it becomes. And I won't lie, the fear of failure is *always* justified, magic or not. Perfectionism is something so many people like you want to achieve. But the truth is, you never will. No matter how hard you try, no matter how well you plan, no matter how great a spell you cast, none of us in this life are perfect. But don't let your longing for perfection be your excuse to not try. You don't want to only dream forever, do you?"

Eric smiled humbly. "I suppose you make good sense."

"I always do," said the Violet Sprite with a wink.

"I'll need a good night's rest if I'm to head to the palace by morning."

"I can help with that!"

"Do you have a sleeping spell?"

"I could give you that. But how boring!"

Eric chuckled, as he understood the sprite's implication. "Apologies, but my heart truly only belongs to my prince."

"All right, a gentle sleeping spell it is." The Violet

Sprite waved his wand. Gentle specs of purple starlight floated down from its end to Eric, who soon drifted into a peaceful sleep. A smile remained on his lips all night, as he dreamt of the possibility that the next day would bring.

****

Eric woke with the dawn the next morning. He slept only a few hours, though he didn't care. He was as excited as a child who awaiting Père Noël Christmas Eve. After readying quickly, but with care, he kissed his mother lightly on the cheek and began his journey to the palace. It would be another long trek on his feet, but with each step, he'd be closer to his prince. He traveled across the seaside path, through the nearby Blue Moon Forest, up the Hills of Abbey Valley, until finally he arrived in the village. The palace sat at the end of the long, cobbled path.

He met his first challenge at the end of the drawbridge, for there stood the guard Evers. Eric was not swayed, however. He took a deep breath and strutted toward the door.

"Good morning," he greeted confidently, attempting to push past.

"Hold on!" Evers ordered. "Where do you think you're going?"

"Oh," Eric replied calmly, "to see the prince."

"You can't do that! Who do you think you are?"

"I'm Eric. I'm going to be the new Royal Scribe."

"The royal what? Don't be nonsensical. Get out of here before I clap you in the stocks."

"Hold on, a peasant can't be the Royal Scribe, but a random guard can clap him in the stocks?"

"Don't question my authority."

"Well, you questioned my ability when you think about it."

"I did not."

"Oh, well that's wonderful. Perhaps we can be friends yet. Once I'm the Royal Scribe that is. Perhaps, I can put a word in for a better position for you."

Evers tensed up. "A better position?"

"*Yes*, of course. Despite our differences, you're clearly a man of devotion."

"Well, it's nice to be appreciated."

"I take it you aren't appreciated *enough* around here. Well, that'll be remedied when I'm scribe—provided I may pass."

Evers stood silent for a moment. Though he kept his lips strong and neutral, his shifting eyes let Eric know that he would be victorious. Without making eye contact with Eric, Evers shifted, and Eric began to make his way through.

"Wait," Evers called, briefly causing Eric panic. He turned to see the guard still standing with his back to him. "You'll have to get past a guard called Nicholas to get into the royal wing…When you see him, tell him you're a friend of Evers. And—that I hope he's doing well."

Eric smiled to himself, for he recognized those words of care. Though he may never have spoken to them to the man of his dreams himself, the power of the sentiment was not lost on him.

****

The palace was even more grand than Eric imagined. He walked the elongated entryway, out of breath by the time he finally got to the stairs. Though he'd traveled paths of seaside and forest, the excessive length of this one room winded him.

"Gracious gods forbid they're ever running late," Eric said. "They'll drop dead of dehydration before they leave the castle." It was then he finally noticed just how many stairs he had to climb to reach the main part of the palace. "You'll be able to bounce a wooden penny off my arse before this day is done," he remarked. However, he knew each step he climbed would be worth the effort, for each step brought him closer to the prince. Indeed, destiny awaited, of this, he was sure.

When he reached the top of the stairs, Eric was greeted with much more commotion. Ladies in waiting were waiting for laundry. Members of parliament paraded around in ridiculous wigs. The court jester was having posset with the executioner in the corner. It was a madhouse of nobility and servants. For one less determined than Eric, finding the prince would seem an impossible task. Luckily, Eric *was* just so determined.

He was careful to ensure he was lost in the crowd, keeping his head down when it was best and blending beautifully amongst the help. The hall seemed twice as long and even more daunting than the entryway. Yet, in the middle of the jostle, his stamina was invigorated by the thrill of his task and the risk of being caught. The latter scared him not, for he'd happily spend time in the stocks if it meant meeting Prince Ti'Louien.

Eric came to a long, cobbled hall. At its end stood a door with a single guard in front of it. His eyes looked sad and his posture only remotely dutiful. He knew it had to be the Nicholas of which Evers spoke. He remembered the words of clear care that Evers had given and decided to approach with sympathy, for he could not help but pity that melancholy guard. He wanted not to hurt the guard, but he knew he may have to take part in some manipulation. Still, it was the least he could do to approach sincerely.

"Hello, friend," Eric greeted with kind sympathy.

"Friend?" Nicholas said in a saddened voice that even he didn't recognize. "I don't know you from Eve."

"Are you Nicholas?"

The guard *stood* on guard. "I might be, but I won't divulge that information to anyone."

"Not even a friend of Evers?"

Nicholas' eyes grew wide, his pupils hollow. "You know Evers?"

"We've met. He seems to care for you quite a lot."

"Well, I don't know about that. He's been cold and uncaring since our positions were changed."

"It seems to me that is the most natural response in the world when one loses their lover."

"Lover? Who said anything about *lover*? The king would never allow such unholy lusting."

"The king. Between you and me, I don't agree with a lot of that nonsense." Eric looked around and leaned in with a whisper. "I'm like you. Both of you. And I'm here to change the way the king sees us."

Nicholas remained silent for a while. He knew not if responding was wise. But there was a part of him that wanted to believe. Thus, he pressed on. "And how does a peasant plan to do that."

"Well, I'm not just a peasant," Eric explained, "I'm a scribe, here to read for the prince. I know that when he hears my words, he will insist that the king and queen make me the Royal Scribe. And furthermore, I know I can change the way people like us are treated in this kingdom, for the written word and the stories people love influence them in far greater ways than any age-old prejudice can."

Nicholas thought over it and thought further still. Then, he leaned in. "You'll find the prince held up in his bedchamber. Ever since his mother returned, his stepfather has ousted him further and further from royal duty. He spends most days hiding in there. It'll be up the rounding stairs on the fifteenth floor."

"Thank you." Eric nodded.

****

The steeply curved stairs proved yet another challenge for Eric, but after a while, he finally found the fifteenth floor. Far less grand than the rest of the palace, with halls dull and quiet, it was cold and unwelcoming, as though the whole corridor was meant to depress whoever passed through. Eric wondered if he'd been lied to by the guard. Perhaps it was a trap, and he was now in great danger. Still, on the chance that he *had* been told the truth, he must continue his quest. At the far end of the gloomy passage, there was a small window, presumably put in out of obligation only so that one could at least see where they were going without maiming themselves. To the right of it, was a small, sad door, the only one on the floor. That had to be the room of his prince. The most beautiful boy in the realm was in there right at that moment. Eric took a deep breath and with a shaking, yet brave stride, he prepared to meet his destiny.

When he came to the threshold, Eric did not find the room he expected. It was small and plain. The royal frivolities that he knew the prince deserved were absent. A single, small bed lay in the center of the room. A dirty window let the smallest amount of light in across it. There were no curtains, no rugs, no tassels. Not even the prince himself. Still, Eric had never been closer to the man behind the crown, and thus, he invited himself to step in for a better look. He strutted through the small, melancholy room with care. As he went to the window, he expected a likewise view. However, the sight with which he was met caused his jaw to drop and his heart to flutter. Beyond the village below, past the forest and valley, lay a perfect view of the very spot on the very seaside road where the prince and the scribe first caught sight of one another many adolescent sunsets ago. Eric was filled with a rush of boyhood excitement. The room may have been drab, and he suspected it was far from the quarters the prince would have wanted, but maybe, just maybe Ti'Louien's heart wasn't so far from his.

"Who are you?" came a voice from behind. Eric knew it instantly, and to him, it was youthfully beautiful beneath its warning. "I'll ask you again, *who are you*? And *why* are you in my room? Come to mock the Deplorable Prince?"

"Of course not. Never," Eric said, finally turning to meet the eyes of his beloved. There the prince was, just a few feet away, leaving Eric truly breathless. But he was not the only one...

Louis too was caught off guard, for little did Eric know, he recognized the scribe immediately. Though the years had passed, and though times had grown harder and darker, he'd never forgotten the day he saw those light blue, brown eyes. So rich with color, they'd looked green that day in the sun, and still, now, in Louis' dark room, they remained ever as enrapturing. They were the only source of beauty the prince had seen in an otherwise dark and gloomy time. The prince caught his breath and recomposed himself. "You never answered my first question," he continued, the harshness in his voice melting away. "Who are you?"

"I'm Eric," answered the blue/brown-eyed boy.

"I see," the prince answered with a tanginess in his interrogating tone.

Eric stood in silence for a moment, completely lost in the sight of his prince. For one who hoped to be the royal master of words, he knew this to be a brittle first "And you're Ti'Louien," he finally blurted. "*Prince* Ti'Louien, that is."

"Oh, how I can't stand that formality," Louis said, with strong, folded arms, as he strode around his room. "That *name*."

"I think it's a *wonderful* name. The sort of name people such as me write about."

"You're a writer?"

"A scribe."

"I see," Louis said, his eyes landing upon the parchments in Eric's right hand. "And is that your collection."

"Yes. I've worked hard on it. Day and night, night and day for weeks, it was my only friend, my only focus."

"I think one would call that an obsession."

"I wrote them for you," Eric admitted boldly.

Louis stopped; his eyes held upon the scribe for a moment. "For me?"

"Yes, for you. You see, you're my muse. You've always been my muse. You surely don't remember but you passed through my seaside village years ago. I was doing what I always did in those days: sitting on a rock dreaming, writing. Hoping that my words would find their way to others. That was the first time I'd ever seen you in person, the famous Prince Ti'Louien. From that day to this, you've been my inspiration."

Louis stood still, cold in his tracks. Chills ran through his veins, for the boy was *not* a dream. The boy he was not sure truly existed was *real*. "Well..." the prince said, "if I truly am your muse, I refuse to let you call me by my birth name. I prefer Louis."

"Prince Louis, all right."

"Oh, for the love of the gods, not *Prince* Louis. Simply Louis. No pomp, no circumstance. I wish not to be associated with the state of this kingdom. They've spread lies and rumors about me for so long. In fact, I didn't become '*deplorable*' until the day you saw me. But my stepfather started the rumors about me long before."

"Louis it is," Eric agreed without quam.

Louis was pleased, but still skeptical. He'd never met someone who agreed with him so willingly. "Let me read those pages," he said.

"Not yet," said Eric.

"There it is." Louis smiled cunningly. "I knew you were too good to be true. You probably just wanted an audience with me and used this as a ploy."

"Oh no, I would never do anything like that. It's just...I don't want to give you my pages and never see you again. I'm after something much larger."

"What then?"

"I want to be by your side always. Forever. But I know that...in the way I want to be...it would never be accepted, so I'm looking for a job."

"It still sounds like you're after what I suspect," teased Louis.

"Not really. If I thought there was a way to tell you

what I really want to tell you, and to stay in your presence without conviction, I would. But alas, for people such as I, we have to be clever."

Louis nodded, for though it seemed impossible that Eric felt the same things that he did, the implications were too precise to ignore. "And what kind of people is it to which you refer?"

"Love, of course. Don't be scared, I know that the kind of love that I speak of is unwelcomed and is treated in the way that one treats a witch. But you must understand that, despite what you may have heard about what I feel, of one man loving another, it's not perverse or unholy. In fact, it is pure and true."

Louis' eyes dropped to his well booted feet. For a moment, Eric worried that he had ruined his chances of obtaining employment near the prince with his honesty. But then, he caught glimpse of the smile that pulled at the dimpled corners of the prince's lips. "Pure and true. I've never heard it put in such a way…" His eyes raised back to meet Eric's, "but I've never agreed with something more whole heartedly. Nor have I ever felt more seen."

Eric was now the one uncertain if he was dreaming. Granted, there were many restless nights where he never imagined he would get this far, but, deep down, he always knew the greatest hurdle would be that of the prince's *actual* feelings. The truth was it mattered not how wonderful or mediocre the collection was, or how charmingly he presented himself. If he did not love on the same way Eric did, it would be fruitless and he'd be doomed to spend an eternity with a pining, aching heart. Yet, here he was, collection in hand, with the prince, and maybe, just maybe, hearing that his feelings were returned.

"Tell me Eric the Scribe, if you truly want to be by my side forever, how is it that employment would help?"

"Well, you see, I know it's been some time since the court held a royal scribe."

"We haven't had one since before my mother left, it's true."

"Now that she's back, I was hoping to appear before the court and recite my words. I'd like to bring that tradition back to life, for with that job, I could admire you always and write poems and stories of your strong beauty. Even if their meaning had to be secret, I would be able to look into your eyes forever."

Though he would never admit it, Louis' heart had not felt this alive in many years. "That's very kind of you," said Louis before adopting a more serious tone. "But I'm afraid my mother is unwell, and any stories you may present before the court would not appease my stepfather. It may be best for you to return home and find a new dream."

Eric could not believe what he was hearing. Surely, he hadn't come this far and achieved the things he thought impossible, only for his prince to reject *him* in fear of the *court's* rejection. Suddenly, the shy, respectful boy he'd been since meeting the prince dissolved and was replaced by a man whose passion and ambition met as one.

"Don't be so quick to dismiss possibility," Eric wisely advised, taking steps closer until he was nearly nose-to-nose with the prince. "Sometimes, the hope of what's possible is all we have."

"Ti'Louien!" barked a deep voice from the hall.

Both men felt all pleasantness vanish from the room.

Louis was familiar with the commanding tone, and, though it was foreign to Eric, he knew that it was one to fear. They both brought their eyes to its source in the doorway where the tall, dark figure of King Desmos loomed.

"What in the name of the Ankou is going on here?" he asked with stern command. "Who is this crofter?"

"Forgive me, Your Majesty," Eric defended the prince. "I mean no disrespect. You see, I'm not a crofter."

"An intruder then. Come to corrupt and destroy me beloved stepson." Though his words were protective, his tone was cold and uncaring.

Louis clenched his jaw, for he knew his stepfather's words were nothing more than ceremony, presented frequently by the king when he and the prince were not alone.

"No, I promise, your excellency, that is far from—what I mean is—I'm here—"

"He's here to become our new Royal Scribe."

Our *scribe*?" Desmos scoffed. "We've no such position in our court."

"We did, until *you* rid us of such art."

"A pointless position to have on our payroll. Commoner nonsense."

"Did you not used to once muck stalls and care for horses?"

"Why you—"

"Besides, the Royal Scribe's recitals were once Mother's favorite way to spend a Sunday evening. Surely, now that she's back she'll want to reinstate it."

Desmos became intensely silent, as his eyes filled with intense thoughtfulness, before finally stating "I'm sure her opinions have changed."

"What's the harm in having him try? In fact, as the heir to the throne, I *insist* that we call a meeting of the court. That is my right. I know you wouldn't argue with me on that in front of the guest I invited here, would you, dear Stepfather?"

Desmos inhaled deeply as he rushed to his stepson, a harsh finger pointed directly at Louis' heart. "Very well," he obliged with disdain in his voice.

"Thank you, dear Stepfather." Louis smiled mockingly.

The king leaned into his stepson's ear and with gruel in his voice, whispered "One of these days, Ti'Louien."

Eric was not sure if he'd truly heard what had passed between them correctly, but he knew regardless of what was said, he knew it was something his prince did not deserve. However, as the king dismissed himself with a huff, Louis looked upon Eric with a grin.

"Well, brave little scribe, I suppose we should get you ready for your recital."

Chapter Six

"The Peasant in the Royal Court"
Published in The Scribe's Collection *under the same title.*

I'm not sure how I feel about this chapter and the title. Most of it was lost in translation. Though the story maintained the same name, it was turned into a weird "poor boy pleases the rich and becomes lucky enough to be a servant" romp. It weirdly reminds me of "Jack and the Beanstalk." However, that—very purposely—misses the point. But I'll let you see what I mean.

****

The court was gathered within an hour of Louis' order, as the prince prepared his scribe in the hall. Already, Eric's nerves were aflame as he heard the muffled congregation of those in pompous dress and ridiculous wigs.

"Worry not," Louis said warmly. "They're really just a bunch of old wind bags. Half of them won't be able to hear you anyway. A quarter of those we only keep out of obligation because they survived the plague, two wars and, in one's case, the carnal revolution festival. You'll do fine. And I'll see to it that you're victorious. Oh, listen to me going on. Do you have any questions?"

Eric had plenty. His mind spun with the whirlwind of information which Louis had thrown upon him. However, his mind could only handle one fear at a time.

"How—how many people *are* there?"

"Oh, about one hundred and fifty or so. It's not nearly as massive as a ball or anything like that. Oh, don't slouch. You'll need to look confident." Louis noticed the fear on Eric's face. He gave the scribe a grin and put a hand upon his shoulder. "You'll be wonderful. Just look to me when the worries seem too much." With that, he strode to the door.

As he made this way into the court, Eric waited with pride in his heart. Try as he might, he could scarcely make out what was being said on the other side in the hall through the thick oak doors, but he *knew* he heard the voice of the prince, his inflections and passion already familiar and beautiful to him.

Before very long, the doors were pulled open with a creak and Eric strode forward. The room was leafed with gold around mahogany panels. Elevated high above the exhibition circle where Eric now stood were what seemed to be hundreds of members of the royal court, all with their elderly eyes peered down upon him. Their dressing robes and wigs were just as nonsensical as he'd imagined. He took a moment to inspect it all. These very serious old men did not seem as though they were *his* audience. Love stories and magical battles were likely something they would find preposterous. He knew not how his tales would fair in such a setting. But then, his eyes landed on Louis, smiling down upon him. Eric looked up at his prince and grinned back. Their warm exchange was interrupted by a booming voice above:

"The prince tells us you are the new Royal Scribe."

Eric spun with fright and confusion to see the Lord Chamberlain staring down directly at him with purpose in his wrinkled blue eyes. His proper inflection and dialect had frightened Eric so, that it took him a moment to process what had been boomed at him. When he *did* realize, it was clear there had been some sort of confusion.

"That's right, Lord Chamberlain," called Louis, causing Eric to twirl yet again. "He's quite a talent and I can think of no one better to bring back such an esteemed position."

"I think there's been some sort of mistake," Eric began, meager of heart and projecting as best he could. "I'm not yet—what I mean is I'm not…"

"One for being anything but modest," interrupted Louis. "I'm sure he would much rather let his work speak for him, Lord Chamberlain." Louis looked down discreetly from his spot high above the floor. Anyone else but Eric would have missed the subtle gaze that urged him to play along with the ruse.

It was then that Eric noticed the far more telling stare that came from the fiery eyes of King Desmos. The fury that he felt was evident. Louis had essentially double crossed him in front of the entire court and had handed the job to Eric. But, if the king wanted to keep up the false image of royal family peace, he would not be able to strike his stepson's words down. Though Eric feared his prince would hear much of it later. Queen Krystal sat between the two and kept her regal, if not slightly too powerful, smile beamed. Strangely, Eric could not read her at all, but he figured he must not disappoint just the same.

"Well, with all this praise," intervened the Lord Chamberlain, "I suppose we should begin. Besides, I don't want to miss my mid-morning brandy with my pageboy, he does so look up to me, you know." Both Eric and Louis had an inkling of what he meant. "Get on with it then, get on with it."

Eric jolted in his boots at the Lord Chamberlain's ordering. It was not a wonderful way to start. He reset himself with a breath, and dropped his eyes to his material. Just the night before, he was not confident that it was great work. Now, he was to perform it before the entirety of the royal court and, of course, the royal family. His stomach was in knots and his spine was chilled. Still, it was a moment for which he hoped and now it was here. Thus, he raised the pages, cleared his throat, and began to recite:

"There once was a boy, a boy they called poor.

But it didn't bother him, for he had all he needed and more.

He had the sea at his feet and the sun in the sky,

And an imagination so grand, when he dreamed, he knew he could fly.

When he wrote his sonnets and poems, he made all the girls of his village sigh,

but there came a day when one far more beautiful caught his boyish eye.

His heart fluttered and his mind, it did soar,

for he'd never seen one nearly so glorious before.

He saw beauty, he felt shame,

for he knew the beautiful one would never know his name.

But soon, it did not matter, not one bit.

He was determined to do whatever he saw fit.

He'd go to the ends of earth, to the end of time.

Any mountain, he would climb. Any river, he would cross,

For the eyes that he saw were too beautiful for loss.

He made a promise that day, that day in the sun, by the sea,

That those eyes and those lips, that feeling that they brought would always be.

He vowed that day, from that day to this, that those lips he would kiss, that the sadness, he would melt.

And someday, no matter how far he must go,

No matter what battles he faced, no matter how the sky stormed and the sea swirled,

He and his far-away love would share the world."

Eric smiled to himself, for he'd completed the first entry. He looked up at his prince and gave him a small, proud grin, which Louis returned. Though he was proud of himself, he knew that this was not enough to convince the court of the legend Louis had created for him. Thus, he read on, reciting passage after passage, each story growing more beautiful and more passionate and, to the prince, more obviously a love letter from writer to muse.

By the time he was finished, Eric felt as though he'd been reciting for days. He expected the court to be exasperated with his words, his reading, and he himself. Slowly, with worry on his shoulders but pride in his heart, he lifted his eyes from the parchment. A great surprise filled his veins, for he was not met with the looks of bother and rashness which he expected. Instead, he found eyes filled with an array of emotions. Some were filled with tears, others excitement. Even the Lord Chamberlain had been enthralled.

"Well," began the courtier with his accent so proper, "I must say it was worth missing the meeting with my pageboy. Well done. Prince Louis, this court is happy to instate young Eric as our new Royal Scribe. Now, let's go. I want to tell my pageboy everything about the tales while they're still in my old, pruned brain." He hammered his gavel, and the court was dismissed.

One by one, the members of the court shuffled out of the hall, practically climbing over each other to get to their next affairs. Eric figured the excitement of such people was short, but he cared not, for he had the job. The eyes of the prince remained on him. As Eric smiled back, he noticed that these were not the only eyes still locked upon him. Next to the prince were two other sets: the fire-filled dark ones of the king and the loving yet hollow set of the queen. Eric's emotions suddenly became mixed. His heart still soared at the thought of his victory, however, he could not help but worry if he'd indeed made life harder for his prince. For a moment, Eric's first step toward victory seemed awash with worry and filled with horrors. The long silence only fueled his worries. Then, the queen drew a fair breath.

"Your collection was quite lovely," she said with the noble affect that Eric had expected.

The king shot her his stern, bloodshot gaze. His fingernails dug into the armrests of his throne. He fixed his posture, attempting to be coy.

"You really think so, ma'am?" Eric asked respectfully.

"Of course, dear. I look forward to hearing more of your tales. I enjoy readings with my supper and my wine. You must get to work as soon as possible. Ti'Louien, why don't you show our scribe to a quiet place where he might do his work?"

Louis perked up in his chair. "It would be an honor, Mother. Scribe, I shall meet you in the corridor beyond the hall."

"As you wish, my prince," Eric said with a bow.

"Wonderful," said the queen. "Dear husband, join me in my chambers. I must pick out my mid-morning dress."

"Very well," Desmos agreed with a deep, tight tone.

Eric could hardly wait to be reunited with Louis in the hall, and Louis could not wait to be close to him. They both enjoyed the kinkiness of their shared secret as they shuffled out to the corridor.

When they were reunited, the prince ran to his scribe. He stopped himself just short of meeting the man in a full embrace. "We did it!" he whispered with excitement.

"We certainly did." Eric beamed. "I'm so happy, I could kiss you."

"Sir," Louis began, taking on a tone of jest, "I've only just learned your name. What kind of prince do you think I am? Besides…" Louis brushed a hand against one of Eric's, "there will be plenty of time for that."

A moment of unspoken heat passed between them through a glance alone. It was the sort of passion Eric had only ever read of in stories, and *never* in those tales was it between two men such as they. But Eric didn't care. For all he knew, they were the only men in the world capable of such lust, but in his heart, he knew that if they could truly feel lust so deeply, so soon, it was impossible that they were alone…

****

King Desmos furiously followed Queen Krystal to their bedchamber, passing far too many members of the court for him to say what he wanted. Not just for the sake of keeping face, either, for the king and queen had a dark secret that not even Louis could imagine. When they finally arrived in their quarters, Desmos closed and latched the door behind them.

"*What* was that?" he barked.

"Oh, don't get your knickers twisted," said Krystal. But this was not the kind, regal voice the kingdom knew. This voice was raspy and strange. Krystal waved a hand, and, in a puff of smoke, she was transformed into a strange and haunting woman. She was of medium height, with curly, blood red hair. Her eyes were lavender, her features sharp and painted with a plethora of strange, inked markings. Her chest was busty in her old, black clothes. Indeed, this woman was not at all Krystal, but a legend long thought dead, lost, or captured. Parents would tell stories of her to frighten their children into behaving. Sometimes they called her a witch, other times a demoness. The older stories claimed she was a fallen, who lured children to her hellish lair in the dark forest with a trail of breadcrumbs, so that she could feast on their flesh. Drunken, unrespectable men would claim to see her in the streets, luring them with her hefty chest and sharp cheek bones. If any men went missing after one such night, his drinking mates would claim that they fell victim to the banshees of Belle Terre. It mattered not how the tales varied, she was a primal fear that all had, whether they believed she existed or not, for the legend of the Celtic Witch struck fear into the hearts of all who lived in the kingdom.

"Don't you know by now that everything I do is part of the plan?" she said with command to the king. Sauntering over to her mirror, she looked over herself before waving a hand and conjuring an image within the reflector. A swirl of sparkling black smoke filled the glass. When it cleared, a manifestation of the prince and the scribe filled the mirror. The king squinted as he tried to make out what was reflected before him. It did not take long for him to recognize the location which his stepson had taken the scribe to work, for they were back in Ti'Louien's bedroom.

"I don't think this is what your mother meant when she told you to find me a place to work," Eric said, looking around the barren room to which he'd just returned.

"Oh, I honestly no longer care what she thinks," Louis said with a wave. "Ever since she left—I don't know her. She's *far* too infatuated by my stepfather to care *at all* about me."

A somberness appeared in Louis' eyes. In the weeks since his mother's return, he'd tried his best not to think about how alone he felt without her. However, it was moments such as these, the sadness he'd been avoiding would pour into his heart like the rushing waters of Pecker Bay.

Eric could see how much his prince hurt. He wondered how appropriate it would be for him to sit next to Louis on the bed. Never one to make bold moves, he hovered for a moment, however, standing over the prince, Eric realized that even the top of his *head* looked sad with the slumped shoulders below. Thus, he sat and placed a hand upon one of the prince's. "I'm sorry you've been so alone."

Louis shifted his downward eyes from the bedspread to his once lonely hand that now had company. "Well, I suppose I'm not so alone anymore." Louis brought his eyes to Eric's and put his free hand atop the pile.

Eric's stomach filled with wonderful, youthful nerves. He'd never truly felt anything like this before, not even when he imagined moments such as these. He looked up at Louis, whose gaze was devoted fully, and *lustfully* to him. Slowly, Louis puckered his lips and began to lean in. Suddenly, Eric was nervous, and his underarms began to sweat.

"Don't—don't you think we should wait a bit?" Eric nervously cracked.

Louis gave a breathy chuckle. "Why?"

Eric smiled greatly, exposing every tooth behind his small, pink lips. With great reassurance and nerve-wracking thrill in his heart, he leaned in and kissed the lips of his prince. It was a kiss so beautiful, so passionate, so wet, so wonderful that Eric immediately wanted more. He embraced the back of Louis' neck and pulled him in closer. Louis returned the grasp with a hand behind either shoulder, slipping his tongue inside the mouth of his scribe, and still it was not enough, for they pulled each other in even closer, and breathlessly melted into each other's passion.

It was a beautiful moment not enjoyed by all, however, for the wicked King Desmos watched from the mirror with disdain and a brewing plan. The witch wiped the image, revealing the fuming king's reflection. His eyes were blood red, and his nostrils flared. He had his suspicions, but seeing them confirmed infuriated him more greatly than he'd ever been before. It was true he was never fond of his stepson, but now he'd committed what the king considered the most wicked of sins, and he was not going to let it go at all.

The witch watched with concern and wonder. She too had never seen the king so angry. "My king, you look volatile," she observed.

"The only thing volatile under the roof of this castle are the acts of my stepson," he said with his voice a near beastly growl.

"What shall we do?"

The king thought for a moment. "The scribe never wants to lose him, does he? Well...then that's exactly what he'll do."

****

That ends Part One of The Prince and the Scribe. *If you've made it this far, you're a decent amount in and I don't see you quitting, but if you're folding now, thanks for coming along for the ride and thanks for the ten-cent royalty. I really enjoy this first part, but the next three get wonderfully wild. Unhinged almost. And that's the kind of camp I love.*

Part Two

Chapter Seven

"The Evil King and His Son"
Published in The Scribe's Collection *as "The Evil Queen and Her Daughter."*

This was one that I just had to roll my eyes at. I was able to get my hands on a decent amount of the original chapter, but you wouldn't believe what it had become in publication. They combined the characters of the Celtic Witch and King Desmos, making the witch a queen and— typical of literature's treatment of powerful women— turned the queen into your typical "I cursed a baby because I wasn't invited to the rave," or "My spawn is prettier than me, and I'm gonna make her choke on some fruit" archetype. I guess you can call this a slight spoiler alert, but the Celtic Witch has way more nuance to her than that. You're just going to have to trust me there. Anyway, rant over. Here's Part Two of the book.

****

The king paced his room all night long, scheming with wicked joy, trying to find the perfect way to destroy his stepson and the newly employed scribe. The Celtic Witch sat up in bed, with her bosoms strapped freely in her favorite leather night ware.

"Are you ever coming to bed?" she asked with annoyance, his pacing on their cobbled floor keeping her awake.

"Not until we have a plan," the king barked.

"Oh, would you stop and rest for the night? I need my beauty sleep. I'm over four hundred years old and don't look a day over twenty-seven. That doesn't happen without work."

"Some things are more important than you," proclaimed the king.

She sighed, knowing that she would never be able to sleep until her insolent lover had a plan in place. "Very well," she agreed begrudgingly. She flung the covers from her body and climbed out of bed. With a wave of her hand, she was transformed out of her sensual nightwear into one of her tight, but practical conjuring dresses. Her make up was harsh and flared, her hair now pulled high on her head in a flowing ponytail.

"What's with the theatrics?" the king asked with irritation.

"You don't expect me to cast a spell without my icon looks, do you? Don't be *daft*."

"What spell?"

"It's a good thing you're handsome." She sighed with a snide roll of her eyes. She stomped her left foot with flare, magically transporting the two to the lair she'd set up below the palace when she began her affair with the king.

"You know I don't like coming in here with all this witchcraft," remarked the king.

"Stop your whining. You must be mindless not to see that the scribe is the perfect way to finally execute our plan to take over this wasteland of a kingdom fully."

"*How* can that little flake help us?"

"The prince is clearly infatuated with the young man. Who wouldn't he be? For a peasant, he's quite beautiful. Those blue-brown eyes that look green and that messy brown hair. Enough to make anyone fall to their—" she noticed the king's disapproving glare, "Well, you get the idea. And the prince has needed someone to believe in ever since he was disappointed by the return of 'mommy dearest.' Thus, our scribe is the perfect pawn. I'll cast a spell that creates an unbreakable prison for, what's his name? Eric? Let the prince go after him. Alone, there's no way he'll be able to get past my dark magic boobytraps. That takes care of our prince problem. You can play the grieving stepfather and with my performance as the queen, I'll hand over the kingdom to you."

"I see," agreed the king. "What of the *real* Krystal?"

"Well, then, then it's time to finish her off finally. Her body will be found, the apparent suicide of the already unstable queen."

King Desmos smiled wickedly. "This," he said, grasping one of the witch's buttocks, "is why I love you."

She laughed with a spine-chilling maniacalness. "Shall we begin, then?"

****

The spell would take at least three days to concoct. The Celtic Witch traveled deep into the dark forest, diving so far in that she reached levels of darkness that not even the bravest of wildlife would dare tread. Protected by her magic, she ensured the king that there was no way the prince would be able to survive the journey, and even if he did, she promised her magic would keep him far from finding the scribe. She cast a spell on the very spot where she planned to imprison Eric. Now, all they had to do was wait for the perfect time to enact their curse. Luckily for the villains, the opportunity to do so presented itself before long…

****

I'm going to make a few cuts here. This chapter gets a little wordy. I figure if I have to rewrite whole chapters, I can at least take the liberty of improving what—to put it bluntly—sucks. What you need to know is that, after a bunch of events that don't lead to anything, Louis convinces the royal court to throw a ball in honor of "The return of the arts to the palace." But it was really just an excuse for him to celebrate and ogle over Eric. Long story short, the Celtic Witch and King Dickhead decide to cast their spell on Eric when he goes to bed that night. I think that's a pretty decent "previously on." Now, here's this week's story...

****

Eric had butterflies in his heart and nerves in his stomach. He'd never been to anything so refined or so proper as a royal ball. In fact, he never enjoyed the idea of attending one. But Louis had assured him that it would be a night which he'd never forget. He had split his time between home and the castle so much that he felt as though he already lived in the palace, though he never brought more than his garment for the day's work with him. He hoped what he decided to don for the evening would be appropriate. As he stared at his reflection, adjusting his clothes, he was shaking like a leaf. Sure, the reading he prepared was fine and he'd grown ever closer with the prince, but still, fear of ruining the blossoming romance caused his mind to race and his most private areas to sweat. He was thankful that his mother gave him some of her "secret potpourri" to mask the smell.

There came three sharp knocks on the door, which he recognized as those of his prince. "Come in," he called.

Louis entered looking more beautiful and more regal than Eric had ever seen before. Immediately, Eric felt his suspicions confirmed. "You look Heaven sent." He gasped with amazement.

"Oh, thank you, darling," accepted Louis with grace. "I don't have much say on what I wear to these things. But I'm glad you like it."

"I-I love it. Sorry I'm so underwhelming and underdressed."

Louis looked him over. "Don't be silly! You're dressed as you and that's all that matters to me."

Eric was certain that was meant to be a compliment, but his anxiety filled gut told him otherwise.

"I should like to prepare you," the prince continued, "this will likely go late. It'll be hard to look at all the couples and not be able to celebrate our love as they do theirs. I may even have to dance with a maiden or two, but it means nothing. Just the duties of a royal. Oh, how I loathe being prince sometimes."

"I understand." Eric nodded. "I'm under no illusions about the kingdom of Belle Terre and how it sees us."

"When I'm king, it'll be so different. Provided my stepfather ever goes to the Underworld where he belongs."

"Louis!"

"Oh, forgive me my sweet. He just makes me so angry."

"I know. But don't stoop to a level as low as his. We have each other at least, and he can't take that away from us."

Louis smiled at his scribe. "I don't know what I did right to have you come into my life. Oh, how I wish I could dance with you tonight or at least hold your hand in mine."

"Well, how about this?" Eric said with a smile. "When we're missing or when we can't be close, I'll hold my hands behind my back, and you hold yours as well, and it'll be as if we're together."

"Oh, gods, how corny!"

"You don't like it?"

"I do. But it *is* corny."

"But you'll do it?"

"Of course, I will." The prince kissed his scribe and left him to finish preparing for the evening's festivities. In that moment, his anxieties melted away and he was certain that, if he lived a thousand years, he'd never find a better match for him than the prince that the kingdom called deplorable. In his heart, he knew they'd last for the rest of their lives.

He took one more look in the mirror. His curls were tightly wound, his garments free of wrinkles. From the nearby end table, the scribe picked up his parchment. There was no further preparation he could employ to delay his entrance. Thus, he gave his reflection a smile, hoping tonight would prove a special one for him and the prince.

What he did not know was what lurked on the other side of the reflection. The plotting eyes of the king and the false queen watched, each with their own agenda of sorts, each agenda filled with something awful for the lovers.

Chapter Eight

"The Scribe's Ball"
Published in The Scribe's Collection *as "The Peasant and the Princess."*

The trumpeters were ready, the dinner placements set. There was no avoiding it, Eric would have to face the whole of the kingdom's nobility now. Louis had gone over the detailed schedule for the evening several times, and yet he was still terrified that he'd ruin it for all. The evening would begin with dinner. Members of the court would be seated first, followed by the royal family. Then, a special guest of honor fanfare would play, and the scribe would be introduced. He was not to be seated presently, though. That royal family would lead the court and other invited attendees to sit, after which Eric would read his latest composition.

He'd worked day and night on the piece, using the tools he'd had left from the Violet Sprite, in hopes that *this* would be his greatest piece. While he loved it dearly, it was not perfect to him and after weeks of rewriting, the night was here, and it was as good as it was ever going to get. He stood behind the great doors that led to the dining hall, his parchments tucked firmly under his forearm. He could hear the muffled announcements of the nobles. Then, before he knew it, came the trumpets for the royal family. It was comforting to know that his prince would be waiting for him in the great hall, but it meant that the next trumpet would signal his entrance.

Without much time at all, it came, and the doors opened. The hall was lit by elegant candelabras and a stunning chandelier. He did not know what he expected upon his entrance: applause, mutters, sound of some sort. However, there was nothing but cold, staring silence. He recognized plenty of members of the court who'd been present at his hiring, and though they had respected his work once they'd heard him read, he did not expect anything more than proper blinking from them. However, it was the cold stares of the jewel encrusted nobles from the extended royal family and neighboring kingdoms that made him nervous. He'd already proven himself to the highest court in his land and it was not an easy task. Should they not approve of his work, or should any of them suspect its true meaning, it could end his career and his romance with the prince. The last weeks had been so wonderful, he promised himself this would not be the case. It was far too great a risk, thus he strode into the dining room with pride.

He stood proudly on his mark. As he removed his parchment from beneath his arm, he worried that his audience would notice the sweat on the pit of his tunic. However, he knew the best way to get through the stain unnoticed was to proceed with assurance:

"What I Knew.

I was young and alone and to me, that was always just fine.

Never knew what I was missing until the day your glance met mine.

Young and bold and dumb,

I knew one thing was for sure,

Holding you so tight was a magic I needed forever

more.

And I made it my quest, my destiny,
Forever I would hold you close to me.
It didn't matter if it took a day or an eternity,
Loving you was to be my life, bold and true.
Different lives didn't matter,
For that future was what I knew.
Sadness in your eyes was nothing I would ever wish
for you.
That day I saw them, there was just one thing for me
to do,
Saving you was something I just had to pursue.
That's what I knew.
It's what I wanted, it's what I knew.
Then came the day I went away.
I left to learn all I could,
From you, I was far away,
But, still, my heart would not stray.
The years at sea were nothing more than a test to me.
It mattered not where I went or who I met,
I knew I would get to love you yet.
And I will forever more,
We'll never part,
I know in my heart,
We will be forever.
We'll never let go.
That's what I know."

His reading was met with silence for a moment, yet he stood confidently. It may not have been the great work he'd been pursuing, but still he was proud. Suddenly, there came applause from a young princess from a neighboring kingdom. Her mother joined in the ovation, then her husband, and her father. Soon, three more groups in the regal audience applauded too. Finally came the approval of the whole room. It was rapturous, and true. It was a wonderful reassurance despite all the fear he'd felt that night. He looked over to his prince, who applauded with equal gusto, though his beaming face told Eric that he wanted to embrace him in celebration and place his tongue. Chills ran down Eric's spine as he watched his secret lover cheer. It was the love which he'd dreamed of for years, and though it may not have been a sentiment they'd spoken yet, all they had to do was look into the eyes of one another to know it was true. If Eric lived to be one hundred years old, he knew that there would be no greater feeling than the love he shared with his prince.

****

Supper was filled with noble conversation that Eric found baffling. The pomp, circumstance and routine that was a necessity was so bizarre to Eric. He knew he and his mother would have enjoyed a good laugh over the excess elegance had she been there. He felt bad she had not heard him recite for royalty; however, Louis made it clear that his stepfather would never allow it. Whilst his mother had made it clear she had no desire to step into the palace, claiming that too many members of the court who recognize her from the night, it was still a dream of his to take her with him for a reading, instead of reading his pieces to her before leaving for the day's work. With how the last few weeks had turned out and with how well the *evening* had gone, tonight, it did not seem impossible to him that there could be such a kingdom where his mother was invited into the palace to hear her son recite his work.

Eric sat close to Louis, his prince instructing him on

the proper manners to use and sharing whispered conversation. Each giggle in the ear or secretive smile that the two gave one another infuriated the king and he could not wait to execute the spell his lover had created. When supper was over, he shot to his feet eager to start the dance, for the sooner it began, the sooner the witch's work could be carried out. "Let the ball commence," announced he bombastically.

The guests immediately pushed back from the table. As they climbed from their chairs and adjusted their wares, the orchestra upstairs on the second level began with a lovely little melody. It built to a beating drum and then an exciting, brash melody broke out. The guests took to the center of the room, waltzing in circles with style and grace. It was a spectacular sight of flashing colors and opulent jewels as they swished around in unison. It was the first part of the traditional splendor that Eric truly enjoyed, his lips forming a childlike grin of joy.

Louis took notice of Eric's glee. He longed to join the crowd with Eric in his arms, leading the waltz for a while before Eric took charge, then he again. Though this was impossible, he was not about to miss his chance to spend a romantic evening with his lover. He placed his left hand behind his back and held his right. Nudging Eric with his elbow, he asked, "Would you like me to show you around the festivities?"

Eric immediately saw Louis' hands go behind his back. With a smile, he too held his own hands. "I would love that," he agreed with a nod.

The two made way for the dance floor, much to the anger of King Desmos. He watched them like a hawk as they made their way through the crowd and around the dance floor. He took notice of how they both stood clasping their own hands and was certain it was some sort of vile secret that unholy men such as they kept. He *had* to break up their flirting before the disgusting display became more sickening.

The couple had made their way up the stairs to the orchestra's level. Eric admired the way they played, and Louis admired watching Eric become lost in the music. Louis was well aware of how he'd allowed himself to slip into prickliness over the many years that had passed since his adolescence, but in this moment, he saw a future beyond being so cold and uncaring. He began to imagine a kingdom where he *could* dance arm in arm with Eric, where he didn't have to be so defensive about his heart, where his passions were not so odd, and where the pursuit of harmony would guide the decisions the kingdom made instead of perceived perfection. And for the first time, he realized that embracing his royal duties instead of rejecting them may be key to a happier future for not just he and his scribe, but for his Belle Terre and its people.

A voice, deep and cold, tore him from the dream. "You're to dance with the Princess of Kinsley."

Louis and Eric both turned to see King Desmos standing incredibly close to them, his stance condescending, and his eyes purposeful.

"Must I?" complained Louis. "She's never liked me."

"And it's the fault of you that she doesn't," replied the king. "You *will* dance with her."

Louis turned disappointed eyes to Eric, who smiled and gave him an understanding nod. He watched as his prince made his way down the stairs; his hands clasped ever tighter in themselves. Behind his back, Eric echoed the strength with his own. The king was growing ever more displeased with the scribe. Now, alone with his victim, the beast decided to strike.

"How are you enjoying the evening?" King Desmos asked.

Eric's attention shifted to the king with a light jolt, for the king had never spoken to him directly, nor did he ever expect him to do so with small talk, let alone any form of kindness. "Oh…" he began. "It's—it's lovely."

"Strange to you, I'm sure. You know, I once felt that way too, coming from my humble beginnings. It can be very arousing in many ways, but you get used to it after a number of them. They may even become *boring* when you've been to enough of them."

"Oh no," Eric said with a grin, looking down upon the waltz. He spotted his prince dancing so elegantly and so proper. "I could watch this forever."

The king needn't follow his eyeline to know what it was that had the scribe so enchanted. It made his scheming all the more pressing. "Well, I'm glad you're enjoying it so. But please take it from an old king who's been in your shoes. You'll need rest. Why don't you stay here in the palace tonight?"

Eric was flabbergasted. Never in all the weeks he'd been the Royal Scribe did he expect such an invitation from the king. His mind raced and the sweat beneath his arms returned. "What?" he asked with flabbergast. "What I mean is—are you sure, Your Majesty?"

"Of course, I'm sure. I'll have my man prepare a room for you."

"Oh, I'm sure that's not necessary. I'm certain the prince wouldn't mind my sleeping on the floor of his room."

The king took pause, using the moment to recompose himself, for the anger he felt building was great. "Sharing the prince's room? Well, don't be silly. I won't hear of it. Allow me the—honor."

Eric could sense a strange shift in the king's demeanor. However, be it out of hopefulness or naïve thoughtfulness, he chose to give the monarch the benefit of the doubt. "That's very kind, your excellency."

"Isn't it? Well, excuse me. I'll see they start preparing your room."

King Desmos left a stunned Eric alone. There was a gnawing feeling in his gut that he could not identify: nerves, awkwardness, or even *fear*. He knew not what it was, but decided it did not matter, for tonight, he'd sleep under the same roof as his prince. He looked down upon Louis lovingly but was met with a concerning sight. The princess with whom he waltzed stomped a foot and stormed away. Louis just shook his head and turned to leave the dance floor.

On the stairs, Louis came face to face with his stepfather. Their exchange was clearly less pleasant than the one Eric had shared with him. He watched his beloved intently. Finally, the exchange ended, and Louis made his way over to Eric.

"It looks as though you've had an interesting half hour," observed Eric.

Louis smirked and shook his head. "I've never liked her, nor she me. But her kingdom has always been after a marriage arrangement between us. She was expecting a proposal of all things." Louis laughed.

"She seems desperate." Eric chortled at the preposterousness of the princess' dramatics.

"She told me that if there was to be no proposal, then she had no desire to dance with the Deplorable Prince."

"Oh, Heavens," Eric continued to laugh.

"I told her she smelt of fish and delusion."

"Louis!"

"I couldn't help it. Besides, the fish part was true."

"What about you and your stepfather?"

"Oh, him." Louis groaned with a roll of his eyes. "You know how he can be. He asked why the princess was so upset, which became him questioning why I couldn't woo a lady. It matters not. He is, pardon my language, one vile ass."

"Maybe not always."

"What do you mean?"

"I think, perhaps he's coming around. He invited me to stay in the palace for the night."

"He did what?"

"He's having a room prepared for me now. It was surprising. Even a little uncomfortable. He said he remembered what it was like when he was in my position. It seemed like he just wanted to make me feel a little less alone."

"I don't trust it. He's up to something."

"Don't be suspicious. Maybe he's not as against people like us as we thought."

"You're being drawn in by his lies. Don't let a flashy promise distract you from who he really is deep down. Too many in this kingdom fall for his fallacious vows and promises to make the kingdom better, when all he's doing is chipping away at what makes Belle Terre wonderful to begin with…"

Eric gave his lover an inquisitive look, for he'd never known him to speak highly of the kingdom before.

"What?"

"*The people*," Louis said with a matter-of-fact tone. "It's always been the people. Everyone who does their best to contribute to the lives of others, those who awake and with the intention of being their best self. But to my stepfather, the best self is something *he* should determine. And if you're not one he approves of, he'll do everything in his power to rid you and your way of life from Belle Terre's gates."

It was a haunting concept, one that gave Eric chills. Deep down, he knew that despite the apparent kindness King Desmos showed him, Louis was right, and it made Eric wonder what the king was truly planning. The orchestra reached the crescendo of their score, bringing Eric out of his icy trance. "Well, there's one good thing about his scheming," he said, clasping his hands together behind his back. "I'm here for the night."

Louis grinned, for he could not argue that the thought brought him great joy. Over the next few hours, he was forced to dance with many more equally unwilling maidens, all the while, his eyes meeting his beloved, who watched with folded hands.

Chapter Nine

"The Boy in the Tower"
Published in The Scribe's Collection *as "The Boy in the Tower with the Long Hair."*

This chapter—this chapter was done dirty by The Scribe's Collection. *It was gutted, pulled, and torn like a twink at Pride, except no one had a good time. It's a shame; this is where the adventure really begins, and yet, the original publisher turned it into a weird watered down "Rapunzel." It basically became a story about a little boy who was stolen from his family by a witch, put in a tower, his hair grew to an unmasculine length until a random nobleman saved him and was rewarded with the marriage to the kingdom's princess. The boy gets a haircut, then falls out of the story. The whole thing reads as a celebration of crotch grabbing manhood. I get why the chapter would draw comparisons to "Rapunzel," but this was a choice.*

****

It was midnight before the last guests were gone. For all the things Eric and Louis had said about the Kingdom of Belle Terre that evening, they could not deny that the realm knew how to throw a party. They waited at the upstairs banister, watching the servants clean below.

"What a night it was," acknowledged an exhausted Eric.

"Did you enjoy it?" asked Louis.

"Oh, yes," Eric replied with a dreamy tone, followed by a yawn. "Even more than I thought I would."

"I'm glad it was so perfect."

"Well, it wasn't quite perfect." Eric said, placing a hand upon the banister across from Louis'. "There's something that would have made it so."

Louis turned a beam to Eric as the two inched their hands closely. For a moment, it seemed as though their clasps would finally meet after the long night, but their hopes were short lived.

"Your quarters are ready," declared a voice from behind.

Immediately, they recognized the deep call of King Desmos. However, absent was his normal gruffness. It was a great surprise to Louis, who'd come to think his stepfather was incapable of any tone other than gruffness.

"Thank you, Your Majesty," replied Eric with a bow.

"Winston will show you the way and see that you're comfortable," the king proclaimed, as he motioned to the elderly butler.

Eric nodded to Winston. Then, turned to Louis. "Thank you for a most wonderful evening, my prince." He bowed, as he secretly longed to take his prince in his arms and give him a sweet kiss goodnight. He'd once again have to settle for clasping his own hands behind his back as Louis followed suit.

The scribe followed Winston down the hall, leaving the prince alone with his stepfather.

There was a long, awkward silence between the two, until the king finally broke it. "Did you dance with many maidens?"

"As many as I could," Louis replied with defense. "I probably could have fit in more if I wasn't busy trying to figure out what it is you're planning."

King Desmos inhaled as he clenched his fists. "I don't know what you mean," the king replied with constraint.

"I think you do. In fact, I *know* you do. And whatever that plan *is,* if it brings any harm to Eric, I will bring you down."

"You don't sound well, my son. But you have my word: *I* will not harm a hair on the head of our dear Eric."

There was something in his smile and his stern walk that sent chills down the spine of Louis. But, it mattered not, for Louis promised himself that he would protect Eric at all costs.

****

Eric had never seen quarters with such frivolity. The large bed covered with silk blankets over a blood red carpet exquisitely matched the drapes over the windows. A mahogany vanity with gold leafing sat across the room beneath an ornate mirror. It was a far cry from his loft, and, sadly, somehow, a further cry from the room of Louis. He wondered why he was given these quarters so kindly, while his prince slept in a baron, depressed room. As he removed his tunic and flopped on to the comfortable bed, he wished he could invite the prince to lie next to him. It was a wish that found its way into his dreams and brought a smile to his lips, even as he slept.

He'd been asleep only an hour when the Celtic Witch appeared outside his window. Before entering the room, she said an incantation to ensure he would not wake while she practiced her spell. She climbed through the window, and landed on all fours, as though she were a creature of the night. Standing with poise, she approached the bed, but tripped on the gaudy rug and fell with a "Shite!" She landed face first into sleeping Eric's chest. With a wave of her hand, the rug disintegrated into ash. "Fecking carpet!"

After a moment of recomposing herself, the witch turned to her victim. Between her bosoms, she carried the vile filled with the spell. Producing the concoction and popping its top, she began to chant in Gaelic. She poured the mixture over the length of Eric's body four times.

After the last pass, she jumped back so as not to be swept up by the spell. A whirlwind of smoke surrounded the scribe, growing stronger and denser as it swished. Then, in a sweeping vortex, the scribe was gone from his bed.

****

The morning was uncomfortably still. Eric was only just drifting into awareness, yet, still, he knew something was wrong. The bed felt hard as stone, the room icy cold. Though morning rays danced across his eyelids, there was no chirping of birds, no croaking of frogs. As Eric returned to consciousness, he realized that he was not where he'd gone to sleep at all. He opened his eyes and flung to a seated position. The new surroundings were stony and strange: a round room, built unevenly from the floor to the walls. One single, small window allowed for the minuscule light he'd seen in his waking form. He'd gone to bed nearly nude, only his undergarment on, but now, he was dressed in a scratchy, hefty burlap tunic. Lost, confused, and scared, the only thing he could think to do was to figure out his new surroundings.

Puzzlingly, there were no doors or stairs, thus he

rushed to the window. For a moment, the confusion continued, for he was met only with sky and treetops. He stuck as much of his thin face through the window as he could to get more of a gander at what lay below him.

He was at least two hundred feet off the ground. His prison was supported by a gnarled, thin tower. Below was a clearing in the center of the forest, covered in dead, brown grass. Across it, moved a figure all dressed in black. It traveled with an unearthly slowness, passing back and forth. It did not seem to stride, but float with a haunting weightlessness. It stopped and slowly turned its head up toward Eric. Though it was far below him, Eric could see there was something peculiar about its face. It was sickly pale and seemed to have no expression whatsoever. As its grimace sent chills down Eric's spine, its form dissipated.

Eric continued to watch, as the mist it left behind vanished. He hoped the strange apparition was gone. He'd heard legends of spirits, both human and unholy, lurking in the dark woods before, wreaking havoc at the behest of witches and warlocks.

There came a spine chilling, low growl from behind. Eric jolted. His heart palpitated; his breathing grew heavy. Though he was terrified of the truth, he slowly turned to face the monstrous sound. His fears were confirmed, for in the shadows stood the creature. Its yellow, decomposing eyes were piercingly on Eric, as the creature huffed through its skeletal nose.

All of Eric quaked from his lips to his bare feet. He wanted not to speak to it, in fear of what it would do, but then, legends of such spirits claimed that they would carry out their evil deeds, regardless. He mustered a brave breath and tried to speak. "Wh—who are you?"

The creature opened its mouth slowly. Its voice seemed to travel from somewhere beyond its body, building quietly from a distance before it arrived, allowing the ghoul to form its words. "...I am but a servant to the master. I was called to this realm to ensure you never leave..."

"C-called?"

"...From the Underworld..."

Eric's heart now felt chilled. "Where are we?"

"...A prison built just for you..."

"Why me? Why here?"

"...I know not that. All you need to know is that you will never leave..."

Eric shook his head. "You're wrong," he said sharply, finding his bravery. "I have my mother, my lover. They'll come looking for me."

"...But, they will never find you. And even if they did. *I must destroy them...*"

With that last chilling statement, the apparition vanished.

Eric looked down out the window, and there it was, looking back up at him, before it returned to its pacing. Eric had never been more frightened in his life. He realized that there was indeed a great chance he'd never be found. However, he refused to let his terror show. He paced away from the window, and sat against the far, cold wall. He wished he had his parchment and pen. Perhaps he'd be able to send a distress note on the foot of a pigeon, or at least pass the time. Suddenly, inspiration struck. He sat up straight, his eyes wide and his jaw dropped. He wanted not to think the idea too loud, for he did not know if the creature could read minds. However, it might be his saving grace. He stood to his feet and began to plan. He didn't know if it would work, but he had to try. He closed his eyes and with bated breath, called out to an old friend.

****

Louis had awoken before first light and readied himself to perfection. He was eager to see Eric and hoped to spend a quiet day together now that the ball was over. When dawn came, Louis decided to ensure Eric had a proper breakfast to which to wake up. The Royal Chef Arnaud was always in the kitchen before the sun, so he knew there would be time to prepare something *spectacular* for his love. When it was ready, Louis let himself into Eric's room, beaming with a boyish charm. The excitement was soon gone, however, for the prince found an empty bed and the lavish rug gone. Louis felt a chill, for it was obvious that something horrific had happened.

He dropped the tray to the floor and rushed to the opposite end of the hall to the chamber of his mother and stepfather. He listened for the vile, irritating giggles and moans that often haunted his nightmares coming from behind their door. It was rarely silent, thus he knocked on the door feverishly.

King Desmos shifted in bed with a grumpy grumble. The Celtic Witch, exhausted from her long night before, did not stir for a moment. The knocking continued. "Hello?" came the muffled voice of Louis. "Hello, wake up. It's important."

The king growled with anger and nudged the witch. "Wake up," he ordered. "Wake up!"

She yawned with a nearly depressed level of fatigue. "Tell him to go away," she whined.

"Oh, shut up. Don't you remember what we did last

night? We *must* deter him. So wake up and change your form."

"*Al—right!*" she barked back, sitting up ferociously. "But don't expect to ogle my cruiscínís today." With an obligated and irritated shoop, she quickly transformed into Queen Krystal. She took a deep breath and called: "Come in, dear."

The door flew open, and Louis rushed in. "Mother, something terrible has happened," began he. "We *must* help Eric."

"What?" King Desmos said without pleasantry. "No 'good morning?' I'm starting to see why they call you the Deplorable Prince."

"I have no time for this, Stepfather. Something has happened to Eric, and we must *save* him."

"My dear," cooed the false Queen Krystal. "What do you mean? Surely nothing could have happened to him within the walls of our palace."

"That's just it, Mother. He's not *in* the palace. He's gone. His bed was empty and unmade, and, for some reason, the rug was gone."

"I knew it!" shouted the king. "He's not missing at all. He's likely a flighty criminal. He sought employment here, just to take our most expensive rug to sell." He shot the disguised witch a quick, irate glance to insinuate his curiosity about the rug. She shot him an equally irate glance that warned him not to push her, lest there be unpleasant consequences.

"He's *not* a criminal!" Louis argued. "He's been taken, I know it!"

"Taken? Don't be ridiculous, Ti'Louien," the king replied with a tone of judgment. "Who would want to take one so common as our scribe?

"Well, what else could it—" Louis' babbling stopped. Suddenly, his stepfather's doubt began to put it all together: Why he'd offer Eric a room in the palace for the night, why he'd been so gentle to the scribe, perhaps why he even agreed to the ball in the first place. Louis did not know how, but his stepfather was responsible. His mind raced with terror and fury. "You..." he muttered.

"*What?*"

Louis was quick to conceal his worry. "Nothing," he replied plainly. "Nothing—yet."

The prince returned to the chambers from which Eric had been taken. He paced the room, diligently looking for some sort of clue. He rummaged through the bed, the windows, the wardrobe. *Determined*, he searched every nook and cranny. Yet, he still came up short. He sat on the bed with nervous defeat. As he shuffled his feet with frustration, something scraped below them. He leaned forward and was met with some sort of sandy pile. He fell to his knees and looked under the bed to find a mess of ash. Amidst it was an unburned tassel from the rug. It was confusing, and he knew not what exactly it meant, but he *knew* it had something to do with Eric's disappearance. There was no way his stepfather was going to help; he would have to ask the queen. Louis only hoped she was not too far gone to assist him.

He brought the tassel to his false mother, who turned it over in her hand as he explained what he found and his hunch. "Don't you see, Mother? Something *did* happen to Eric. And if this ash is any sort of indication, time is of the essence."

"Darling, even if something *did* happen to him, we

have no idea how to find him or what we're up against. How do you think we'll be able to find him and save him?"

"With our army, of course. By land and sea, we'll begin our search, and together, we'll find him."

The false queen stood silent for a moment, then shook her head. "My sweet boy, it's blind optimism you have. Besides, your stepfather would never approve it."

"What? Why does he get a say? It's our army, not his."

"But, of course, it is. It's the army of *all* of us. And, as the king, he *oversees* such affairs."

"Such affairs? What do you mean?"

"Oh, come now, Ti'Louien, really. You don't expect *me* to handle matters of war."

Louis stood silent, for he knew what this meant. He'd long suspected his mother would fall for his stepfather's tricks and turn over control of the kingdom's powers to him, but now that his gnawing fears were a gnawing reality. "What happened to you?"

With that, Louis left the queen who was not in silence. On his own, he would not waste any more time on those who stood in his way.

****

Eric paced, hoping his call was heard. After an hour and a half, his feet grew weary. Defeated, he gently placed his forehead against the back wall, closed his eyes, and let out a discouraged sigh. Would Louis ever know what happened to him? Would the prince think Eric had abandoned him? Or would he move on with his life and find a new lover, perhaps a new scribe? Perhaps one who could write that perfect piece that seemed to evade Eric.

"Oh, feckin' hell," called a light, familiar accent. "I know you're a writer, but there's no reason to get dramatic on me now."

Eric spun the see the Violet Sprite leaning on the windowsill. "You came!" cried Eric.

"Well, don't be daft, of course I came," he said, hopping to his feet.

"I wasn't sure. I didn't know if you would hear me, or if you would break the rules once again."

"Now wait just a tit. Am I not all-powerful and whatnot? *Of course,* I heard you. And as for breaking the rules, I *make* the rules. I just keep up all that hocus pocus for clout. Besides, what kind of 'good sprite' would I be to let you suffer?"

Eric smiled. He knew that he was special to the Violet Sprite, and despite his tempered explanation, he cared very deeply.

The Violet Sprite made way toward the window and looked down at the undead guard below. "Who's the barrel of laughs down there?"

"He's the guard."

"Oh, to do better than that if they want to keep you in here."

"I don't know. If anyone tries to save me, he threatened to kill them."

"Pfft. Whoever put you in here obviously didn't know you had a fare folk friend. My magic is pure, his isn't. I can whop him in two minutes, *tops…* Who *did* put you in here?"

"I don't know. I have my suspicions about the king. He invited me to stay in the palace after the ball last night. Next thing I knew, I woke up here."

"Yes, he is a bit of a twat."

"But he doesn't have magic. And this is *clearly* a magical prison."

"*Clearly*. Well, how about this? I'll go do some exploring and see if I can't figure out who might have done it. Here," he waved his wand and a small piece of parchment appeared with a simple pen, "write to your loved ones. They'll want to know you're all right and I'll fetch them for you."

Eric's mind immediately went to Louis and his mother. Though he knew not where he was, he detailed his location as best he could. He finished the letter with heartfelt declarations of love for both and wishes to see them soon. He wondered if he *would* see them soon or if he was doomed to remain in the tower for the rest of his ever-limiting days. It was a harrowing thought, and as the emotion within him built, he felt tears rushing toward his eyes. However, before they could wash down his cheeks, the sprite returned.

He flew through the window in his minuscule form to avoid being caught by the guarding demon. Once through the window, he landed in his full shape. "Phew." He exhaled. "That wore me out. There are better ways to tire me and work my glutes at the same time."

"What are you talking about?"

"Never mind. I flew the length of the forest, and you'll never believe it. The person who put you in here used a barrier spell. It's an old incantation that prevents anyone who doesn't know how to break the spell from being able to get here."

"So...so you're saying I really *am* stuck here?"

"Have you got mutton in your ears? I said anyone 'who *doesn't know the spell*.' I could de-spell this in my sleep. Or at least in bed with my legs—well, never mind.

Anyway, I have a feeling I know *exactly* who put you in here." His tone changed from his normal lightheartedness to one of knowing concern. "I just hope I'm wrong." The sprite recomposed himself and took the letter. He read over it and raised an eyebrow. "You sure do like your mum."

"We're close. What's wrong with that? And I see you've skipped over the loving words I wrote for Louis."

"No, I read them. Cute, but could have used some more spice. Don't tell me that dribble gets him in the sheets."

"No, we haven't yet—oh, why are we doing this? Shouldn't you be rallying my rescue?"

"Yes, yes. You're right about that." The sprite tucked the letter into his belt loop. "I'll be back as soon as I fetch them. Sit tight and stay out of the ghoul's way." The sprite spun with a flair, returned to his shrunken form and flew through the window.

Eric watched him go, and longed for rescued. As he looked down at his haunting guard, he felt doubt creep in. What if the spell wasn't unbeatable? *Worse*, what if such a rescue would put his loved ones in danger? Many more questions such as this rushed through his mind, causing great fear. But then, as he watched the sprite soar, he chose to have hope that his love would find him and that they would return to the Kingdom of Belle Terre, safe and together.

****

If you couldn't tell already, this chapter gets a little wordy. However, I can't really cut or edit it down, because this is when the tone for the rest of the book is set. Instead, I decided to split it into two. Think of it as "a very special episode."

Chapter Ten

"The Boy in the Tower (Part Deux)"

Louis roamed the streets of the kingdom in disguise. If he could not use the royal army, he was going to form his own. He was not sure how, though, for he approached the armorer, the architect, the blacksmith, the barber, the butcher, the baker, even the chandler. None wanted to join the Deplorable Prince on his quest. He wished he'd spent his formative years being more pleasant to Belle Terre's denizens, as he began to fear he would not have the means to find and rescue his love. Defeated, Louis trudged down an alley, and with a sigh, slid his back down a nearby wall, landing on his firm, fleshy bottom.

"My *Eric*," he cried to himself. "How will I ever find you?"

"You're not so easy to find yourself, you know that?" proclaimed a sharp, yet exhausted voice.

The prince turned his eyes up to see the Violet Sprite. Though he'd seen plenty of vibrant and peculiar dressing at many balls, he'd never seen a man wear a dress, but something about this just seemed so right to the prince. However, he did not focus on his style, for Louis' eyes were quickly drawn to the sprite's floating feet.

"You—you're *flying*!" Louis exclaimed.

"Actually, I'm hovering. But you understand the idea."

"Who are you? *What* are you?"

"My, my, you royals are bold as brass. If you must know, I'm a *sprite*. The Violet one to be specific."

"Aren't you supposed to have a whole bunch of rules for summoning?"

"Oh, I don't have the strength to go through this again. Listen, aren't you the least bit worried at *all* about Eric?"

"Eric?"

"Yes, you know, lots of curly hair. Blue-brown eyes that look green. A little thin, but, damn, he's just a sexual *beast*!"

"Yes, I know who he is! I love him."

"Well, enough questions. He's awaiting our rescue."

"Do you know where he is?

"Oh, yes. I know *exactly* where he is. I'll be taking you there. But we have another stop to make first."

"I don't want to stop *anywhere*! I want to go save my love."

"Well, we can't do that alone. You know that. Why else were you trying to gather an army? You may have clout, and I may have magic, and a *fantastic* bum, but that doesn't mean we won't need all the help we can get."

"Who do you suggest we take with us then? Because I've tried, and no one wants to help the Deplorable Prince."

"Ridiculously uncreative name but worry not. I know *exactly* who we're going to get. Someone who would *never* abandon him, even if it meant working alongside you." The sprite gave a playful glare that brought Louis comfort.

"All right," said Louis, as he stood with determination. "Let's go save my scribe."

****

The prince had not been by the sea since the first time he saw Eric. Outside of seeing his scribe, it was not a day filled with pleasant memories. There was an irony to his mission today that was not lost on him: Here he was, returning to the same land where he learned he was losing his mother, to retrieve the mother of the lover, whom he'd first seen here and lost less than three hours ago.

He felt strange on the journey. Louis had always thought that, when he came to meet Eric's mother, it would be by the scribe's side. An array of emotions, nerves, guilt, anxiety amongst them, filled his heart.

As he and the sprite looked upon Eric's hovel, Louis felt jealous. His home was many more times the size of this, yet the family he shared it with seemed lost and not his own. He'd trade it all to live in the crowded hovel with Eric, Ruth, and his mother, far away from the stepfather who'd ruined it all.

The door opened and out came a tall, middle-aged man. He stopped in the muddy ditch just outside the door and adjusted his pants.

"Oh, who's that?" asked Louis. "It can't be Eric's father. I know he's not around. Is he family?"

"I guess you could call him an uncle," remarked the sprite.

"His mother's brother?"

"I hope to the Heavens he's not."

As the man wiped his nose and released a healthy spit, Ruth came out behind him. She was wrapped in an old shawl that covered her bobbling bits. The man handed her a small bag of coins.

"Oh?" Louis asked curiously. "*Oh!*" he repeated,

finally understanding.

The man was then off, and Ruth shuffled back into her house.

"Well, I suppose we should break the news to her." Louis sighed.

The two made way for the door. Once they arrived, Louis raised a nervous fist. It hovered for a moment, shaking from both pressure and nerves.

"What are you waiting for?" asked the sprite. "You afraid to see her knockers?"

"No! It's just—it's my fault her boy's missing."

"Oh, none of that. I can't abide the dramatics."

The Violet Sprite pushed past the prince and banged on the door.

"If you're not my Eric, I'm closed for the day!" Ruth called from behind the door.

"We're not Eric, but our business isn't with bosoms," the sprite returned. "It's serious, and it's *about* Eric."

Without hesitation, she threw the door open. Still in her corset and straps, Louis felt his cheeks blush.

"Well?" she asked with urgency. "What *about* my boy?" In her nervousness, she didn't notice the Violet Sprite, but once she did, her jaw dropped, and she knew that this was indeed a most serious matter.

"Ma'am," began Louis, "I'm sorry this is how we're meeting, but I have reason to believe that our boy…was taken.

"*Our* boy? Just who the hell are you?"

It was then that Louis realized he was still wearing his cloak. He removed the hood to reveal his face to her. Her jaw was now twice as agape, and she shivered.

"My gods," Ruth respired.

"May we come in?" asked the prince.

Still in shock, Ruth could not form further words and thus, only gestured to invite them in. Louis told her of the ball and his suspicions when it came to his stepfather's invitation, how his room was empty and how the king refused to offer any help. The Violet Sprite then took over the story, filling in the two about his visit with Eric in the tower, the ghoul that guarded it, how it was protected by a spell. It was an intense whirlwind of information for Ruth.

"How—how did this all happen?" she asked, struggling to form the words. "What I mean is, the king doesn't have magic, *does he*? How could he have concocted such a spell?"

"I've been wondering that myself," Louis agreed. "My stepfather may be many things, but magical isn't one of them."

Both the prince and Ruth turned their eyes to the Violet Sprite, who looked down with anxious eyes, and worried, pursed lips.

He sighed. "I didn't want to say anything in case I was wrong. But I know the truth. I know this magic all too well. Now, I want you both to brace yourselves. This won't be easy to hear."

After all the insanity they'd had to deal with already, they felt as though they were ready for anything. Still, they did as the sprite suggested and prepared for whatever was about to be revealed.

"Magic is not something that is simply black or white," began the sprite. "It's a whole hue, *a spectrum* if you will. Some practice pure, wonderful enchantments…magic that has the power to help and align the world around them."

"Like you," said Louis with confidence.

"Not exactly. You see, pure white magic can only go so far. It can help things along. But it can't create change, not really. There is a gray area of magic, practices that have the best intent but are eager to produce the change that white magic cannot. Those such as I, we would never use our magic to harm anyone, or cause misery, but we know the reality of playing solely by the rules. Without that gray area, our world would be a far drearier place for many. Then, there is the *dark side* of magic.

"Those who practice this have only the most selfish of intents. They enjoy flexing their power for others, often proclaiming that they're solely out to help the greater good. But it's a ploy—a wicked trick that even the smartest of people fall for as the liars spread superstition for those who truly want to help *everyone*. These practitioners are out for one thing and one thing alone: *Power*. And none are so fearsome or dangerous as the one I suspect captured or dear, sensual Eric…"

Ruth and Louis waited with bated breath. A few moments passed, but there came no answer. A few more passed and, still, there was nothing.

"*Who?*" Ruth demanded to know.

"For the love of the gods," the Violet Sprite jolted with surprise. "I was taking a dramatic pause."

"Time is of the essence," Louis remarked.

"Right," continued the sprite. "I don't know how or w*hat* he promised her to do so, but I believe that the king has employed the magic of a most dangerous adversary…The Celtic Witch."

"Dear gods, it can't be true!" Ruth exclaimed.

"I thought she was nothing more than a story," Louis

said. "A night terror used to scare children into behaving."

"I assure you she's very real," the Violet Sprite admitted in a strange tone, one that suggested both fear and knowledge.

"How are we ever going to break *her* spell?" Ruth asked.

"Now, don't get your titties in a twist, my dear. I have a plan: The witch's spells are always cast out of darkness and maniacal intent. Naturally, we'll use the very opposite of what she practices.

"What?" Ruth and Louis asked in unison.

"Truth and love."

****

Eric had waited patiently for some time. He could not rest and tried not to pace in fear of conjuring the creature, thus he sat trying to lose himself in the hope of seeing his loved ones again. He imagined holding Louis tightly in his arms as his mother sobbed joyfully at the reunion. Eventually, such wonderful daydreaming drifted his body into a sleep where the blissful images continued. He dreamt of a kingdom perfect and pure one where he could share his love with the prince openly, hand in hand.

The miraculous vision was soon washed away by a frightening darkness. Amidst the void came the face of the creature and from its skeleton mouth, a warning: "…Her spell is too strong, and I will kill if I must…"

Eric was jolted awake. *My family.* His heart palpitated at the thought of his loved ones being ambushed by the undead guardian. He could not allow anything terrible to happen to them. Thus, he devised a plan: They may have been his rescue, but he would meet them halfway.

****

The Violet Sprite led Louis and Ruth through the thickness of the dark forest. The deeper they traveled, the harder it seemed to see, to walk, even breathe.

"Will we be there soon?" Louis struggled to ask as the heaviness of the forest consumed him.

"Who can say really?" the sprite replied rhetorically.

"Don't you know where we are?" Ruth asked impatiently.

"That's the point of the dark forest, dear," the Violet Sprite explained. "*No one* knows where they are once they've entered."

Ruth and Louis stopped in their tracks, exchanging terrified glances.

The sprite turned over his shoulder with a playful grin. "I'm just teasing you lot! We're here." He waved his hand, and with a rushing gust of wind, the trees and bushes parted to reveal the foreboding task that lay ahead. The sky was black; the *trees* were gnarled as though they were filled with evil intent. In the distance was the tall, uninspiring spire. Seeing the prison in which his love was kept took Louis' breath away, but the prince was determined. He wanted Eric back *now*.

As the rescue party drew closer, they kept low to the ground, tiptoeing quietly, making their way through the dark, gnarled paths of the cursed wood. Haunting hoots from unseen owls and snarls from mysterious creatures warned them to turn back, but it was fruitless, for the trio had no weakness of heart among them.

Suddenly, the sprite came to a halt and nearly toppled the group. He turned with foreboding eyes and proclaimed in a whisper: "Someone's here."

The sprite's eyes shot wildly from left to right and he spun around, worried the creature was upon them. His mad spinning came to a stop when he caught sight of the monster, not more than a few hundred yards away, moving with a frighteningly slow pace through the trees.

"Do you both trust me completely?" asked the Violet Sprite.

"Yes," the two answered without hesitation.

"All right. I'm going to use a bit of magic on you now. It may feel strange. But follow my lead."

Ruth and Louis nodded vigorously, for they dared not question the wisdom of their guide with what was at stake. The sprite raised a hand and muttered something under his breath. A gust of sparkling violet smoke surrounded the trio. They felt their bodies contort, and move in ways unfamiliar to them.

Louis felt dizzy as the magic whirled his being around. Ruth was used to bending and cracking, but this was far from pleasurable. Finally, the smoke cleared, and they found themselves on all fours in the dirt, having fallen from the cloud.

"Gods in the heavens!" exclaimed Ruth.

"What happened to us?" Louis asked.

"Look around to find out," the already upright sprite said.

The two stood and were shocked by what they found. The trees and shrubs now towered above them as though thousands of stories high, as the calls of the wild echoed with a boom.

"Are we *small*?" Ruth asked.

"Indeed," confirmed the sprite. "Welcome to my world, part of the time. This should keep us safe from the creature. But 'safe' isn't enough. We'll use our size to our advantage."

"How?" Louis asked.

"Surprise attack. You two will assault with practical cunning, and I'll use my magic. And then we'll send that thing far away from here."

Louis looked around at all the trees that surrounded them. An idea born from painful memory came to him. It was extravagant, but with the help of Ruth and the magic of the sprite, he *knew* it was possible. "Then let's get to work."

****

Eric was terrified as he looked down below. He didn't know if his plan would work, but if there was a chance it would save his loved ones, he *had* to do it. Thus, he took a breath and reached out past the windowsill, reaching for its lip with his feet, he began to climb through. Suddenly, a force pulled upon his tunic, and he was thrown back into the tower.

His captor stood over him. "...I told you that you would never leave!" it shrieked.

The scribe stood, rubbing the back of his head, where his skull met the cobbled wall. "Can't I at least explore the land if I'm going to live here for eternity?"

"...You are a prisoner...Prisoners do not explore..."

"Well, that doesn't seem fair," Eric stated firmly, crossing his arms. "I've got so little to live for already. I have no family or friends here other than you."

"...We are not friends..."

"Not *yet*. But I shall grow on you, as you've grown on me."

"...Don't be foolish..."

"Who's being foolish? Not *I*. I speak the truth. Besides, if we're to be stuck together until my death, and mind you, I keep good health, it seems to me that I'll be your only company."

"…I shan't fall for your tricks…"

"Tricks? What is it, you're up to anyway? Should I be worried?"

"…Intruders, you fool… Intruders must be destroyed…"

"Well, if you just didn't give me a brilliant idea! Let me prove to you that I mean what I say. Take me with you, and I'll show you that I am out to comply with your orders."

"…Why would you *want* to help me keep you prisoner?"

"Truth be told," Eric began, rubbing the back of his neck, "I've nothing much to live for at home. I am but a common peasant, a poor man with no one to love. This prison isn't exactly a prison. It's more of an escape. *Please*, let me come with you. Let me obey and protect what little I have."

The creature stood, quietly gasping for air as it pondered. "…If I find you betray my trust…" it said finally, "…you will find a fate worse than this tower awaits…"

Eric held back his grin, so as not to give himself away. Instead, he gave a simple nod.

With a wave of its cloak and a heavy, quick gust, the guardian whisked the scribe away. Eric had been successful so far. Now, he just had to execute the rest of his plan without being doomed for eternity.

****

The trio had set up an ingenious weapon, using bark and sticks. Louis modeled the build after the cart he'd help destroy in the village. He and Ruth had gathered plenty of supplies for the sprite, who used his magic to construct the contraption.

"We'll have to coordinate our moves carefully for when the monster returns," Ruth stated.

"I know exactly how we'll do it," assured Louis. "I have experience."

Ruth grinned, for she knew that day in the village had been a fateful one for her son, and it brought her wonderful joy knowing that it would continue to serve him well.

Louis led the planning, while Ruth added tricks that would keep them cunning and discreet. The final piece of the puzzle was the Violet Sprite's spell to exorcise the creature from the land. He explained the precision it would take and the focus he would need while the others physically battled the guardian. It sounded complex and risky, which caused the sprite's human companions to worry.

"Are you sure you can do it?" asked Ruth.

"Oh, don't worry. It just takes determination. But I—"

The sprite did not finish his thought, for he was suddenly ill at ease.

"What is it?" Louis asked. "Is it the creature?"

"Yes," whispered the sprite. "But something's different. It's moving strangely."

"Should we be worried?" inquired Ruth.

"Always, but let's give *it* something to worry about, shall we?" The sprite gleefully raised his wand. A bright light slowly rose up the shaft, stopping at the top and edging back and forth from the tip for a moment. Finally, it shot skyward and exploded loudly.

Louis and Ruth both jumped at the blast, while the

sprite giggled with joy.

"Always a thrill," he said.

"What good did that do, other than create a mess?" asked the prince.

"I liked it." Ruth shrugged.

"Don't worry, your hineyness," the sprite reassured. "I'm just setting that thing into motion. Which reminds me: assume the positions! It's on its way."

A chilling fear suddenly filled the air. The three heroes shivered with fear as the monster drew near.

"Are you ready?" asked the Violet Sprite.

"We are," they agreed.

The silhouette of the guardian cast an unnatural and frightening shadow across the forest ground as it approached. Ruth nodded to Louis and Louis to Ruth.

They assumed their positions and the sprite pointed his wand at them directly and released his magical explosion. The two were once again put through a strange mix of pleasure and pain until they were returned to their normal size. Immediately, they jumped into action, throwing the now enlarged cart toward the monster. It cascaded toward the demon, but with a wave of its hand, the weapon broke into small shards, flying every which way.

The creature glared at the two with its poisonous eyes for a moment, before its thin, barely existent lips stretched into a horribly wide smile that revealed shark-like, yellow teeth.

"...Did you really think *that* would defeat me?"

Suddenly, Louis' look of despair turned to one of cunning. "Of course not," he teased. "It was nothing more than a distraction, while *he* set up your real demise."

"Hello there," the now enlarged Violet Spite gleefully called with a near sing.

The creature turned to see the sprite's spell surrounding it.

"…You're a fool…" it said without movement. "…I cannot return to the Underworld while *she* controls me…"

"I have a more unique punishment for you. A realm ruled over by one just as cruel as your deity. And one that won't let you go. The depths of ocean should keep you nicely, don't you think?"

The demon laughed. "…It's a shame it won't be me it keeps…"

A chill, worse than any that had haunted the sprite before, ran down his spine. He knew not what the creature meant, but his stomach turned at the monster's vague threat. With another wave of its hand, a flash of blue surrounded the monster. When it faded, Eric stood in the center of the vortex, and the creature appeared next to the sprite.

"Eric?" exclaimed Louis.

"My boy!" Ruth called.

"Stop the spell," Louis ordered the sprite.

"I can't!" the sprite bellowed with fear in his voice and wide, frightened eyes. "It—it won't stop."

"…I warned him, and now—he'll be gone from your reach forever. My job is done…" A flume surrounded the guardian, a pyre in which it vanished.

"Eric!" called Louis. "Come to me! Run!"

"I-I can't," returned a terrified Eric. "I'm stuck!"

The cloud built and bubbled around the scribe, all parties watching helplessly. Soon, the entire spell consumed Eric, with a loud, violent rage.

Then, it was quiet. The cloud was gone completely and so was Eric. The heavy, stunned breaths of the Violet Sprite, Louis, and Ruth were the only sounds that filled the void of the forest.

Louis began to shake and quake. First with shock, then with fury. Finally, he broke the silence:

"Where is he?" Louis shouted.

"He—he must have gone where I meant to send the creature," said the Violet Sprite, still in shock.

"Where is that?" Ruth shivered.

"The bottom of the sea," the sprite blurted with fear.

"But, *how*, how could he survive that?" Ruth asked.

"I don't know," admitted the sprite.

"So he could be…" Louis began, an iciness on his breath as he struggled to form the words.

It was harrowing to realize no one knew of Eric's fate. What they *did* know was that they would do anything to save him, and that time was of the essence.

Chapter Eleven

"The Divine Lady of the Bay"
Published in The Scribe's Collection *as "The Divine
Lady's Husband."*

Most who made the journey to Pecker Bay never
returned. It lay at the foot of the foggy, treacherous
Man's Peak Cliff. The stones were uneven and
infamously crumbled, sending its trekkers to their deaths
in the deep, icy waters below. If one attempted to reach
the bay by sea, the risk was equally as great, for the reefs
were known for causing shipwrecks that left no
survivors. The more superstitious citizens of Belle Terre
claimed that it was not the *reefs* that brought sailors to
their demises, but the legendary Lady of the Bay, a
malevolent deity who ruled the ocean.

It was in this very bay that Eric landed, face down
in the water. He was in a strange place in between life
and what comes after, his soul drifting farther and farther
from his body. His mind was incoherent, his body felt
drained. Indeed, it seemed as though it was the end of the
scribe. Before his soul was completely gone, he faintly
felt something below his nose. At first, he thought it
seaweed, but then, it wrapped around the back of his
head. It was far too thick to be seaweed and grasped him
as though it were on purpose. An intense feeling of
suction grasped his neck.

Fear brought Eric's life force back. His eyes flew

open, salt immediately stinging them. Whatever grasped him seemed to come up from the depths. And now, with its full force around, it pulled him into the terrible blackness below. He felt his lungs grow empty, his head dizzy, and he was certain he would return to his near-death state at any moment. Suddenly, his journey came to a slamming end. His vision had only worsened, but he *did* make out a glaring, frightening pair of eyes staring directly at him.

A booming, yet murky voice filled the water around him, followed by a cackling laugh. His vision worsened, and his head grew light. He was certain that the end was upon him, and he began to say his prayers.

Suddenly, something strange began to happen to him. He felt his lifeforce returning, rushing back so quickly that the sensation was intoxicating and nauseating. Suddenly, he was able to draw a long, crucial breath. He closed his eyes, enjoying the gasp. As he let it out, he noticed the sting completely gone from his eyes. It surprised him so that his eyes instinctually blinked open. They were blurry for a moment, but soon, his vision became clear, despite the murky heft of the sea. The slimy serpent around his neck released its grasp. He watched it retract and realized it was a long, green tentacle. It moved farther and farther back, until it arrived at its source, the same source from which the eyes had glared at him.

Not at all was this creature a Kraken or a sea monster, but a woman, olive of skin, with dark hair and eyes. She had wide, plump red lips over a small, sharp chin. Her body was covered in leathery skin that resembled a dress. She stared at Eric with a cunning grin, her hands on her hips as she eyed him up and down.

"Well, well, well," she said with a deep, entrancing voice. "It's been a *while* since we had one of your kind fall into the depths."

Eric shivered in the cold water, as his mind raced. Who was this frightening, yet beautiful creature? How was he now breathing when, just moments before, he was near death? *Where* was he? How did he get here?

"What's the matter?" the woman asked. "Catfish got your tongue? Oh, that joke was old when I was a guppy. I didn't save you to float there like whale blubber. Who are you? Speak up."

Speak up? Eric did not know that he *could* speak underwater. Then, again, up until a few moments ago, he could not breathe either.

"I…" he began with ever growing confusion. "…You *saved* me?"

"Well, *of course*! You didn't think you grew a fin and learned how to breathe under the sea at random, did you?"

"A…*fin*?" Eric looked down to discover his tunic gone, exposing his thin, toned torso. His glance continued down until he saw that the thin trail of hair below his bellybutton no longer led to his humanly, private regions, but to a shimmering, scaley, long, blue fish tail. "Oh my—oh my! I'm—I'm a merman!"

"You don't need a reef to fall on you."

"How—*how*?"

"Well, let's see, sweetheart" began the creature, as she commandingly floated around him swishing her black tail. "You belly flopped into my waters. Now, normally, I'd let your kind drown, or I'd have a little fun; you know, siren seduction, followed by strangling and feasting. But the second I saw that cute face, I knew you were the one."

"The one?"

"Yes, sirens are far more complex than stories give us credit. We're a kingdom with certain traditions, especially for me, as I'm sure you've gathered."

"I-I'm not sure who you are."

"*You're not sure who I am*? Damned be the day the humans forget one of their *gods*. Fools you all are."

"You're a god?"

"Not just any god. Say hello to Morgana Marina." She placed a hand on her hip and once again showed him her sly grin.

Using his new skill, Eric took a breath, drinking in the shock he felt as though it was the water around him. "The Divine Lady of the Bay," he uttered.

"Yes, that's what your people call me. I prefer Queen of the Sea, Aquatic Empress, Illustriousness of Marine Life. Well, you get the idea. With my status of the sea, I have certain royal obligations. Obligations that have kept our kingdom thriving for thousands and thousands of years. I've fulfilled most of my duties, *except for one pesky* little law."

"What is it?" Eric bravely asked, as the sea witch circled him domineeringly.

"Let's call it an issue of breeding. My family has ruled the seven seas for seven thousand years. My father was king before me, his father before him, and his father still. Do you notice anything peculiar about that?"

"You're the first queen in many generations."

"In *all* the generations. Each king would steal a bride down from the land above and transform them for the purposes of continuing the family."

"Why from the land?"

"How do you think half-fish, half-people are made? What are they teaching up there these days?"

"Not that. That's diabolical."

"Thank you. Anyway, running the kingdom better than my ancestors was time consuming, and I enjoyed it. And, frankly, any young man from the world above who dared venture into my bay proved to either be a fisherman, after the subjects of my kingdom, or worse, a terrible bore. It always seemed far more fun to kill them than marry them. That is, until you found your way here. How *did* you get here? My reputation has proceeded me for some time now. It's been a while since one of your kind ventured into the depths."

"I don't know how I got here. I was a prisoner of King Desmos."

"The loudmouth with the hair so hard it might as well be a conch shell hat?"

"I guess that's one way of describing him. You know him?"

"He's been an enemy of the sea and the forests for quite a while. Always looking to destroy in order to build. Why were you his prisoner?"

"I think—think he wants me dead, or at least out of the way of his stepson."

"Oh, yes, that grouchy little man. The Deplorable Prince they called him last I heard."

"He's not deplorable!"

She stopped her under water acrobatics, for the young man demonstrating his backbone both surprised and intrigued her. "Why would a peasant like you be protective of a royal like that?"

Eric did not want to broach the subject and thus sought distraction. "What makes you think I'm a peasant?"

"What am I, *blind*? Anyway, it matters not. Any enemy of the king is a friend of my anemone. You'll make a perfect husband. Come with me."

She began to lead him toward a cave that lay ahead. However, follow he did not. He floated, nervously, trying to find the courage to confront this intimidating divinity, and ask her to send him home.

"Actually," he called finally, stopping the queen in her swish. "I was wondering, perhaps, maybe, your excellency, you could use your powers to...to..."

"Get on with it! Nobody likes a kissing guramis."

He took a deep breath. "I was hoping you would send me home."

The Divine Lady did not believe what she'd heard for a moment, for no one had ever been brave enough to ask *her* for anything. "That I can't do, angel fish. I need a husband to continue my bloodline. And I'm a picky girl. Besides, being royalty isn't so bad. You can force the dolphins to perform for you and sick sharks on your enemies."

She began toward the cave once again, but Eric mustered even more bravery this time. "What if I don't *want* to marry you?"

She turned, more slowly this time, revealing a look of extreme displeasure.

"Come again, dear..." she ordered with a low, ferocious tone.

"What I mean is...I don't want to marry you. I don't care if you're the Divine Lady of the Bay. You can't force me."

"I think you'll come around," she said, her voice even more chilling.

"I've been through things today that you wouldn't believe. What makes you think you can break me?"

A frightening, wicked grimace contorted her mouth and filled her eyes. "Because," she groaned in a deep rasp, "I can be very persuasive."

With a jarringly fast thrust, she arched her back up. Her head moved to one side with a sickening crack. Then, it shifted to the other with a resonance even louder. Her fingers cracked too as they wrapped around each other. Her arms snapped out to four times their length, and her olive skin turned ash gray. With every crack and pop, her body continued to grow, morphing into something entirely different. When the transformation was done, Eric found himself staring into the eyes of a monster many only thought to be a legend. It had sharp teeth, horribly lifeless eyes, tentacles, *and* a tail. It was five times his size and even more terrifying than the monster he'd face at the tower. This was the legendary leviathan. It released a low-toned growl from its throat, causing Eric to shiver as though he were not already in cold water. And worse, it caused him to agree.

"A-all right." He trembled. "I'll marry you."

Quickly, the monster returned to its bodily form. "I thought you'd see it my way."

The frightened merman followed his apparent bride-to-be into the cave. He knew not what lay within awaiting him, but he knew he had to find a way out of this new, harrowing prison and return to his prince and family.

****

Ruth had barely spoken since Eric disappeared. Her eyes were distant, her skin white as a sheet. Though Louis had not known her long, he felt a connection to her through their shared love for Eric. He approached gently to comfort her, though deep down, he still needed comfort himself.

"Ruth?" asked the prince. "Are you—all right?"

"No, Your Highness." Ruth struggled. "*I'm not all right.* You see, I've always put my faith in magic, thinking that it was pure and wonderful when used for good. And now, that magic I put all my faith in just lost me my son."

"Ruth," said the sprite, approaching with a sympathetic tread, "you must not give up faith. Right now, it's all we have. We will save him. I'll do everything in my power—"

"Your power's done enough!" Ruth shouted. "My son is at the bottom of the most dangerous body of water in the world, with the vilest deity this side of the underworld, *if* he's not already dead. All because of *magic*!"

"I was trying to help him! You think I don't know this is my fault? You think I wouldn't do anything I can to get your boy back?"

"That's enough, both of you!" Louis intervened. "Do you think the three of us turning on one another does him any good?"

There was an ashamed silence between Ruth and the sprite. Confident that he had their attention completely, Louis asked the fairy:

"Can your magic get us to the bay from here?"

The Violet Sprite waved his wand, but no magic was expelled. He tried hand magic and not even a spark would appear. "I can't. That monster must have neutralized my magic to keep us from following."

"Bastard zombie!" Ruth exclaimed.

"Wait, if it wanted to stop us from getting him," the prince pondered aloud, "perhaps, perhaps that means he's still alive."

All three became intensely silent as the hopeful prospect washed over them. It would indeed make sense. Eager to find out, they began their journey on foot with furious passion. It should have taken nearly a day, but the brave and determined trio made it in less than half the time. They stood at the edge of the village, Ruth and the Violet Sprite uncertain of what Louis was planning, but they could tell his mind raced intensely.

"So what's the plan?" the Violet Sprite asked.

"If my stepfather is truly in league with the Celtic Witch, we can't risk him finding out what we're doing, or that Eric might be alive."

"Your stepfather has a powerful ally on his side," the sprite expressed. "How are you going to gather help if you're not able to rally anyone?"

"I'm not. *You* are."

"What? You think they're going to listen to a Gaelic fairy in pumps? Very stylish pumps, but *pumps*. In the Kingdom of Belle Terre? I think not."

"You're probably right. Is your magic back?"

The sprite waved his hand. Still, there was no sign of enchantment. "I don't think so."

"Very well, you'll just have to see who you can convince. You'll both go."

"Fine crew, a fairy of no specific sexuality, and a prostitute."

"It's probably better than the Deplorable Prince," said Louis.

"Don't be silly, dear," Ruth replied.

"No, he's right," the sprite acknowledged. "They

really hate him."

"Thank you for that," huffed the prince, " I'll find us a vessel while the two of you gather a crew."

"How will you do *that* without getting caught?" asked the sprite.

"I have a plan. It *is* risky, but it's worth it for Eric."

"Dear?" asked Ruth with motherly concern.

"It'll be all right," Louis stated with a forged strongness. "Let's form our army, and then we take to the sea."

****

Eric's stomach quaked as he continued to follow his new captor farther into her strange, dark domain.

"Keep up with me," the sea witch ordered. "We're almost there."

The cavern grew darker, becoming a frightening void. Eric wondered if it was too late to flee. But he knew the goddess to be all-powerful, thus he would have no chance. Besides, where would he go if he *did* escape? For now, he'd have to comply with the witch.

Suddenly, a faint light danced along the cavern walls from around the corner, barely noticeable but unmistakable in darkness. It grew brighter and brighter the closer they swam. Finally, a beautiful cluster of light blinded him. The silhouette of the Divine Lady cut through the middle of the circular illumination.

She turned to him dramatically, crying out, "Well, come along and see the kingdom."

The Divine Lady of the Bay dove down out of view. Whether it was the promise of light or the fear he felt from the siren's orders, he followed. His stomach tingled as he dove down into the clear, beautiful blue water.

He followed the lady deeper, attempting to keep up

with her, for as much as she frightened him, getting lost in the vastness of the sea would be a worse fate. He finally caught up with the deity when he found her stopped at the edge of a reef.

"It's about time you made it." She grinned over her shoulder.

"I hope I haven't kept you waiting, your excellency," replied Eric with feigned kindness to hide his fear.

"Only slightly. Come, there's something I want you to see."

The merscribe took a subtle gulp, for everything about the lady frightened him. The legends he'd heard were vicious, but there was something even more terrifying about her in person. Reluctantly, he joined her. "What is it?" he asked, attempting to hide his caution.

"Why it's your new home," she said, motioning beyond the rocky coral of the reef. "*My kingdom.*"

Eric turned his eyes from his captor toward what lay below. After seeing the horrific monster she could become, traveling through the terrifying cave, and having to unwillingly follow her to the depths of his new prison, he expected the sight to match the terribleness of the day. But, lo, this was not the case. It was a shimmering city of pearl, amethyst, and gold. A palace that glistened in the waving rays of the sun attempting to reach the ocean's depths. There were homes of shells and gemstone. It was, indeed, a spectacular sight of enchantment that Eric believed only existed in his fairy tales.

"Don't you just adore it?" asked the Divine Lady. "It's better than those drab palaces on land. Don't you think? I asked you a question!"

"Oh, sorry. I thought it was rhetorical. Um, I supposed, yes, it's quite magnificent. You've been to our palaces?"

"Well, not in the flesh and scales. However, I'm the best singer of siren songs there is."

"Siren songs?"

"Don't tell me they don't tell the stories of my *songs* up there anymore! What are myths coming to these days? Yes, my siren songs. I can send my voice farther than any other of our kind, even into the palaces if I so choose. That's a skill that comes in handy whenever I have a craving for royal flesh."

An idea began to brew in Eric's head. He knew he'd have to be clever as he inquired, proceeding with as much boyhood innocence as he could muster. "Your song can be heard across kingdoms?"

"You don't need an anchor to strike you, my dear," teased the Divine Lady, brushing a scaly hand across Eric's cheek.

The sensuality of her touch not only frightened him but reminded him of what his life might become if he did not escape the enchanting domain of Pecker Bay. "Do you think you could teach me?" Eric asked.

"*Teach you?*"

"How to sing a siren's song—dear," he answered with a gulp, as he attempted to flirt.

"*You* want to learn to sing a siren's song?" she asked, crossing her arms and raising one of her dark, arched eyebrows.

"Why not—angel fish?" He knew his attempts to flirt were as transparent as the water in which they floated.

This was only confirmed by the Divine Lady's

smirk. "You understand that a siren's song is typically sung by mer*maids*?"

"Oh, does that really matter down here too?" groaned Eric.

"It matters quite a lot. Mermaids have always been the ones to lure men to their demise. It's tradition."

"Is it not tradition that has left you having to settle for me?"

The Divine Lady grinned. "Don't sell yourself short. I may be forced into marriage, but I'm not exactly complaining." She winked temptingly and gave his forearm a squeeze.

He wanted to shudder in disgust, but he managed to keep his composure. "Well, that may be, but it's a very human idea to think that mermaids and mermen can't *both* sing a song. You see, uh, my love, humans have very prosperous ideas about who can say what, who can wear what, who can marry who—who can sing certain songs. Very old age and naïve, don't you think? I don't see why *our* kingdom can't be better."

The Divine Lady cackled with zeal. "Let's get one thing straight, angel fish: This isn't *our* kingdom, it's *mine*. And as for the marriage, I wouldn't have kept you alive if I didn't want you."

Eric's stomach churned with nerves, as his plan seemed as dead as fisherman's chum. But then, the arched beam of the Divine Lady returned.

"But I *will* teach you the siren's call," she said with a deep-voiced enthusiasm.

"You *will*?" Eric exclaimed enthusiastically. He corrected his bearing. "You will?"

"Yes," she agreed. "If nothing else, I like the idea of my kingdom being superior to that of the humans, and finally getting the recognition I deserve for being the greatest ruler in the eight realms."

"Yes," he agreed with forceful and convincing passion. "No doubt of it! Our kingdom—*your* kingdom will, without doubt, blow the rest out of the water."

The Divine Lady gave him a look of unamused eyes and pursed lips.

"Oh, right!" Eric corrected. "It'll—*keep* them out of the water?"

"We'll work on your sea puns. After all, now that you're merfolk, we have hundreds of years to correct them. Now, come along. I must introduce you to the royal court."

Another royal court he had to impress. It was not a prospect with which Eric was pleased, nor was the idea of being a merman for hundreds of years. Still, if there were any chance his foolish plan might work, he'd have to obey. Thus, he followed the lady to her beautiful and baffling palace.

****

The Violet Sprite and Ruth were exhausted. Though they knew it to be an uphill battle, amassing a rebel army was far more challenging than they ever imagined.

"I don't understand it!" Ruth cried. "We've asked every qualified, strapping young man in the kingdom who was not already committed to the king's army. I even offered them half-off services, and *still* not one of them bit!

"For what it's worth, they'll regret turning you down the next time they meet a nice girl in a chastity belt."

"My boy, my dear boy stuck with a dangerous sea beast, and no one wants to help!"

"Well, don't forget, it could still be worse. At least

we're rather sure he's not dead."

For the first time since they'd met, Ruth did not bother with fronts of bravery, or strength. As the day's frustrations pulled at her heart, she wept loudly and painfully. The Violet Sprite became uneasy. Giving as he may have been, he was not well-versed in the art of counseling.

"There, there," he awkwardly attempted, barely tapping one of her shoulders. "It'll be all right—someday."

Ruth released another sob, causing the sprite to jolt. "Oh, for the love of the gods," he whispered. He needed to find some way to help her, though he knew that his attempts at comfort would only prove futile and cause even more bawling, but it seemed as though there was no way for them to forge the army they needed.

It was with that very thought that inspiration struck: What if the army they *needed* wasn't the one they'd attempted? *Of course* those brawny fools were never going to help their crew of misfits. They were far too easily bamboozled by the king to believe what was true and decent. Indeed, these unlikely heroes needed an even more unlikely army, and the sprite had a decent idea where to start.

****

Louis stood both beneath his cloak and behind a wall at the rear of the courtyard. The clustered guards in the courtyard were due for supper duty at any moment. He would have to get Evers alone somehow before he too followed the shields in for serving. Evers was the proudest guard the prince had ever known. Yet, Louis could not help but notice that Evers now stood with a sadness that Louis had only seen him carry once before, many years ago, when they were but boys and they carried a warm, lustful secret.

Finally, the grand bell high above the courtyard rang, calling them to their duty. The guards began for the door inside. Luckily for Louis, Evers was last in the line to enter. Louis would have to time his call just right, but he knew he could do it. When the moment presented itself, he wasted no time in executing his chase.

"Evers," Louis called softly.

The guard stopped before crossing the threshold, turning with a stunned glance. "Your Highness!" he exclaimed with a jolt. "Where have you been? Everyone's been worried about you."

"Have they really been *worried*, Evers?" Louis asked, though he already knew the answer.

"Well, more concerned really. How may I serve you, Your Majesty?"

"You can cease with the formalities. I'm not here to talk to 'Evers the Guard.' I'm here to talk to the Evers from long ago, but who I hope is still in there."

The guard understood what the prince meant. Experimental memories from years past returned vividly.

"I don't know what you mean," he lied.

"It's only you and I here, Evers. Let's be honest."

Evers stood silent and uneasy. "Your Highness," he finally spoke. "You know your stepfather would never allow such talk."

"To hell with my stepfather! What good has he ever done for anyone? Evers, there are lives at stake. And...I know I hurt you all those years ago when I broke your heart after my mother was put away. Please allow me the chance to make it right, and you'll be rewarded handsomely for your help."

The look of a simple man plagued with a thousand difficult thoughts danced across Evers' face. He was once again at a loss for words. He knew that his employment to the kingdom meant he had a duty to uphold its values set forth by King Desmos. However, as the guard looked upon the prince, all he saw was the boy he knew and once loved.

"Well, you are the prince." Evers smiled. "It is my duty to serve you."

Louis' eyes began to tear, and a beam of gratitude stretched across his lips. He could not allow himself to dwell for long, for time was still of the essence. "I won't lie to you," he explained, "what I'm asking of you is risky. And if we get caught, the ramifications we'll face are great."

"I have a feeling the risk is worth the reward," Evers reassured with a grin. "It's the scribe, isn't it?"

"How did you—"

"I've met him before. The care he has for you is clearly as strong as the care you have for him. And he once spoke of ideas for a better kingdom. And I've known you all my life. I'd like to see if the two of you can do it."

Chills of amazement and gratitude raced down Louis' spine. "We must get to the harbor before the others realize you're missing."

"Why there?"

"We're going to steal my stepfather's most prized ship and sail it to the ends of the earth."

****

Evers led the prince safely through town to the royal dock. Each berth was filled with a ship from the royal fleet that had not seen action for some time. This was not due to lack of need, but due to King Desmos' lack of empathy, for any cries of help that came from neighboring kingdoms when war broke out were ignored by the king. However, he never had any sort of issue when it came to taking his favorite ship, *Le Grand Garçon* out for a pleasure cruise.

"There it is." The prince motioned toward the grand vessel. "We must come up with a plan so we're ready when the rest of the cavalry arrives."

"Oh, I already have one," Evers claimed.

"You do?" asked a surprised Louis.

"You know, everyone sees me as a bumbling fool, but let me ask you, how often are you down here warding off attackers and pirates? Just trust me, all right?"

Louis was both stumped and surprised by Evers' assertion and gave him an agreeing nod.

"Keep your hood on and *don't talk* to anyone."

The prince followed the guard's orders. As they came to the ship, Evers started up the slipway, followed by Louis. When the prince came up on deck, he was met with no discernment. He found Evers holding the small crew of three at double sword point.

"…So you're either going to help us or abandon ship right here, right now," Evers was barking with a command that Louis had never before heard him use.

"What are you doing?" Louis barked in as hushed a tone as he could manage to not be caught.

"Stealing the ship," Evers whispered calmly back to Louis. "I told you not to question the plan. Shut it and be ready."

"Be ready for what?" Louis whispered.

"And who are *you* to command *us*?" asked the smug

captain.

"Oh, I'm nobody," Evers continued without fear. "But he's the prince." The guard nodded back toward Louis with matter-of-fact ease. "By law, you have to listen to him."

A terror ran down the prince's spine. This plan had gone from insane to deranged.

"No one has seen the Deplorable Prince for at least a day," the captain mocked. "You expect me to believe that *wraith* is him?"

"Your Highness," cooed Evers, "be a lamb and remove your hood."

Louis would not normally entertain such arrogance, especially those that involved the horrible nickname, but he was *desperate* to get under way. Thus, he decided to embrace it, and removed his hood to reveal a horrible scowl.

"Who are *you* to question my identity?" Louis roared at the captain. "I should have you keelhauled!"

"Your Majesty," the captain pathetically cried with a bow. "My most sincere apologies."

"Don't grovel. You look like an ass. Stand up! I want to look in your eyes when I fire you!"

"Oh, please Your Highness," begged the captain as he rose pathetically from his bend. "I *need* this job. I've got a wife who's sleeping with the farmer next door, and nine children, all who want to become jousters. Do you know how expensive it is to send that many children to knight classes, and—wait a moment! You're the prince, why are you *stealing* the ship?"

"Oh, there you go again," demeaned Louis, not missing a beat, "questioning my authority! That's enough! I won't even allow you the dignity of walking off this ship. You must jump into the harbor to leave. Get to it, or I'll have your manhood turned into earings for your wife's lover to give to her."

The threat was enough to convince the captain, who immediately and fearfully made way for the side of the ship.

"And take your crew with you!" the prince ordered.

The captain stopped. "Well, come on, you bilge rats! My goods are at stake!"

The crew followed and one by one, they plummeted into the harbor, and with humiliation, swam for the dock.

"You were *wonderful*!" Evers beamed.

"You weren't so bad yourself," claimed the prince. "I'm sorry I ever doubted you."

"You were always stubborn." Evers shrugged.

"Now see here—"

"Oh, I'm only teasing you. So we have the ship. Now what?"

"Well, I've sent my allies out to gather our crew. It's time we reassembled. And then, we go save my love from his watery hell."

****

The Celtic Witch stared at herself in the mirror. She donned her Queen Krystal disguise, and while the queen was indeed beautiful, she was tired of hiding.

"Why must I wear this ridiculous disguise?" she asked. "The prince has been gone for a whole day. He's not coming back. I made that prison foolproof."

"But there lies the problem," King Desmos warned as he lay in their bed. "My stepson is no fool."

The fake queen rolled her eyes as she scoffed. "You haven't had a restful moment since I made the scribe disappear."

"Can you blame me? You were sloppy. Burning that rug—It was as though you *wanted* us to get caught."

The witch took a deep breath in, her neck tight and her eyes filled with annoyance. "If I wanted to get caught," she growled, turning to face the king, "do you think I'd keep up this nonsensical charade?"

"Don't take that tone with me," the king defended.

"Oh, Desmos, I'll take whatever tone I'd like with you. Don't forget where you'd be had it not been for me."

The king was suddenly silent as memories of hardships returned. He employed a debonair grin, for though he did not want to agree with the witch, he was reminded what he could lose should he cross her. "Now, see here, my pet—I only—"

"Quiet!" the Witch ordered suddenly, snapping her eyes off to somewhere in the distance. "There's something I must take care of. I'll be back soon."

She vanished before the king could protest, an act she knew would restoke his fury, but there were far more pressing matters elsewhere in the kingdom.

A mile east of the castle, Ruth and the Violet Sprite had managed to persuade a few denizens to join their quest. Eager to introduce the colorful band of misfits they'd inducted to their leader, they'd begun their journey to the royal dock. A quarter of the way there, however, the Violet Sprite stopped. Ruth took immediate notice of his concern.

"What is it?" she asked.

"Continue on without me," replied the sprite, only giving half of his attention to his partner.

"It's a long trek, and we must be underway soon."

"I'll be there, I promise, but trust me, you don't want to be here when what's coming arrives. Just get yourself and the crew to the ship. And—if I'm not there before the evening—shove off without me. This is bigger than me, and you must save your boy."

Ruth stared for a moment, as a terrified chill ran down her spine. Leaving the sprite to face whatever was coming was a harrowing thought.

"Ruth," he uttered softly. "Please go."

Reluctantly, Ruth returned to the group and led them off, hopeful that she would see him again.

When she was gone, the atmosphere around the sprite began to change. The sun vanished behind clouds that appeared as if from nowhere. A cool, ominous breeze gusted with a haunting howl. As the apparition began to materialize, the Violet Sprite found himself confused, for the being he expected was not the being that appeared. Surely, he was mistaken. Surely, this was not Queen Krystal who stood before him.

"Hello, dear," the queen cooed, only confirming for the sprite what he suspected.

"You don't have the voice quite right," he said, folding his arms.

The faux queen transformed into her true form. "I've done well enough to fool her son and the kingdom."

"How long have you been tricking him?" asked the sprite. "Is she even still alive."

"Yes, she's alive. We're not barbarians."

"Oh, of course not. You wouldn't *kill* her, just imprison her, am I right?"

"Don't act so high and mighty. You're no better than me."

The Violet Sprite scoffed. "How do you figure that?"

"Well, let's see. You've had your suspicions for

some time now, and yet you said nothing to him."

"He has enough to worry about without my uncertainties making it worse."

"You're helping him find that scribe. Don't you know what that'll do to the king?"

"With any luck, it'll put him in his grave."

"Oh, yes. The good little sprite wishing death upon the king. How benevolent."

"I wish the king punished somehow. It's evil preachings such as his that tear apart friends, siblings, mothers, and sons."

The Celtic Witch grinned her haunting grin. "You weren't going to wait long for that, were you? Is that the real reason you stayed behind to face me?"

"Oh, no. No, not in the least. I wanted to see your face when I told you that no matter what you do, no matter what spell you cast, no matter what curse you create, I'm going to see to it that those boys are together. You may have stopped my love story, but I'll be damned if you stop another's."

"Interesting choice of words. You really are like me, my son."

"Like *you*? That's something I'll never be."

The eyes of the witch tensed for a moment. Her emotions were unclear, and replaced with a grin far too quickly for the sprite to figure out his mother's emotions.

"Stay safe, *dear*. I suppose I'll see you when you get back—if not sooner."

Before the Violet Sprite could respond, she vanished, as did her storm clouds and the frightening wind that came with her. Why she appeared to him, he did not know. Perhaps to scare him, or spy, or perhaps to just rouse his anger. Her intentions were never clear. He only hoped that whatever his mother was planning would not prove doomful.

Chapter Twelve

"The Kingdom of the Merfolk"
Published in The Scribe's Collection *as "The Little Merman."*

Or, as I like to call it, the laziest, watered-down rip off in the whole original collection. If you can't tell by the name, the published collection was riding Hans Christian Anderson's, "I know it's the period but how was fashion ever this gay without anyone knowing it?" coat tails. I can't go on about this one, or I'll burst a blood vessel, so let's just say that almost all of this chapter except for the concept of Eric being a merman was morphed into the rip off of a far better story.

****

It was quite the swim across the village to the shimmering sea castle. Eric followed the Divine Lady to the grand doors and watched as she had a word with the two anthropomorphic fish guards. They were not quite merfolk but had all the expression of curious men. They used their pectoral fins to open the coral doors. The Divine Lady waved for Eric to join her. His stomach still filled with nerves, for his plan was still young, and he knew swimming into the palace would leave him with no choice but to see it out. He decided it would be wise to learn about the confines from which he must escape, thus he struck up conversation:

"I've never seen fish like them before."

"Asian Sheepshead Wrasse fish," explained the Divine Lady. "They're not common to this area. But those two owed me a favor, so they're working it off."

"They're strange to me."

"Don't be rude," she ordered. "They're the closest relatives that merfolk have."

"Oh, really?"

"Yes, nearly as intelligent, but not as attractive."

"Can they sing the siren's song?"

"No, they don't possess much in the way of magic, but I did give them enhanced strength. No good having guards without muscle." She whirled with style as she swam.

As she showed off her skill, she gave Eric a tour of the palace. He made note of every nook, cranny, door, and window. He asked endless questions, determined to know *everything* about the kingdom in order to escape it. Though the throne was magnificent, and the concert hall ornate, it was all nothing more than a prison to keep him from his prince, and one he hoped would not dwell in for long.

****

Louis and Ruth waited at the bottom of the slipway, hopeful that the Violet Sprite would soon appear.

"How much longer do we have?" asked Ruth.

"The sun is nearing the West...Not long," Louis replied dauntingly.

It was then both noticed a glimmer that shot madly across the sky. It was far too early for shooting stars, and their hearts fluttered with relief when they realized the sparkle could only be that of their friend.

He landed with a thud and a chime as he returned to his larger size. "Oh, how frustrating it can be when you must deal with magical nonsense," he declared in his lighthearted tone. "Have you met the crew yet, Your Highness?"

"Not yet," replied Louis as he and Ruth exchanged confused glances. "Isn't there something you should tell us?"

"No, don't be silly." He tried his best to hide the thousands of anxieties with which his mother had burdened him. "Now, shall we go aboard?"

It was clear that the sprite was not going to explain whatever it was that had made him so fearful, and with evening soon approaching, they had to make way. Ruth followed the sprite up the slipway first, tailed by Louis.

"Feast your eyes!" the sprite exclaimed with grand showmanship. He was certain Louis would be pleased with the gathered misfits of Belle Terre. But the glance Louis gave was filled with uncertainty. "What's wrong? You look like you've seen a ghost."

Louis eyed the line once again. At the far end was a withered old geezer, in a captain's coat, brandishing a leather hat that looked as though it had been tarnished by the sun one thousand times. "I'm not sure I haven't."

"Don't be an arse," the Violet Sprite scolded. "They're willing to help, and they're more than capable. Come and meet them before you judge so harshly."

"All right, all right," agreed Louis, as he followed the sprite and Ruth toward the line.

The first candidate to whom he was introduced had gorgeous, clear, golden-brown skin, surrounded by a thick crop of cascading hair, over a striking, emerald, green waistcoat.

"What's your name, sir?" asked the prince.

"If you'll pardon the interruption, Your Majesty,"

chimed in the sprite, "they aren't called 'sir,' nor 'lady.' "

"I can speak for myself," said the being, giving the sprite a poisonous, impish glance, before turning their attention back to Louis. "You can call me Yvonne."

"Yvonne it is," the prince agreed. "What skills do you bring to our crew?"

"Well, besides keeping my fellow practitioners in their place, I'm quite versed in the magical arts."

"Are you a sprite, as well? Or a pixie. I'm sorry. I'm not sure which to call you."

Yvonne lightly chuckled. "Worry not, dear. I'm not either. I'm a soothsayer."

"How come I've never seen you around my kingdom before?"

"Well, besides the fact that the Deplorable Prince likes to keep to himself," joked Yvonne, "your stepfather outlawed my kind many years ago. I was your age when my mothers and I were forced to move underground to survive."

"I'm so sorry," Louis offered with sincerity.

"You needn't be. I know it was not your doing. However, the Indigo Fairy, over there—"

"Violet Sprite!" corrected Louis' guide with full Celtic rage.

"Yes, *you*, promised me that this voyage would really stick it to the king, and I would like nothing more than to *royally* bend his fat arse out of shape."

"You've come to the right place," Louis smiled. "I'm honored to have you onboard." Already the prince had begun to warm to the idea of this crew, thus he moved on to the next recruits.

He was met with a pair of twins one of brown-blond

hair, one of black, but both boasting the same beautiful faces. Though he'd only just begun to build it up, Louis felt his confidence challenged. The young men did not appear to be more than nineteen. Practically children, the prince wondered how they would fare on the rough seas and in a domain as dangerous as that of Pecker Bay.

"And what are your names?" Louis asked.

"We don't know," said the brown-blond boy.

"What?" Louis asked, with an arched eyebrow and uncontrollable uncertainty in his voice.

"Don't be brainless, brainless," the dark-haired boy corrected his brother. "What he means is we don't know our *actual* names. We were abandoned as babies."

"Tragic stuff," the other chimed in.

"But we made the best of it," continued his brother.

"We were adopted by a traveling actress. She was wonderful."

"'Till she drank herself to death," acknowledged the black-haired boy.

"She decided to give us names that would make us stand out in the crowd. She called me Glacé," the blond explained.

"And me Zest," said the other.

"I see," replied the prince, overwhelmed by their hijinks. "What are your skills?"

"Well, we may look young and pretty," began Glacé.

"And we are," Zest added.

"But we can brandish a sword," continued Glacé.

"And run a man through." Zest grinned proudly.

"Before he even knows what hit him," Glacé finished.

"All right," said the now annoyed prince. "As much

as I don't want to prolong this performance, I'll need to see proof. Frankly, I don't believe—"

Before Louis could even finish his sentence, Glacé and Zest both drew their swords and hurled them toward the old seaman. Louis' heart practically blew out of his chest as he was *certain* he was about to watch the old man meet his death. With a boink, the blades landed: One in the very top of the man's hat, the other in the collar of his coat, over his left shoulder, both swords trapping him on the mast.

"My gods!" cried Louis as he lurched to help the captive old man. He stopped short and looked over his shoulder at the boys. "Welcome aboard!" He continued his sprint.

Louis removed the sword from the man's collar, but before he could reach for the hat, the man plummeted to his knees on the deck. "Oh, sir!" cried Louis with embarrassment. He removed the sword from the still-stuck hat, sending the cap falling upon the poor old man.

"Ye really be testin', boy," growled the geezer.

Louis dropped the sword and fell to his knees to help the man up. "Forgive me. I'm so sorry for all this mess."

"I've been treated worse. But that don't mean I want this to be habit on my ship. You understand, boy?"

Louis looked inquisitively upon the man. "Your—your ship?"

"Well, yes," the sprite intervened as he stepped forward sheepishly, "every ship needs a captain. And, despite what the stories say about his temper, drinking, smoking, herb use, and, that undeniable sensuality—you won't find a better captain in all the kingdom."

Louis felt uncertain about where this was going. "Who is this?"

The Violet Sprite took a deep breath. "Prince Louis, meet the most celebrated and feared commander in all the kingdom, the infamous Captain Armand!"

Louis had never felt such fear. His eyes grew wide as he wildly snapped his head toward his magical ally. "*What*? You can't be serious!"

"Of course I am. Have you ever known me *not* to be serious? Don't answer that."

"I can't believe," Louis began, before looking to the captain, "excuse us a moment..." He huddled closely with the sprite and Ruth.

"Oh, don't get panicky on us now," said the Violet Sprite. "We need a skilled captain, and you won't find one more skilled than he."

"I've no doubt he's skilled," Louis whispered frantically. "How else would he have become the *most wanted pirate in the kingdom*?"

"*All* the kingdoms, boy," came the voice of Captain Armand. "Don't be sellin' me short. I worked my old arse too long to be disrespected."

Louis' heart thumped hard as he turned over his shoulder to see the looming pirate. "I meant no disrespect, sir," Louis explained. Though he'd faced the tyranny of his stepfather and battled a ghoul from the Underworld, the legends of the bloodthirsty Captain Armand he'd heard in his childhood had haunted his dreams his entire life.

"Aye, you royals never did have any manners," growled the old captain. "But perhaps if you give me a chance, I'll charm the pants off ye like the rest of this colorful crew."

Louis took a breath and considered the captain's sentiment. Perhaps he was right. Perhaps Louis had judged Captain Armand as he had the others upon *their* introductions. His stepfather had spread vile stories about those such as Yvonne. Maybe the captain had been just as much a victim of his stepfather's deceitful slander as well.

"My apologies, Captain," Louis began with a new calmness about him. "It seems I have many age-old lessons to unlearn. I apologize for any lies my stepfather may have told about you over the years."

"Lies not be the issue. All them stories ye heard be true. I've run men through just to watch 'em die. I've pillaged. I've plundered. I keelhauled me own brother because I didn't be likin' his attitude one mornin'. And I don't be doin' anything without the promise of treasure and upfront payment. And those who can't pay me, I cut off their toes and add them to me special necklace." The dastardly man put a hand on his worn, leather satchel. "You wanna' see?"

"No!" shouted Louis. "Heavens, no! Is that what smells so *ghastly*?"

Captain Armand glared at the prince for a moment with a greatly insulted scowl on his chapped, thin lips. "That be me," he snarled.

"It's lovely," Louis said with a grin, trying to win back the captain's favor, for he realized they had a bigger problem than the smell of salty sweat. Without access to the palace, they had no way to pay the frightening man. He turned back to his coleaders with fear. "How did you two think we were going to pay him? I can't exactly walk into the royal treasury and withdraw without anyone knowing."

"Don't worry about that, dear," Ruth said calmly.

"I already paid him," explained the sprite with a

wide, satisfied grin.

"You did? How did you…"

"I used *nature's* treasury."

Louis' eyes went wide. He turned to the captain, who gave the sprite a wink. Disgusted, Louis turned back to the enchanter, who was making eyes at the old seafarer.

"What?" the sprite quipped "I'm a fairy, not an angel."

"I still think it's dangerous," Louis explained, a childhood fear in his eyes.

"I know, my boy," said the sprite. "This whole *mission* is dangerous. But need someone who's willing to lead us into the treacherous waters of the bay."

Louis' expression remained uncertain and, what's more, *frightened*, a guise not lost on Ruth. "My dear Louis," she uttered softly. "I know it's scary. *I'm scared too*. But I also know how much you love my Eric, and I know how he loves you. When you have a love like that, I don't believe there's anything that can destroy it. Not pirates, not ghosts, not villains. And if this is going to work, we don't have to like each other—but we do have to work together."

Louis gave a deep sigh, knowing Ruth to be right.

Without a second thought, Ruth placed her right hand softly upon his cheek and the other on his shoulder. "We'll bring our boy home," she assured with the lovingness only a mother could give. Her tenderness made Louis long for the relationship he once had with *his* mother and served as a reminder for *all* they were fighting.

"All right." Louis exhaled, choosing bravery and love over his learned prejudice and fear. "Let's chart a course."

****

So I have to confess something: I made a little change to this part. I know, I know, I should have warned you, and I fought myself over it, but I just couldn't let it slide. I talked to one of my research partners, who said I shouldn't make the change, that it was just a product of its time. An editor told me I should rewrite the whole sequence to make it more sellable. After a few days of going back and forth on the topic, I had coffee with the one person I knew would give me a definitive answer: Professor Sherman.

Let me explain a bit: The relationship between the Violet Sprite and Captain Armand was portrayed slightly differently. Originally, the sprite tangoed with the captain purely out of obligation. There was even a lowbrow joke in there about a "pain in the ass." I'm not one for censorship, but I'm also not one for stories being so blatantly uncomfortable that it makes me feel like I'm back in high school gym having to run the track.

I considered removing the reference altogether, but that still didn't seem right. When I met up with Professor Sherman, I asked her what she thought I should do. She gave me a long, thoughtful stare. I had absolutely no idea what she was going to say. The longer the silence went on, the more nervous I became. Had I asked something so ridiculously blasphemous? After all, this story was very special to her. The silence continued, but just before I could apologize for being a snobby, literary wannabe, she simply said: "Why don't you go with your instinct?"

She took a sip of her vegan latte. I sat, staring at her with abyss eyes. At first, I was confused. This couldn't be the same professor who always knew the perfect direction to give, the one I thought walked on water and could make the moon bow down.

"Wh—what?" I asked.

"What do you think would work? You want to be a screenwriter, don't you? Think like a screenwriter."

I hadn't thought of it from that angle and wondered if it would allow me too much liberty. "I don't know if that's such a good idea."

"Sure, it is. Why do you think I gave you this story?"

"I'm still trying to figure that out."

"Well then, this is part of the process. Part of being a good screenwriter is to look back at the materials that came before you, to know what works, how to make changes the right way without losing the story. Just trust the process and chart your course."

"Chart your course." It was so obviously intentional that I almost got the feeling she knew *I'd be asking this question. Maybe she was magic, or maybe she was just that smart. Either way she knew what she was doing. I went home that night and decided the joke had to change, and it became the one you read above. I can't quite say it was censorship, but I also can't say it didn't need the change for stories like this to last. Regardless, this is one retelling. The book could very well come back again in the future, unedited, warts and all. And I think that's the point Professor Sherman was trying to make that day. I definitely learned something about "thinking like a screenwriter" that day, and it's something that has stayed with me ever since. But more on that later.*

****

Time worked differently in the kingdom of the Divine Lady. Though it had only been a day on land since Eric was taken from his loving rescue, it had been a week below the waves. Every moment that he was away from his prince felt like an eternity. From his first night under the surface of the sea, he badgered the Divine Lady for lessons in a siren song.

"Be patient," she would order. "We have an entire lifetime together."

After a week, Eric decided enough was enough. He swam into the Divine Lady's bedchamber with the power of Poseidon's waves in his heart. He found her floating above her coral vanity, fixing herself into the vision of fishy sensuality in which she took such pride.

"My dear," she greeted with her a loud gusto. She turned from her bubble mirror to face him. "Barging into my private chambers before we're married? What kind of mermaid do you think I am, and how did you guess so easily?"

"I've decided not to marry you," Eric said bravely, folding his arms across his bare, merman chest.

The Divine Lady leered at him for a moment. Surely, he hadn't been so bold, so daft, so *senseless* with his order. She forced a chuckle but put no effort into making it sound convincing. "I don't appreciate land dweller wit. It's all so—well—fishy."

Inside, Eric's nerves were aflame, but determination gave him the strength he needed to face the terrifying creature. "Humor has nothing to do with it," he boldly commanded. "You made me a promise that you would teach me the siren's song. Have I not upheld my promise to live here, and serve you until our wedding day? And yet you can't keep the one promise you made *me*? I see no reason why I should marry you."

"Listen here, *boy*. I've done you a multitude of

favors already, the first being *keeping you alive!*" She swam toward him with rage as vibrant as the Red Sea building in her eyes. "If you think I am in any way indebted to you, I can take away that tail and those gills and let you die a slow, brooding, painful death before I slurp down your flesh and crunch your bones! *Now, does that sound like a better alternative than marriage?*"

The Divine Lady was now upon him, her piercing eyes glaring directly into his. The silence that followed her shouting was intense and dominant. It made the resonances of the ocean ever more prominent, from the heavy tide above to the bubbles that pushed their way through Eric's thick, wet hair. Not a minnow nor a shred of seaweed had the courage to float through the domain after the queen of the sea displayed such rage. Still, terrified as he was within, Eric floated strong with arms folded tightly over mernipples as he arrogantly proclaimed: "It's better than being *lied* to. I'll take it."

He positioned his strong, proud eyes upon those of the Divine Lady. She met them with a flabbergasted stare. This was the moment of truth, and Eric knew it. When her astonishment faded, he knew she may very well carry out his destruction. Still, if there was even a *chance* of learning the song, he had to risk it all.

Finally, she released a full-body chortle, boisterous and booming. "Well," she declared, "I've never met anyone, human or merman, with gilly gonads quite as strong as yours...All right, my sweet." She stroked beneath his chin. "I'll teach you the song." She swam toward the grotto cavity with pride.

"You will?" asked Eric with disbelief in his voice that he tried his hardest to hide. "When?"

"Why, *now*," she turned back over her shoulder.

"But you must promise me one thing—our marriage must occur on the eve you sing your first song. I uphold my end of the bargain, you uphold yours."

This alternative deal was risky, and Eric knew that. However, risk had gotten him this far and he could not turn back now. "It's a deal."

Eric spent day and night learning his song. Often, he would wake before the sun's rays began to break through the sea's surface. He would enter the Divine Lady's chambers and wake her lovingly in hopes of stirring her for the day's work all the earlier. They'd work at breakfast through luncheon, and if he could convince her, until at least the early evening. Following the day, he'd stay up 'till the latest of hours to practice what he'd learned.

After a particularly successful day, the Divine Lady ended their work with a sly grin.

"What's got you so happy, my dear?" Eric asked.

"You did very well, my sweet," she proclaimed. "In fact, I'd say this was the most wonderful you've ever sang your song."

"Really?" exclaimed Eric.

"I believe you're ready to truly sing tomorrow evening."

"You mean it?" It was the first true hope that Eric had felt since the ball with his prince. But hope was soon matched by fear, for with his victory came the duty to fulfill his promise. He'd have to be smart and sleek to execute his plan. It was the greatest risk he'd ever taken, but nothing scared him more than the thought of never seeing Louis again.

That night, he swam far, past the reef that separated his kingdom from Pecker Bay. As he'd been taught, he beached himself upon a rock. He looked to the moon, hanging at its highest point, surrounded by a million stars. He closed and folded his hands around one another. The sound of waves caressing the rocks of Man's Peak relaxed his soul, and he began to picture his prince. As was often the case with memory, Eric had begun to worry that he'd forget the beautiful details that encased Louis' even more beautiful soul. He needn't worry. The moment he closed his eyes, every detail of the dashing prince appeared to him, from his brown-blond hair, to his hazel eyes, to his built physique, to the way his glance lingered far into the distance when he was deep in thought.

He inhaled deeply and exhaled slowly. As he did, the waves around the bay began to follow his breaths. The trees swayed as though a distant storm had only begun to caress them with a gentle wave before violent destruction. With everything as it should be, Eric began to sing:

"My love started years ago,
I was sure you'd never know,
Know my face,
Know my name.
I was sure it was all just a game,
One I'd play 'till I died.
Now matter how hard I tried,
How could there ever be a world,
For the prince and the scribe?
But suddenly you found me,
You took me in your arms.
Suddenly, you loved me,
I'm surrounded by your charms.
I'm convinced I found an angel,

I know I've found my muse.
And despite those who would tear us apart,
To give up on you I refuse.
And so, I ask you on this night,
To follow my song,
To make my voice as your guiding light.
Bring me home,
As you did before,
Bring me home and forever more,
I'll take you in my arms,
I'll surround you with my charms.
And the prince and the scribe shall forever thrive.
And never again will I let you go.
And, together, we'll let our love grow,
Our love that started years ago."

As his song came to an end, the magical winds of the bay blew away from Man's Peak and through the trees of the forest that surrounded it. The bay was now calm. Eric closed his eyes and held his folded hands in each other behind his back. He'd done all he could. Now, he'd just have to hope that his love would hear his call. Reluctantly, he dove back down to the depths and prepared for the long night ahead—a night filled with dreams of rescue and the sweet kiss of his prince.

****

Night was falling over the ship, and they knew they had to shove off lest they be caught. However, attempting to find the right course was not an easy task. As the Violet Sprite pointed out, if they attempted to cut directly through the bay, they would surely be shipwrecked by the rocky bottom the cliffs provided. Captain Armand would not allow them to go around the back, as the small town on the forest's end had a bounty on his head. Two other routes were recommended and ultimately dashed for dangers of the legendary sea creature, the Divine Lady's pet, that guarded the waters.

Louis was growing impatient. He knew their time was running out, and thus so was Eric's, *if* he had any time at all. Frustrated with the arguing of the others, he pulled himself away from the group and went to the rail. The Violet Spite soon took notice and joined the prince in his frustrated sulking.

"Are you all right, Your Highness?" asked the sprite.

"How can I be?" Louis intensely questioned. "Everyone's arguing about courses and monsters, while my Eric is out there somewhere. Perhaps he's suffering, drowning, or already...*gone*. We're never going to find him this way."

"You must have faith. Don't give me that look, dear. I know how wretched such advice sounds in times such as these. It's one of the most sickening parts of being a fairy, mind you. But—it is true. You simply can't believe we'll never find him. The fates and the gods know your true feelings. Prove your faith, and *we will rescue your Eric*."

As the words of the sprite lingered on the pallet of the prince, a gentle breeze swept over his cheeks as though it were a gift from the sea. It grew stronger, rousing the waves below and shaking the mast above. Something within Louis told him to close his eyes, and in the wind, he heard the gentle, enchanting voice of Eric. Though Louis did not understand the nature of the beckon, nor did he understand how it came to him, there was no mistaking that it was indeed Eric.

After the wind passed, Louis' eyes snapped open.

He was breathless for a moment but finally managed two words that brought him the greatest joy of his life: "*He's alive*."

"What was that, Your Majesty?" asked the sprite.

"He's alive!" exclaimed Louis. "I know he is. And I know exactly how we're going to find him!"

The Violet Sprite grinned as Louis rushed to the bickering group.

"Enough arguing!" Louis commanded. "I know what we're going to do." He pushed through the group to the captain's map that was laid out on the table. Several seas and channels had been coursed on the wrinkled map, but Louis was not interested in them. He ran his fingertips over a blank area of the ocean, one that had not yet been charted. "Here," he proclaimed. "Here is where he is, and here is where we'll sail."

"Don't be so daft, Your Highness," Captain Armand ordered. "These waters not yet been explored by man. Any creature or demon could drag us to Davy Jones' Locker. And besides, if ye spell took him to the bay, that be leagues away."

"Don't ask me how I know, but he's there, and *don't* argue with me again, Captain, or I'll happily turn you into the many bounty hunters who'd fight over your head."

The prince's threat rang in the ears of all, and they knew it to be true. No one dared argue with him further, despite how dangerous and unpredictable the passage may seem.

Even the fearsome Captain Armand was quiet for a moment before nodding with the declaration: "Aye, chart a course to waters unknown. This ship be under the command of the prince, and we best better listen to him!

What are ye staring at ya cockroaches? To your positions!"

With that, the crew eagerly scattered to make way as Louis watched with amazement. Though he was royal and had lived his life in a palace, he'd never before known such loyalty and respect from his subjects. Perhaps, his place had been with these wonderful misfits all along.

The Violet Sprite watched the prince with pride, for he'd grown just as fond of the young royal as he had the scribe and longed to show it. With a wave of his wand, a cloud of sparkling purple smoke surrounded Louis. When it cleared, Louis found himself in a strapping, leather tunic that was both striking and presented command. It was far more feminine in style than what a prince was supposed to wear but was built perfectly for his body.

"What was that for?" Louis asked.

"Well, you are the leader of our little crew of rebels," explained the fairy. "I figured you should look the part."

Louis smiled, for he truly felt at home in these clothes and with these people. All that was missing was his love. An unfortunate truth that would soon be remedied, of that he was determined.

"We're shoving off, Your Highness," Captain Armand said with newfound respect.

Louis nodded to him and made way for the tiller's end. From there, he looked out over the sea that lay past the harbor. The uncertainty of the voyage ahead weighed on his mind, but the determination to rescue filled his heart. He held his own hands behind his back, deep down knowing that Eric was doing the same. As they slowly began for the sea, the breeze once again caressed his face, the scribe's song once again called to him. Quietly, he spoke to the wind, in hopes its magic would carry his promise back to his beloved:

"You can never know how lonely I was the day our eyes met all those years ago. My life was the most miserable of existences and I wanted nothing more than to escape this horrid kingdom, until that day. Your gaze and your smile saved me from drowning in my sorrows; they sang to me as you sing to me now. I never knew if I would know your name, nor if I would see you again, nor if you were real. But the hope that you were and that you would someday be mine kept me from fleeing this kingdom when it seemed as though it was my only freedom. But now, now I flee to save you. Eric, my love, my life, I won't rest until we're together again. And this time, no man, nor beast will separate us. I don't care how long I must chart these waters. If it takes one hundred years, I'll see to it I live longer to hold you in my arms again."

The ship sailed from the harbor, putting more and more distance between the crew and the kingdom. But Louis did not care. His eyes were on the open waters that lay ahead. He climbed the ladder that hung against the mast, his sight on the last ray of the setting sun. The breeze became a wild bluster, gusting through his thick, well-kept hair. He inhaled the gust's sea salt, the sweet words of his scribe within it, and spoke aloud one final promise for it to carry back:

"If it takes the rest of my earthly days, I'll find you, again, and I'll bring you home forever more."

Part Three

Chapter Thirteen

"The Pirate and the Prince"
Published in The Scribe's Collection *as "The Pirate and the Princess."*

Congratulations on making it to Part Three! You must be really committed, or Drag Race *is on hiatus. Anyway, if the name change isn't indication enough, this chapter was changed into yet another run of the mill hetero-fairy tale romance. While the name makes it sound like some drug store paperback porno, it could not have been more boring and more sexless—neither of which the original chapter is. Because of that, it was not easy to piece back together, but it* was *easily one of the most fun. I hope you enjoy reading it as much as I enjoyed discovering it.*

****

The three guards stood dripping wet in front of the king and queen, who were seated high upon their thrones.

The king had been frighteningly silent since the men told him of their overthrow at the docks. He tapped a finger on the gaudy arm of his chair, impatiently glaring down upon them. "They got away?" he began finally. "*With my ship?*"

The leader of the trio took a deep breath. "Unfortunately—yes," he admitted.

The fire in the king's glare was sweltering, as it

landed upon the guards. Still, there was a fate worse than its burn. "Kill them," Desmos told the false queen.

She looked upon the king with disbelief. "What?"

"You heard me, *kill them*. And do it in your true form. I want the last thing they know in this world to be terror and dread."

The witch was reluctant to shed her regal shape. "My love," she whispered, "it's too great a risk. What if the screams call others before I can return to my disguise?"

"Then you better kill them quickly!" The king's order was filled with horrific anger.

The queen shivered and reluctantly stood. She rolled up her sleeves and descended the stairs. She looked upon the terrified and confused faces of the men, an eerie feeling of regret in her heart. "I'm sorry, boys," she said, dropping Queen Krystal's voice to use her own.

"Queen Krystal?" questioned the leader.

She inhaled; her eyes grew tense. "I'm not Queen Krystal," she proclaimed chillingly.

A plume of fire surrounded her. When it dissipated, the Celtic Witch stood in her full, frightening form in front of the men. Before they could scream, she waived her hands, and the trio crumbled into dust. The witch kept her regretful eyes upon the piles for a moment, as King Desmos smiled behind her.

"See," he called from behind with a wicked glee in his voice. "It wasn't so terrible, now, was it? Now, come along." He rose from his throne and descended the stairs. "We must find that ship."

The Celtic Witch lingered in her regret a moment longer, for unbeknownst to the king, there was more to their relationship than met the eye; a truth that she worried had pulled her in too deep.

****

The seas had not been kind to the crew of misfits. Rocky waters, dangerous reefs and strange sea life continuously threatened the voyage. It did not help that Louis insistently pushed Captain Armand to pick up the pace.

"We'll get there when we get there, boy," argued the captain. "These waters be treacherous and unpredictable. We must take the course slowly."

"That's not good enough!" Louis barked, slamming his hand upon the nearby rail.

"Listen here, yer majesty, just 'cause you threaten me doesn't mean I won't show you how I got me reputation. I can still run you through."

"Good luck avoiding mutiny!"

"I'll show them all what becomes of mutineers!"

"That's enough," called an approaching Yvonne. "We can't allow our differences to make us like our enemies. We have one goal here. Do you think arguing will bring us some sort of magical solution?"

"Magic." Louis beckoned with epiphany in his voice. "That's it. Where's the sprite?"

"He be in the captain's quarters," Captain Armand said with a sly grin.

"Lovely" Louis shuddered. He rushed down the stairs and made way for the doors to the captain's private room.

Without warning, Louis threw the door open. "I have an idea!" he called as he barged into the room. The sprite stirred beneath the sheets, and sat up, his eyes squinted from slumber.

"I'm so sorry," Louis apologized.

146

"Worry not. It's only the exhaustion of a sprite who did well satisfying his lover."

"I-I have an idea," Louis continued, too excited to concern himself with the state of the sprite. "A way to get us to Eric faster."

"Pray tell," the sprite requested.

"Magic!" Louis explained. "You're the most powerful being I've ever met. You were going to banish that ghoul before it intervened to the depths. Can you use your power to get us there faster?"

The Violet Sprite sighed. "I'm afraid I can't."

"What? Why not?"

"It's not so simple, dear. You see, we knew we were sending the creature to meet his climactic end in Pecker Bay. But, where Eric is now, we don't know. Without guidance, the spell would run rampant. We could end up at world's end—if it had one. For future reference, it's round. But anyway, I'm afraid it is quite impossible."

The prince stood intensely silent. The Violet Sprite nodded, letting Louis know he was ready for him to shout his frustrations. What came from the prince, instead, was far from what the sprite had prepared for. Instead of a lashing, or unreasonable reasoning, Louis' eyes filled with tears of fear, frustration, and loneliness. Tears that broke the heart of the sprite as Louis fled from the room.

The Violet Sprite had long been proud of his work. He'd always managed wishes granted, spells that pleased, and wit that educated. However, for the first time, he felt like a failure. As misery filled his being, there came an eerie and familiar voice from behind:

"It's so hard when the mortals misunderstand us, isn't?"

A chill rushed up the sprite's spine. He needn't turn around to know who it was stepping out of the shadows.

"No one ever said being magical was easy," the Celtic Witch proclaimed as she approached her son.

"What are you doing here?" he asked with a cold, viciously low tone. "How did you even *find* us?"

"Don't be so distraught," she gleefully ordered as she passed around to his front. "Seems to me that location spell is just what you need."

"Oh, I need a spell from you like I need a kick in the arse."

"From what I gather, you've already had one of those tonight from that dirty pirate."

With a cloud of smoke, the sprite shrunk himself down and began to fly away from the witch.

"No, wait!" she called, a strange, unfamiliar tone in her voice stopping the sprite in his path.

Reluctantly, but unfortunately curious, he turned back to her.

"I didn't come to argue or insult you."

"Fine job you're doing."

"Well, old habits." She grinned. "Hard as it may be to believe…I came to help."

"*You? Help?* Good gods, Mother. You expect me to believe such do-lally?"

"I know I've given you very little reason to since we—since we?"

"Fell out because I was in love with another sprite instead of a pixie?"

"Yes. Believe it or not, I want to make it right. And this may not be the time for that yet, not completely. But I'm hoping this is a start. You see, there is a great war on the horizon. Something even bigger than this battle. This is much larger than just the prince and his poet."

"He's a scribe."

"I know that! Dammit, will you just give me a chance?" She breathed in the silence as she prepared, then released it. "I was shite as your mother. That I know. But my alliance with the king, it's about something more. Something that's been years in the making. And today, today he forced my hand with a task that confirmed what I've been sensing. Believe it or not, for this battle, I—the kingdom—need the prince and the scribe united. The fate of all depends on their union."

"You expect me to believe that the woman who couldn't handle my little romance wants the prince's to work? The woman that is taking a ride on the crown every chance she gets?"

"We're far too much alike for you to judge what I do in the night. Besides, he's a means to an end. *His* end. He's on the hunt for this ship, but if you'll allow me, I'll see that you get to the Divine Lady's Kingdom and back home before he and the navy can even get within a thousand miles of you."

"You speak well, Mother. You always have. But you've given me no reason to trust you. Besides, any spell you cast is that of dark magic. It's messing with such nasty work that lost you your wings. I may not be the best sprite as of late, but falling from grace as you have, that's something I'll never do."

"Then let me prove to you that my intentions are true, and let me protect you from such a fate."

The Violet Sprite could not help being intrigued. "*How?*" he asked with a raised eyebrow.

"With this," she said, pulling a vile of potion from her garter. "I've bottled the spell you need. Do as I did to you and neutralize my magic. Send me back to the kingdom, so you know I can't cause mischief. All you have to do is smash the bottle on the bow, and it enacts the spell without it affecting your soul. You can save the scribe and safely get everyone home."

The Violet Sprite glared and stared her down. He would not show any sign of emotion other than suspicion as he thought over her offer. His mind told him not to trust the woman who'd rejected him and ruined his life. But his gut said something different. There was something both frighteningly unfamiliar about the look in her eyes, as well as something that reminded him of home. A home he hadn't known since he was a boy, and a home he'd always been afraid to admit he missed.

"If this turns out to be a trick," he sternly stated, "I'll see to it you spend a thousand eternities in the pits of the Underworld.

To this warning, she simply gave an honest nod. "I'm not so sure that isn't the fate I will face already."

The Violet Sprite knew not what to believe, but the offer was better than any he could conjure on his own. With caution, he reached out his hand. She brought the bottle to him gently. He snatched it quickly and did not allow their fingers to touch.

"I wish you the best, my son."

Before she could say another word, he waved his wand, and in a puff of magic, she was gone. The sprite took a moment to himself before joining the others on deck. His mind and his heart were locked in a battle of logic, emotion, and confusion. Time, however, was of the essence, and he was forced to reconcile with his sensitivities, at least temporarily.

When he emerged on deck, he found Louis sitting

sorrowfully with Ruth, Yvonne, and Evers. He took a breath and ignored the troubles within him.

"Why the long face?" the sprite asked Louis with a forced but well-played enthusiasm.

"You know why," answered a defeated Louis. "I'm sorry I forced you all out here. I should have come alone."

"Don't be sorry, my dear," Ruth comforted with a mother's touch.

"You didn't force us at all," Evers added.

"Except for the captain," called the twins in unison.

"All right, all right," the Violet Sprite interrupted. "*Enough moping.* It just so happens I've got something that'll fix it all."

"Unless it's Eric, I don't think that's possible." Louis sighed, his spirit growing weaker by the moment.

"Well, as much as I'd love to have him tucked away in my belt strap, what do you think of *this*?" the Violet Sprite asked, producing the vile his mother had given him.

The group gandered at the small jug, curious and confused.

"What is that?" Louis asked.

"Follow me, and you shall see," the sprite sang.

Louis and the group followed him to the ship's bow.

"Steer us straight, captain," called the sprite.

Captain Armand gave the fairy a wink with one of his wrinkled eyelids. The Violet Sprite shrank himself and soared out to the ship's buffly carved, merman figure head. With nerves and a glimmer of hope in his heart, the Violet Sprite smashed the bottle on the pecks of merman. As the liquid morphed to blue steam, the sprite fluttered back, and landed in his full-grown size on deck.

"Everyone, grab onto something!" he ordered.

The crew did as they were told, folding their arms in and around ropes and rails. Captain Armand tightened his grip on the handles of the wheel.

"Well?" asked Zest.

"When's it going to happen?" continued Glacé.

"Oh, it's going to happen," the Violet Sprite sang, trying to keep up his gleeful persona, though deep down, he was beginning to worry that he'd been tricked by his mother. However, before his anxieties could become too great, the hull beneath them began to rumble.

"What is that?" asked Evers.

"It's a Kraken!" exclaimed Captain Armand.

The rumbling grew louder as the deck planks creaked. With a jolt, the ship began to rise, throwing the unsuspecting crew as they fought to hold onto their respective safety. Higher and higher it hovered. Some members of the crew were amazed, others were shocked, and in the case of Evers, one was sick.

"You can *really* tell how high we are now," Ruth said as she watched the guard hurl over the side of the ship, the discharge traveling quite the distance before it hit the cresting waters below.

"Thanks for that." The sprite gagged.

Finally, the ship stopped its upward path. It hung in the air, creaking still as all waited to see what was next to come. Then, with a violent thrust forward that knocked the entire crew back, the vessel cut through the wind so quickly that their surroundings just appeared as a vast, consuming haze of white.

"Woo!" Glacé gleefully screamed.

"This is fantastical!" followed Zest.

"I'm going to be sick again," complained Evers.

"Don't even think about it!" remarked the Violet Sprite.

The ship continued to pound its way through the nothingness until Louis saw a light at the end of the tunnel.

"There!" he pointed. "Do you see that?"

"What ye see, boy?" asked Captain Armand, trying his hardest to keep the ship steady.

"A light! We're heading straight for it!"

"I hope it's death," cried Evers.

"It's the place we've been looking for," Louis proclaimed. "This is it! I can feel it!"

As they approached the light, they were met with the unmistakable gust of a sea breeze, the squawks of gulls fighting over a meal, the mist of the ocean caressing their cheeks.

The ship burst through the brightness, onto a morning-lit ocean. It skidded forcefully across the sea, before Captain Armand was finally able to bring it to a halt. The sudden stop threw the Violet Sprite forward into the rail.

"Perfect," he said with muffled voice, his face still pressed against the banister.

The sprite adjusted himself. "Well, let's get to business."

"Yes," intervened Louis. "My sweet Eric is here somewhere. And it's time we found him. It's time we bring him home."

****

I thought this might be a good place to check in. This is by far one of the more eventful chapters so far, and it only gets more eventful from here. In fact, I would say as the rest of this all plays out (the rescue and everything) it gets sort of bizarre. Not in a bad way necessarily, but it does start to take on some vintage Tim Burton. I sort of feel like this was Author Eric's way of setting the tone for Part Four, in kind of the same way he set up Part Two by slowly introducing the witch earlier. But I'm getting ahead of myself, considering you just started Part Three. Anyway, just wanted you to be prepared for some of the oddities that were coming and—I guess spoiler alert— *some of the downright insane solutions that come out of the arc of the hero's quest. Don't say I didn't warn you.*

****

"Rise and swim, sleeping beauty," called the gruff, full voice of the Divine Lady.

Eric's eyes immediately snapped open. He need not clear them to know she was there with her clever grin and a plan.

"Good morning," he greeted nervously. "You're up early."

"Well, it is our wedding day, after all. There's much to do."

Eric had been so overjoyed by his prince's response that he'd all but forgotten about his bargain. "*Our wedding?*" he exclaimed. "I mean—of course, our wedding."

His correction was quick enough for the Divine Lady, whose suspicions were raised, as was one of her curious, arched brows. "Now, now, my catfish, you didn't put our special day out of mind, did you?"

"Of course not. It's only—so early. I'm not quite awake."

The lady's cunning smile turned to one that was chilling. "Well, perhaps if you hadn't spent your night swimming to the surface, you wouldn't be so waterlogged."

A chill greater than that of the icy ocean rushed down Eric's spine and all the way through his shimmering, blue tail. Despite the fear within him, he kept his composure. "Oh, yes," he softly agreed. "Sometimes, when it's hard to sleep, I like to go and make certain our kingdom is safe from humans."

"Is that so?" she asked, her smile remaining eerily unmoved.

"Of course," responded Eric.

"Then, why did you sing your song?"

Eric floated with flabbergast. He didn't know how to respond. Telling the truth would only anger her, whilst lying would anger her more. "I-I," he stuttered.

"I'm the queen of the sea," she reminded him sternly. "You think you could sing a siren's song, something I *taught* you without me knowing? And *why*? So you can call your prince here?"

Eric's jaw dropped, and his fear grew.

"That's right," she continued with a menacing glee. "I know *everything*! I know the betrayal you planned; I know about the rescue. And I'll see to it that your *prince* never sees you *again*."

Eric felt his heart palpitate wildly as his mind raced for some way to warn Louis of the sea monster's wrath. However, his anxieties were only raised when the grimace she laid upon him became a wild and devious beam.

"You're wondering how to save him," she gleamed. "Perhaps you're foolish enough to even try calling to him again. But, *my angel fish*, it'll be hard to do that without your voice."

She snapped her eyes shut and reopened them

quickly to reveal her stunning brown eyes were now lifeless and like those of a viper fish. It was a horrific image. One that made Eric's stomach quake. But this was not the end of the unnerving sight, for her human lips disintegrated and turned to that of deep-water species as well, spiking teeth and all. Eric tried to swim away slowly, but the Divine Lady released one of her tentacles, wrapping it around his left side and then one around his right, the feelers meeting in the middle of his back. With horrible, unescapable force, she pulled him back toward her until his neck was less than an inch away from her jaws.

Her lips parted with a crack, and she cocked her head to one side, slowly moving the gaping, needled doom to Eric's neck. He was certain he would find no rescue and that the last thing he would know in life was the bloody, painful sensation of his throat being ripped from his neck. Still, this was not nearly as horrid as the demise she'd threatened Louis. For that reason, he fought with the only part of his body that he could move: his head. He pulled it farther and farther away, but soon one of the tentacles moved it closer. He could feel the sharp edges of her teeth wrapping around his throat, ready to clamp down. He closed his eyes, unwilling but readying himself for death. However, he was not met with the gory, horrific death he expected. Instead, there came a hefty breath followed by a sucking of air and popping of fish lips.

Eric opened his eyes, confused and intrigued. The sight with which he was met was somehow both comical and disturbing. The Divine Lady's jaw was indeed but a bite away from ending Eric's earthly existence. However, hover above his throat was all they did.

Suddenly, his throat began to feel tight and dry. That's when he remembered her threat. His vocal cords began to throb as though they were about to explode. The taste of blood lingered on the back of his tongue as it bubbled up from his distressed voice box. It was a painful concoction of horror, one that Eric was not sure he could survive.

Then, the chaos ceased. The blood in his mouth slid back down his throat, and the pain in his vocal cords vanished. But all was not well for long. Soon, the painful horrors of the unholy spell were replaced with an ashy dryness. Eric could feel his vocal cords shrink and disintegrate. It was slow and almost monotonous, which made it all the more horrific. Desperate, he gasped and tried to sing one last song to warn his lover. However, all he could manage was a minuscule, fleeting "Ah." Try as he might, no other sound would come from him. As she'd warned, the Divine Lady took his voice.

When she pulled back from Eric's neck, her features had returned to that of a lady.

"You probably thought I was going to kill you, didn't you?" She grinned.

Eric opened his mouth to shout at the woman, though, deep down, he knew it was futile.

"Oh, yes," she viciously teased. She released him from her tentacles and looked him over. "You know, when I found out you loved the prince, I was worried that our marriage would be bumpy seas. But, without your voice, it looks like an eternity of smooth sailing. Now, I have to pay a visit to your prince, and his friends. And don't you even *dream* of swimming away. I'll know, and I'll be left with no choice but to serve your prince on a plate at the wedding."

The Divine Lady began to swim from the chamber. Desperate to save his lover, Eric swam after her with fury, reaching to grab her tail. His swishing was like blood in the water to Morgana's shark-like senses, and she turned, ready for the attack, freezing Eric in his path with a wave of her hand.

"I warned you," growled the Divine Lady. "Now you'll see how wrathful the seas can be."

She cast a spell that sent a mess of conch shells, sand, and dead fish cascading down, defying the laws of water and blocking Eric in.

Still, he would not give up. He swam back across the room, geared up his tail, and rushed the barricade, meeting it without success. He did not let this failure deter him. He stretched his fin and once again made way for the clutter that kept him trapped. Still, the wall stood firm. He tried once more, this time injuring his good writing hand in the process. It was a shattering pain, only made worse by the fact that he could not shriek, swear, or sigh. Defeated and pained, he sank to his fins.

He longed to cry out to his prince, to beg for help, to warn him of the coming danger. However, he feared that doom was imminent. Eric deeply sighed and began to weep. Little did he know, he'd already sent a message up to the surface. Small and minuscule, but one that would still serve his prince nonetheless.

****

Louis stood at the railing looking over miles of sea. He ran his hand around the hilt of his sword as frustration built within. They'd been sailing the strange waters for an hour, yet there was no sign of any sort of life—not a whale, not a fish, and certainly not Eric. He tore himself from the rail and paced to Captain Armand at the helm.

The Violet Sprite stood at the captain's side, his wand drawn and held out proudly.

"What are you doing?" Louis asked. "Is this some sort of strange game I don't wish to know about?"

"No, no!" called the sprite. "Although, you've just given me an idea for later."

"Aye," agreed the captain.

"This is a location spell," the Violet Sprite explained. "My wand is searching for any sort of magical life. It will glow the closer we get to it, and *that* will lead us to the scribe."

Louis took a deep breath, his anxieties racing as he realized more patience would be required of him. He decided to climb the crow's nest for a better vantage point of merlife. When he reached the top, he found Glacé flipping through a book and Zest asleep, his head propped up on the rail.

"What are you two doing up here?" Louis exclaimed.

"Keeping a lookout," explained Glacé.

"Nothing to report so far, Your Highness," added Zest, his eyes still closed.

"How could you tell when you're both up here lollygagging?" Louis asked.

"We're not lollygagging," Zest defended.

"We're still virgins," added Glacé.

"That's not what I meant. What I mean is, Eric could be out there right now, and we wouldn't have any idea—"

Suddenly, a cry in the wind stopped Louis' scolding. The last sound Eric had made before the Divine Lady had taken his voice found its way to the prince. Though but a small call, Louis knew his lover's voice so well.

"Eric," he said to himself with a shiver.

"What was that, Your Majesty?" Glacé asked.

"I think he called us hysterics," explained Zest.

"Please," interrupted Louis. "I must listen." Louis closed his eyes and concentrated on the echoes of the ocean and wind, hopeful that they carried a further message. Sadly, there came only lonely gusts and cresting waves.

"What is it, Prince Louis?" asked Glacé without a hint of the normal regimen for which he and Zest were known.

"It was Eric," the prince sorrowfully explained. "He's in trouble."

Before Louis could say another word, there came a call from below: "Your Highness!" It was the Violet Sprite.

Louis looked over the side to see the Violet Sprite's wand glowing bright. Without hesitation, Louis climbed down the latter with haste, landing on deck with a thud. "Is it him? Is it Eric?" asked the prince as he stood from his mooring. However, once his eyes met the fairy and the captain at the wheel, he knew it could not be his scribe, for their jaws were dropped, and their gaze was wide.

"It's not Eric." The sprite shivered.

Louis turned to see the rest of the crew gathering on deck with equal awe and fright. A large wave rose in front of the bow in a manner which waves did not behave. It was slow, large, threatening, and growing by the second. Once it reached a height greater than that of the crow's nest, it hovered threateningly above the ship. All stood back aghast at the leering sight, wondering when it would smash down upon them and destroy the vessel.

However, as it floated, Louis squinted. He saw something *else* coming their way, something moving *within* the wave itself.

"What is that?" Louis exclaimed.

"Whatever it is," began the Violet Sprite, pointing his wand directly at the mass, as it glowed intensely, "it's merfolk magic."

Suddenly, the figure within approached and stepped out of the wave. She waltzed across the deck with a frightening confidence. The eyes of all remained locked on every step she took. For a moment, none were brave enough to address the enchantress, until there came a call from the captain:

"You *devil*. Get off me ship. I won't have any of your evil aboard."

"Evil?" Morgana teased in a guileful voice. "Now, now, how could one think that of a *Divine Lady* such as I?"

Her words sent chills down the spines of all but that of the prince.

Louis stepped forward with caution. He was not about to make the same mistakes he'd made at the tower. "Please," he began politely, his hands held up, defenseless, "we don't want to fight. My love is in your kingdom, my lady. We've just come to save him. I can give you anything you want. But, please, *please* just let me have him."

"Oh, well isn't that lovely?" she grinned. "But, you see, that boy is no longer your love. *He's mine*. We're getting married this evening. I'd invite you, but I don't think you're the sort of influence that would do him good. You see, I gave him a place in my palace, and I taught him to sing a siren's song. I've treated him very well—much better than I've ever treated any human before…And yet, he betrayed me by calling you here. So I suppose I just have to kill you."

It was with that threat that Louis stripped away his compassion. He drew his sword. "Don't challenge me. There's nothing I won't do to bring my scribe home. And if you're not going to bring him to me, *get off my ship*. And I'll find him myself."

"I'll get off your ship," she said with a snaring smile. "And I'll take your ship off my *ocean*."

She ran backward to the railing and, with unearthly agility, she grabbed the banister and threw herself leg over leg back to the sea.

Louis ran to the side and searched the waters for any sign of the lady. For a moment, there was none. Then, something began to rise from the depths. Initially, it seemed miniscule. Then, it grew to the size of a shark, then a whale, then more and more as it rushed to the surface. Nothing that Louis imagined could have prepared him for the creature that breached.

A monster greater than that of anything the crew had ever seen sailed through the air with horrific velocity. The lady had transformed into her full leviathan shape. She roared with power that shook the ship more than the waves her breech had caused.

"She's got a monster under her command!" exclaimed the captain.

"That's no monster!" Louis yelled back. "It's her!"

The creature floated on its tail, looking down upon the vessel.

"You've got that right." The voice of the Divine Lady boomed from the beast. "Now, I suggest you sail far, *far* away from my kingdom, or I'll be forced to murder, maim, eat all of you.

"Eat us?" cried Zest.

"No one said anything about being eaten," Glacé stated.

"Only potential death," agreed Zest.

"Nothing about being eaten, though," Glacé said, turning his nose up at the idea.

"Shut up, or I'll devour you both first," ordered the leviathan.

For the first time, the twins were completely silent.

Louis turned to the Violet Sprite. "Can we win?"

"She and I both have magic," he explained. "We both have armies. But only one of us has a heart."

Louis grinned, then turned back to the monster. "I'll give you one last chance to surrender my scribe," he demanded. "If you don't, I promise you, your throne will be cold by battle's end."

The creature released a robust chortle. "You humans truly are the most arrogant creatures. But have it *your way.*" With the ominous threat delivered, the creature slowly sank back into the ocean. An eerie silence followed, leaving the crew on edge.

The glow from the sprite's wand faded away, even though they all knew it couldn't possibly be over.

"Where is she?" asked Louis.

The Violet Sprite looked around, he too uncertain.

Yvonne moved across the deck, spying something in the distance. "There." They pointed. "Over there, it looks like a storm cloud."

"Aye," agreed the captain. "But that's no normal rain. When ye been on the sea as long as I, you know the threat of a summer storm or a hurricane. That…that's magic."

The suspicion was confirmed when the sprite's wand sparked back to life. The storm soared across the waters, ready to destroy the crew. The waters beneath the ship churned wildly and soon the vessel was pulled in a circular motion.

"What's happening?" cried Ruth.

"I'm going to be sick again," complained Evers.

"I've seen enough," Glacé said to his brother.

"Me too," agreed Zest.

The two hurried down from the crow's nest, as the ship pitched and turned.

"It be a whirlpool!" shouted Captain Armand. "Everyone, grab on to somethin' firm, less ye wanna be washed to the devil's triangle!"

Zest and Glacé each grabbed onto one of Louis' muscley buttocks.

"What are you doing?" the prince demanded to know, while breaking free from their grasp.

"He said grab something firm," explained Zest.

"So we did," furthered Glacé.

"Not like that you idiots," called an onlooking sprite, before turning his urgent eyes to Louis. "Your Highness, look!" He motioned toward the sea on which they now spun with his ever-brightening wand.

Louis rushed to the side to which the Violet Sprite had pointed. The leviathan was rising from within the whirlpool, a horrible screech echoing upward.

"Everyone, to the bombardrums!" ordered Louis.

The crew did as they were ordered and manned the weapons. As the creature once again breached with horror, the cannons were fired one by one. While most struck vigorously, they caused no harm to the Divine

Lady. She fell back toward the sea, creating a massive backsplash that pulled them farther into the whirlpool.

Captain Armand held the helm strongly against the ocean's grasp, as the sprite shrank himself down and flew over the abyss to strike the monster with magic. While the spells did indeed affect the lady, they did not *defeat* her, but *angered* her. She rose for another attack.

"Keep hittin' her with ye blasts!" ordered Armand through the waves, rain, and thunder.

The monster was again airborne, and with a swish of her tail, she took out part of the deck, pulling the vessel closer to a watery hell. The crew fought gallantly, the sprite continued his spells, yet it seemed to Captain Armand that they were fighting a losing battle. He'd not come this far in life and had not outrun a thousand royal navies, nor survived three hundred execution attempts to be defeated by a fish.

He let out a scream and declared "Enough of this shite!" The captain motioned for Louis to take the helm.

"I don't know how," argued the prince.

"You know how to not trip on ye own bollocks? It be the same thing, now take it!" ordered the captain.

Louis did as he was told, and watched the captain draw his sword. Armand made way for the mast. With one free hand, bravely and alone, the old seamen climbed higher and higher, past the crow's nest to the topmost sail. Across it he trekked until he came to the very end.

"I ain't going down without a fight!" Captain Armand bellowed at the beast below. "Ye be hearin' me? If you want to eat me crew, me ship and meself, it be on me own terms. Open wide, and taste this!"

The leviathan was once again rising from the depths, its jaws gaping and its eyes bloodthirsty. Without hesitation, or sign of fear, the captain plummeted from the sail, sword first. Louis, the sprite, and the crew watched in disbelief as the old man soared closer and closer to his approaching death. Gleefully and madly, he chuckled as he fell into the mouth of the monster.

At the height of her breech, the captain was gone, and for a moment, so were the crew's dreams of victory. That was until the Devine Lady's climax was ceased by a loud, gargled, cough. Then, a heave. The monster writhed with pain, as she clumsily fell back into the water below.

As she vanished into the depths, the whirlpool began to fall in on itself, dragging the ship and its crew with it. Louis fought to hold the ship steady. Ruth and Yvonne joined him in the effort, but the powers of the wave that dragged them were far too strong. To their great, astonished relief, the ship came to a sudden, rocky, yet safe halt. The trio looked to see the Violet Sprite hovering overhead, dropping a spell upon the vessel. He floated down and returned to his human size as he joined them on the deck, as the storm above cleared.

There was a moment of silence from all, as the crew caught their collective breaths. No one was quite conscious in the moment as they recovered from the horrific excitement they'd endured. Finally, the sprite took it upon himself to break the quiet:

"What the *feck* was that?"

"Where's the captain?" Glacé asked.

"Is he dead?" wondered Zest.

Louis motioned for the sprite and Ruth to join him away from the group.

"This isn't over," Louis told them with flustered frustration.

"That beast choked on my lover and the storm went away," explained an exasperated sprite. "It's over."

"It isn't though!" Louis shouted.

"He's right," Ruth agreed. "If it's over, where's Eric?"

The question weighed heavily on the three. They wondered if the consequences of the captain's actions had doomed Eric to a life away from them, or worse. The chilling thought brought fear to Ruth, regret to the sprite, and agony to Louis. However, their respective worries were soon interrupted, for not a moment after, two waves gushed over the side of the ship, leaving behind two bodies. The first the crew immediately recognized as that of Captain Armand.

"It's the captain!" cried Yvonne.

The whole of the crew rushed to see if he was still alive, but not Louis, for the prince's eyes were on that of the other cadaver. He knew it was that of the Divine Lady. He drew his sword, and waltzed toward her blade first. As he did, the crew huzzahed with joy as the captain coughed up water and sat proudly. None of this caught any of Louis' attention, for he was concerned with making the witch pay for what she had done to his scribe and was determined to force his return.

Yvonne and Ruth both took notice of Louis' fury and rushed to him.

"Your Highness," cooed Yvonne. "Didn't you hear? The captain's alive."

"So is *she*," the prince growled through gritted teeth. "And now, now she's going to take me to Eric—or she'll meet the sharp end of my sword."

To the startle of all, the Divine Lady sat up, and to their further fright, a sharp end of a sword she'd already met, for Captain Arman's blade was stabbed into her mouth.

"Oh my—" began Zest, before he made way for the rail, over which he intended to get very sick.

"I think what my brother meant was—" attempted Glacé, before he too dashed to join his brother.

"Well, you know where I'll be," admitted Evers as he completed the line at the rail.

The Divine Lady looked around with flustered, vexed eyes, motioning for someone to help her.

Captain Armand released a healthy belly laugh. "It does me heart good to know I can still leave 'em speechless."

The Divine Lady muttered angrily and flayed her arms like a mad person.

"All right, all right," said the captain, standing and limping over to the sea witch. "Don't get your tentacles in a twist."

He grabbed the sword's hilt and pulled it from her mouth. The heroes who remained with their stomachs strong all shook with shock.

"Well, I think I shall be joining our friends," declared the sprite.

"Me as well," agreed Yvonne.

The two made way for the rail, leaving only a stunned Louis and Ruth with the captain and the witch. The Divine Lady hacked several coughs with a hand on her neck and the other rubbing her jaw.

"You stabbed me in the uvula." The Divine Lady coughed.

"I got nowhere near your lady bits," replied the captain.

"You mindless fool," the lady began to bicker.

"Don't you know—"

"Stop it this instant!" Louis commanded. He pointed his sword at the lady's throat. "*You've* lost. Now bring me to my Eric, or I'll see this blade is the last you swallow."

The Divine Lady chuckled. "You really think that scares me?"

"*Yes*, actually. *I do!*" He pushed the sword against her neck. "You see, your excellency, you're not only outnumbered, you're *outloved*. No matter what trap you've set for him, Eric's love for me and mine for him is stronger than your magic. That's why you're lying on the deck of my ship, defeated by humans for the first time in your immortal life. You want to fight again? Be my guest. But it will only get you back here. Bring me to Eric and I'll spare you. Wage further war, I'll still find him, only this time, you'll be dead at the bottom of your own kingdom."

The Divine Lady glanced side to side at the crew that surrounded her. The determination and unassuming loyalty to the prince was evident. Somehow, she knew, despite all the powers she possessed, she was no match for the band of strange and loving warriors. Still, there was tradition and law in her own land to consider. She sighed. "If only it were so easy."

"What do you mean?" Louis questioned firmly, his sword still drawn, and his guard still strong.

"There are laws in my kingdom," explained the Divine Lady. "Laws just as there are in yours. It is my age-old duty to marry one from the world above in order to continue my reign."

"Oh, gobshite," the sprite expressed. "I have *laws* too, but I break them all the time."

"How wonderful for you," the Divine Lady said snidely. "*I* am not so lucky. I must have your Eric, or my kingdom, my subjects, *everything* will be lost to me."

"Find someone else!" ordered Louis.

"Do you know how long it took me to find *him*? My time's running out. Where am I supposed to find a replacement for which I lust on such short notice?"

There seemed to be no bargaining with the deity. Then, an idea struck Captain Armand, one that was bold and could lead to further battle, but one that, too, might just work.

"Seems to be such sad ideas you carry down below the sea," Captain Armand began. "Much like the ones in *his* kingdom," he continued with a nod to the prince.

"How dare you!" barked the lady. "I'm *nothing* like the arrogant rulers of the land."

"Perhaps you're mostly different, me lady, but you've clearly got some overlappin' morals."

"You stab me and then you insult me. A real charmer you are. It's no wonder you're wanted in every kingdom on the coast."

"Aye, that do be my burden in life, different but just as heavy as yours." The captain thought for a moment, his eyes locked on his dueling partner. The old, wrinkled grin of his idea stretched his lips and squinted his eyes. "Perhaps, your fishiness, our *own* burdens can unburden each other?"

"How do you mean?" the Divine Lady asked with a suspicious glower.

"What I be meanin' is simple: Runnin' on land and sea be gettin' harder and harder on me old, dying body. I can't run much longer. And you be needin' a human to rule with you."

"You expect me to entertain the idea of marrying *you* after you *stabbed me* in the *uvula*!"

"For the last time, if I stabbed you in your bits, we'd both know it. And I not be suggesting marriage. But I say you should challenge the rules. Trade me for the boy, and I won't force you to marry such an old sea dog. I'll fill the position; let ye run yer own kingdom. And, once in a while, when you be wantin', I'll help you with that ubula."

"I think I'm going to be sick again," said the Violet Sprite said to the group.

"Ubula's not even a word," commented Yvonne.

"Who cares?" Louis whispered. "This could be the key to rescuing Eric."

The group turned their attention back to the Divine Lady and the captain. Her face remained stoic as she considered the proposal. It was indeed intriguing, and it was clear she was not quick to make a definitive decision. Still, she was considering, and Louis could not help feeling a glimmer of hope in his hardened heart.

Finally, the Divine Lady's formidable grimace turned to that of a crafty grin. "You've got yourself a deal, old man."

The captain offered the Divine Lady a hand, one which she refused. She pulled herself up, a powerful notion the captain appreciated.

"Well, then," she continued, "No time like the present, is there?"

She led the captain to the railing, climbing up first, before helping the captain.

"Wait!" Louis called. "What about Eric?"

The Divine Lady turned back to the prince. "You don't think I forgot my end of the bargain, do you? Oh, you humans are so simple."

"I'm gonna' fall," warned the impatient Captain Armand.

The Divine Lady shook her head and threw him over the edge. The old man fell with a yell and a belly flopping splash.

"Check the Captain's Quarters," the lady told Louis. "And *thank you*. I hope everything works out for you, as it just may for me."

Before Louis could answer, the Divine Lady gracefully dove off the railing, leaving behind a much more calculated splash. The crew ran to the side, looking down into the waters below. For a moment, they saw nothing, and the group wondered if their dear captain had been tricked.

"Look, there!" Ruth called as she pointed to the waves below.

Indeed, in a breaking crest emerged Captain Armand, splashing upward to reveal a shimmering gold tail. "How about that?" Armand called up to his former crew. "Looks like this old bastard may live for near ever!" He released a hearty chortle as the Divine Lady emerged alongside him.

She watched him splash about with a roll of her eyes and a smile on her lips.

"I've been alive for quite some time," expressed the sprite, "and this is the most bollocks thing I've ever witnessed."

Louis chuckled. He could not help but grin as well, for he knew that, together, they had a strange future, but a future that would work; a thought that brought him to his own. His smirk dropped and he peeled away quickly from the side. Ruth and the Violet Sprite took notice and followed in suit. Without hesitation or preparation, Louis threw open the cabin doors. The glimmer upon the sea had been so bright and the darkness within the cabin was so dim, he was blinded for a moment. That did not stop him. He rushed into the cabin, his gaze rapidly shooting from side to side. They came to a sudden, frozen halt, as they focused firmly upon the bed. He squinted, as his vision returned completely. Beneath the covers laid the outline of a tall, thin body, with a thick mop, of brown curls peeking out.

Louis shivered as a chill rushed down his spine. After so much struggle, after the tower, the sea, the demon, the lady, his Eric was finally in front of him. He did not savor the moment, however, for he would not be happy until he was *certain* it was not a trick. He rushed to his slumbering lover. Without hesitation, he jumped atop Eric and rolled the scribe onto his back. The covers were gone, revealing the thin, chiseled face that the prince had so missed. He lay shirtless, allowing Louis to see that his scribe was drawing breath. It was perhaps the greatest relief Louis had ever felt in his life.

"Eric!" Louis called as he eagerly shook his scribe's shoulders. "Eric!"

Eric stirred in his grogginess, his eyes slowly opening. Eric took a deep, waking breath, as he tried to make sense of his surroundings. When he saw the eyes of his prince, he flung upward "Louis?" he exclaimed.

"Eric!" cried the prince, as he pulled his scribe into a tight embrace.

"Is this a dream?" Eric asked, hopeful that it wasn't as he rested his head upon his lover's shoulder.

"No, no, my dear! It's very real!"

"You're here," Eric said breathlessly and near tears

as he took in the beautiful sight he'd so missed. "And my voice. It's *back*. *How* did you?"

Both men began to stream tears as they held each other tightly.

"There will be time for 'how' later," explained Eric. He had to pull himself away from Eric's arms unwillingly, as he motioned toward Ruth. "Look! Look who's here."

Eric turned to see the beaming face of his beloved mother.

"Mum," he cried.

"My dear boy," Ruth returned with equally emotional fanfare as she rushed to embrace her son.

"I'm here too, but I'll let the lovers and the family feel you up first," jested the sprite.

"Get over here, this *instant*," Eric ordered.

The Violet Sprite grinned and joined in the happy reunion.

"But I still don't understand," Eric began. "Last thing I remember was being trapped in the Divine Lady of the Bay's palace."

"Oh, it's a long story," Ruth replied. "Come outside and we'll explain everything."

"All right," Eric said, initially joining the others in their rise from the bed, before stopping short with realization and pulling the sheet farther up his body. "On second thought, I don't believe I should. It seems when I returned from the sea, I returned without my tunic."

"Oh, worry not," Louis said. "See this getup? The Violet Sprite made it for me with his magic. He can certainly do the same for you." He turned his attention to the fairy. "Here, spin him something befitting a prince."

"Actually," interrupted Eric, "not just yet." He

reached his hand out for Eric. "We've been apart for so long, and as lovely as it is pretending to hold hands, I'm ready to for much more…that is…if you are."

Louis grinned bashfully, as he took Eric's hand in his own and slowly followed the guide back to the bed. He sat upon his knees, his eyes on their grasp for a moment. He took a deep breath, then took his hazel eyes to Eric's blue/browns. "I am," he admitted softly, but with an undeniable passion.

Eric turned his eyes to the others with a gentle cunningness on his lips. Ruth and the sprite exchanged glances and quickly excused themselves, closing the door softly behind them.

"You really risked a lot coming to find me," Eric acknowledged.

"For you," returned Louis, "there's no risk too great. I'd follow you to the underworld and beyond, so long as we remained hand in hand, arm in arm."

Eric slowly moved his hands to Louis' cheeks, and pulled him in for a passionate kiss, perhaps the greatest they'd shared yet. Louis allowed the naked body of his scribe down upon him. Each held the hands of the other as the kiss grew stronger, more heated, and more wonderful. Eric began to make love to Louis just as the sun set on the sea on which they sailed. Passion turned to them gently holding each other throughout the night, as their loved ones steered them home to a future they hoped would be filled with days as lovely as this one.

****

I really don't understand that this chapter was called "The Pirate and the Prince," considering that Louis and Captain Armand and Louis spent very little time together. I thought it maybe should have been called

"The Pirate and the Divine Lady," or something like "The Battle on the Seas." I don't know. But when I brought this up to one of the professors who helped me work on it, they brought up the point that without the title, it likely would have been mutilated further. Anyway, I love this chapter, despite the odd naming and I'm very glad I was able to put it back together in full, after the way it was handled.

Chapter Fourteen

"The War of the Misfits and the King"
Published in The Scribe's Collection *as "The King Saves the Day."*

Oh, how this poor chapter suffered in translation. I don't want to give too much away, but that revised title says it all. In short, this went from being a story about misfits and heroes finding themselves targeted just for their existence to a story about a good king saving his kingdom from riff raff. I can't go on, or I'll have an aneurysm. So instead, enjoy the chapter as it was meant to be: Honest and thoughtful, with a necessary amount of rebellion.

****

The ship had been carried gently on the back of the sea, its smooth sailing a gift from the Divine Lady. Louis and Eric stood in each other's arms at the helm, watching the morning stretch across their home. It was a most welcoming way to return to the kingdom. However, the closer they sailed into port, the closer they were to the consequences awaiting them.

"He's not going to be happy." Louis sighed.

"Your stepfather has a lot more to worry about than his own displeasure," Eric acknowledged. "He dabbled with darkness, and the kingdom won't accept that."

"Perhaps," agreed Louis. "But he knows how to fool his subjects. We have a long battle ahead of us."

"We've already beaten him once. And we did it with love; something I don't think he *truly* understands. And *that's how we're going to win.*"

Louis gave his scribe a childish grin filled with optimism, and one he hadn't worn since he was a boy. He looked to the kingdom's coast. Whatever battles may come, he knew they'd win, as long as they were together.

The Violet Sprite waltzed in the captain's cabin, reminiscing on times gone by. He sat upon the bed, a part of him missed the salty old seaman, but the sprite knew he'd find a new lover before long. Still, it was exciting to recall such thrilling and squally times. He remembered one such liaison when the seas were so rocky, they were thrown from the bed and rolled under. They'd hit the floor with such a thud that night, the sprite had released a small bit of magical spark that burned the floor. He was curious if the mark was still there. He crawled down and looked beneath the bedstand to see the crispy plank.

However, a stain left behind from a wild night's passion was not what caught his eye. Instead, there was a small, wrinkly piece of parchment placed very deliberately under the bed. He reached and pulled it out. It did not take long to recognize his mother's handwriting. It would be just like her to ruin a wholesome memory. He knew it was for him, and he thought it would be better to toss it into the sea. However, after their last interaction, he had to admit he'd been curious about her intentions. They'd been estranged for so long, and bitter with each other for longer than that, yet there was something peculiar about her visit to the ship; something strange in, not just her magical aid, but in her very being.

It did not take long to read the note, for the note was

only composed of three lines:

Be vigilant. Stay safe. See you soon.

The Violet Sprite knew his mother was a trickster, but he sensed honesty in this warning. He pondered whether it was time to tell his traveling partners the whole truth. It seemed the right thing to do, but when he came up on deck to see Louis and Eric watching the sunrise together, he thought it best to finally allow them the time they'd been denied. Should any threats arise, the crew had beaten them before, and the sprite knew they could again.

Besides, there were more pressing matters about which they should worry. No one knew what legalities awaited them now that they were back in Belle Terre. They had indeed pirated a ship. Even with the prince, it would still be a political circus to sort out.

Whatever *did* await them was still a concern for later, for now, they were home, and all they could do was live their lives in the best way they knew how.

When the whole of the crew were once again landlubbers, the Violet Sprite called Eric and Louis to a quiet end of the dock to inform them he was returning to his own realm.

"You're leaving us?" Louis exclaimed.

"It's time for me to return home, I'm afraid," explained the sprite. "I've been gone too long, and I'll be damned if I find out the Blue Sprite became more popular than me in my absence."

Louis grimaced as his eyes drifted downward.

"What is it, *now*, your princelyness?" teased the sprite.

"It's only…I'd hoped you would stay around with us for a while. I've come to depend on you."

"I won't be far. Besides, *you have a whole new life to start.*"

It was a promise warmer than the morning sun. Before anyone had a chance to say goodbye, the sprite shrunk himself down to his petite size and flew upward toward the heavens. It was a charming move that made Eric chuckle, and Louis rolled his eyes with a grin.

Alone, Eric turned to his prince and cupped his royal hands in those of his own. "He's right, you know? We can finally go home and be together."

"Though it was only a few days," Louis began, "it seems we've been apart for a century. And perhaps by some miracle, I'm wrong. Perhaps it is over."

"I'm afraid—it's not," called a stern voice.

Both of the lovers turned to see the guard Nicholas waiting below on the dock.

"Hello, Your Highness," the guard greeted coldly. "The king and queen have been worried about you. I'm afraid you'll both have to come with me right away."

These words brought no comfort to anyone nearby. Evers approached his former partner and the man who had his heart with a frightened stare, for Nicholas looked as though he'd just been to hell and back, drained of all human emotion. "Nicholas, what's happened? What is this about?"

"Piracy," Nicholas coldly stated, casting his glare upon the crew of misfits who had gathered to investigate. "A crime against the crown that will end in a hanging for all of you."

The threat riveted through the group of misfits, who all cast eyes upon each other. One by one, all fled from the ship in creative ways in different directions, all except Evers who stood in stunned disbelief.

"Nicholas, what are you doing?"

"Following orders."

"You know there's more to the story. Let us all go to the king and queen together. Then we can explain—"

"The only way *you'll* be seeing the royal family will be strapped in a noose. But seeing as we were once friends, I'll allow you the courtesy of a running."

"Nicholas—"

"I said *run,* boy!"

Evers shivered at the order. He looked to the couple, who nodded to him to run. Though it broke his heart, the now disgraced guard forced himself to retreat off with his crewmates.

"As for you two," Nicholas commanded, drawing his sword, "you're both coming with me to see the king and the queen. And if you fight me on it, your friends will never see another dawn."

The lovers looked at one another, both with fear in their eyes. Louis wanted not to allow his scribe to appear before his stepfather, for he knew it would only mean losing him again. Eric, on the other hand, was terrified of the consequences that awaited his prince. Before either could speak, Nicholas had further orders:

"And let go of each other! You've disgraced the crown enough without displaying such perversion."

Eric knew there was something much deeper going on with the guard other than just loyalty to the crown. But he would not put his prince at risk. Thus, reluctantly, he removed his grasp from Louis. "It's all right," explained he. "We'll come with you…and give you no trouble." As Eric completed his surrender, he stepped in front of Louis and folded his hands within one another.

Louis caught the sight right away, and as he too

stepped forward, he followed suit. "Yes," he agreed. "We'll come with you Nicholas and give you no trouble."

"Come along then," Nicholas ordered. "We're wasting the day."

The two followed with brave composure, though inside, their hearts beat rapidly. Still, they knew not to allow their courage to falter, just as they knew not to let go of their hands.

****

Nicholas ominously creaked open the throne room door. Eric and Louis stood behind and exchanged glances of concern.

"He'll see you now," the guard coldly informed.

With strong demeanor, the brave men stepped through the doors. On the other side, they found King Desmos and the false Queen Krystal. The lovers stared up at the rulers seated high upon their thrones, uncertain as to whether they should continue their journey across the hall.

"Come in properly, boys," Queen Krystal invited.

The two squeezed their own hands tighter and proceeded across the hall. The silence of the room, filled only by the clicking of the men's shoes, was not at all comforting. When they arrived at the dais, both mustered enough courage to keep a powerful glare in their eyes as they looked upon the monarchs.

Silence hung in the air, for a moment. Then, Eric bravely took a breath. "Before you say anything, your excellencies," he began, "I want you to know that Louis' actions were only out to save me. Any retribution for him should be my burden to bear."

"*Don't be ridiculous, Eric!*" Louis ordered.

"Stepfather, I've kept my suspicions at bay for some time, but now I must speak: I know Eric's exile was your doing. I know you're working with the Celtic Witch. You may think you can punish us, you may think you can destroy us, but I promise you...if you so much as *attempt* to harm Eric anymore, I will tell my story to all the powers on my side...powers you can't even comprehend."

The eyes of his stepfather and the woman who was not quite his mother peered upon him for a moment. The silence was even more deafening than any that had proceeded. Finally, the king sat taller, preparing to speak, the moment of truth eminent.

Instead of the stern command that they expected, there came only a chuckle. "My dear boys," King Desmos began, "I don't know what it is you think you know, but I can assure you I had *nothing* to do with the disappearance of the poor scribe. And I certainly would never conspire with such a devilish creature! Horrible thing, magic. We must outlaw it. Anyway, I'm glad you're home safe, Eric. Of course, you'll have a few hours off, but then you must get back to work. We've been without enjoyment for days now, and the court will want that remedied as soon as possible."

None present could believe what they heard, not Louis, not Eric, not the witch in Krystal's clothing. Louis was awaiting a trick, the witch a secretive plan, while Eric was sure he was dreaming.

"Well, why is everyone standing around here with mouths agape?" asked the king. "We've things to do. Welcome back home, boys, and don't worry about the ship. I'm sure you've brought her home in excellent condition. Go on, now. Get some rest, the both of you!"

Nicholas approached to lead Louis and Eric from the room. While Eric at first obliged, Louis stayed behind.

"Yes, what is it, Ti'Louien?" King Desmos asked with a pleasantry that Louis didn't trust in the least.

Louis inhaled with great irritation before boldly stating: "*I know you're lying.*"

The king looked down upon his stepson. His demeanor changed for less than a moment; a mysterious glare flashed across his face, one that was missed by all except Louis. The prince needed not study the quick grimace, the furrowed brows, or the soulless eyes of his stepfather to know his suspicions were right.

"Dearest son." The king forced a tone that *still* did not convince the prince, "It's a shame you feel that way. But I promise you…I will not harm a hair on the head of our scribe."

Louis took a deep breath. "All right, *dearest* Stepfather…See that you don't."

Louis and Eric followed Nicholas from the room, the prince giving his lover a nod of acknowledgment along the way. He knew another battle was on the way, and this time, he was determined to win once and for all.

When the door closed, the witch stood and shed her Queen Krystal disguise. "What is it that you're planning?" she asked.

The king remained seated, a wicked sneer on his lips. "I've only welcomed my stepson home," he explained with a vileness on his tongue.

"Don't treat me as you treat everyone else. We've been in this together from the start. It was my power that got you here. And with my power, I could take it away just as easily."

"Your power—it was *you* that was supposed to keep

the scribe banished from my kingdom. And yet, he's waltzed back into my kingdom on *my stolen* ship, captained by a herd of undesirables. Your power…it's wonder anyone's ever feared you."

"Don't be so quick with your insults, or I'll show you what my power truly *can* do."

"Is that a threat?" asked the king with a cruel chuckle. He stood a towering height. "Perhaps it is *you* who should face the wrath of your own power."

The Celtic Witch glared suspiciously at the king, refusing to surrender her stance. "What does that mean?" she asked strongly.

"Well, you see, when you went out yesterday without explanation, I invited myself into the vault where you keep your spells. You see, I've had my suspicions. And I knew I had to be prepared just in case you were up to anything. The return of my stepson and that queer little writer only confirmed that for me. I'm very glad I decided to take *this*."

From beneath his robe, the king produced a spell book bound in black leather, its cover sealed with a long constructed of wolf's fang. The Celtic Witch recoiled at the sight of the book she knew far too well. It was the Book of Tellers, an infamous collection of the most wicked and dangerous spells known on the Irish shores. Over the centuries, the volume had been used to murder, curse, and destroy all sorts of souls. Its power was so great and so terrible that even one as powerful as the Celtic Witch herself had rarely used it.

"*You don't know what you're dealing with,*" the Celtic Witch growled through gritted teeth.

"Oh, I believe I do," the king claimed with arrogance. "You see, this book is filled with *wonderful* spells that reach beyond *our* realm and into the next."

"I'm aware. It was with such a spell that I conjured the demon from the Underworld."

"Yes, yes, but you didn't tell me there was so much more one could do. You never mentioned the spell that allows you to *send* a living person to the realm of the Ankou body and soul."

"That *spell* is forbidden! Those who cast it are doomed to meet a damnable end."

"Well, my love, I must disagree. You see...I've already used it."

The Celtic Witch stood in stunned disbelief for a moment. She knew he had to be lying and decided to call his bluff. "That's not possible. A soul that is sent to the Underworld cannot return unchanged, for the horrors in that purgatory rip the humanity from any who dwell there."

"Of that, I'm well aware. Have you noticed, dearest, that the guard Nicholas has been acting much less like an undesirable lately?"

What remained of the Celtic Witch's heart grew tight. "You didn't," she argued with cold shock.

"I should have done it years ago, really. He spends far less time with that *ridiculous* friend of his and has finally been getting work done."

"You sent him to the Underworld, so that he...so that he wouldn't..."

"Don't act like you never considered it with your own son. After all, was it not the same vile desire that caused the rift between you both?"

"You're going to use it on the scribe?" the witch asked with a challenging tone.

"Oh no," the king began. "You see, if there's one

thing my stubborn, *disgusting* stepson has proven, it's that he'll stop at nothing to save that boy. The scribe, on the other hand...what resource, what power, what knowledge does he have apart from his quill and his parchment? He wouldn't be able to rescue...*a soul*, let alone the body that goes with it."

"You can't do that to Louis, Desmos. You'll never get away with it."

"His name is Ti'Louien, you ridiculous woman."

"You really think a trip to hell will change that boy? If anyone can make it there and back with his spirit well and his heart still strong, it's him."

"Oh, yes, I know. That's why he won't be *coming* back."

"He can't survive there for eternity. The spell won't sustain him. He'll become nothing more than a ghost, lost in the river of souls. You don't think the people will miss their prince?"

"On the contrary, I think they'll celebrate the demise of the Deplorable Prince at last!"

"It was *you* who made him that."

"With your help."

Guilt pulsated through the very veins of the Celtic Witch. She clenched her jaw, as well as her fists. She'd gotten the prince and the scribe into this unholy nightmare. S*he'd* be the one to get them out of it.

"I may have played a part in all this, Desmos. But there's more to the story than you know. And I'll see that it comes to a happy end. I'll help you no more."

The witch quickly backed away from the king, and transformed into a giant, thundering cloud. She swarmed around him, gusting him from the dais. He clutched the book tightly to his chest, as his back landed upon the cobblestone.

With a thunderous boom, the cloud raced down to the king. The witch transformed back into her true self and marched toward King Desmos.

"Next time you challenge me, you won't live to see the end," she stated with tense eyes and grimaced mouth. The Celtic Witch reached for the book and ripped it from his hands. She held it to her chest and looked down upon the king. She expected to be met with his anger. Instead, the king chortled wickedly.

"*What are you so smug about?*" she asked through gritted teeth.

"Do you really think I'd surrender that book so easily?" he rhetorized, as he lifted himself on his elbows. "That book may be filled with some of the world's most powerful spells, but without magic it's nothing but pages…or so I thought. You see, I realized that, if I'm to remain king, I'm going to have to do this all myself, no matter the cost."

A shiver rushed down the witch's spine. She wanted nothing more than to believe it wasn't true, but deep down she knew that Desmos was mad enough to go to any length, even if it meant giving up what he considered most Holy.

"You sold your soul," she said with breathy fright.

"And, now…I'm more powerful than you. And I won't need your silly book to cast that spell."

"You're not as powerful as you think. And it's ironic, you think your stepson so *vile*, and such an insult to the gods, that you'd rather spend an eternity in darkness, *away* from those gods you worship, just to rip him from his love."

"I made the sacrifice I needed to in order to protect

my kingdom from perversion."

"This won't end the way you think, Desmos. *That I can promise you.*"

The king sneered at his now former lover. He inhaled through flared nostrils and called out: "Guards! An unholy witch has entered the kingdom! Seize her!"

Without a moment lost, the guards led by Nicholas threw open the doors. Spotted, but quick, the Celtic Witch discharged attacking serpents from her hands at the guards. All the men, except for Nicholas, screamed and ran from the room, giving the Celtic Witch enough time to disappear in a cloud of smoke.

An irritated king cast eyes upon the loyal, emotionless guard.

"Orders, Your Majesty?" Nicholas asked plainly.

"Send those feeble men to find that witch and *kill her*," ordered the king.

"And what shall I do, your excellency?"

"Oh, Nicholas. Your job is simple. Tell my stepson supper will be an hour earlier than normal. And make sure he isn't late."

Chapter Fifteen

"The Sprite and the Witch"
Published in The Scribe's Collection *"The Wizard and the Witch."*

If you can't tell by now, this was another chapter that had the nuance sucked out of it. This is, maybe, one of the most important chapters in the whole book and it was reduced to a weird, quirky battle between a strong, masculine wizard and a shrill, evil witch. It took about three weeks, but I pulled this chapter together fully, so I hope you enjoy it. It's far better than what it was.

****

The Violet Sprite roamed the streets of Belle Terre without his normal glamour. He kept a low profile, so no one would know he'd not returned to the belt of Orion. After receiving the letter from his mother, he knew he must remain in town, ready to face whatever darkness was on the horizon. He walked for what felt as though an eternity, determined to find his mother, no matter how unpleasant their reunion may be.

After three hours of mindless walking, the sprite moved away from the populated streets of Belle Terre and ventured into the alleys of crime and despair; the same alleys that were populated by those who helped save Eric from his watery doom. It was not the style of the mother he knew to dwell in such undesirable quarters, but with the secrets she carried, it might have been the only place to find her.

As he passed the poverty and rejection along the way, guilt tugged at his heart. It was clear there were many more of these misfits within the kingdom than he realized, and he could not help but feel he should be doing more with his power to remedy their despair.

Finally, at the very dead end of the darkest alley, he saw a hooded figure. It was a figure that should have frightened the Violet Sprite, but he knew who lay in wait beneath the hood of the hide. He took a deep breath before approaching. No matter her intentions, he knew it best to approach with caution. Then, he made his way toward her.

"I see you got my letter," came the voice of his mother from beneath the cloak.

"What is it you want?" asked the sprite.

"Your help," she admitted.

"That's very rich. I suppose you think I owe you for getting us to the Divine Lady's kingdom. Realistically, you're still in debt to *me,* however, for the emotional toll you've placed upon me, and seeing that therapy won't be invented for a few centuries yet—"

"This has nothing to do with anything like that. This has to do with something *far* more serious and far more dangerous than I could have ever expected."

"Way to play down my issues."

"I'm serious! It's the king. He's sold his soul for the most unholy of powers."

"You expect me to believe that moron has any idea how to do such a thing?"

"You *must*! You see, I've just taken *this* from him." From below her robe, the witch produced the horrible, black book.

The Violet Sprite stepped away and shivered. "The Book of Tellers!" he exclaimed. "Keep that infernal thing away from me."

"Oh, enough of the dramatics! You have no idea what's coming, and time is of the essence."

"How do I know this is not some trick? One good deed does not redeem for a lifetime of sin."

"Rich coming from the fairy who's been nude for the masses."

The Violet Sprite sprouted his wings, ready to fly away, but the Celtic Witch called with desperation:

"Please, wait!" She drew a breath and prepared herself. "I know I was far from the mother you deserved. And perhaps it's too late for an apology."

"You've only had a couple of centuries to give me one."

"I'm aware. But it's not my fault. It's the Celtic blood we share. *Still*, that's not enough. If I can't say I'm sorry to earn your forgiveness, at least let me show you how determined I am to make things right."

The Violet Sprite thought silently for what seemed an eternity, before finally proclaiming: "Very well. Tell me your plan."

The Celtic Witch prepared herself to share every detail of the quest she'd been on for some time now. "I suppose I should start at the beginning. Many moons ago, when my infamy had left me ever most lonely, a young, pathetic man ventured into my domain. You wouldn't know him from what he is today, but that man was Desmos. He was not yet the royal blacksmith, nor was he considered at all important. This was right after the passing of the old king, Louis' father. He and Queen Krystal had implemented laws they hoped would make the kingdom of Belle Terre the greatest in all the realms. Laws that would bring about unparalleled acceptance and love. Indeed, many said they would have made for the perfect kingdom. However, not everyone felt it so.

"Many feared the changes to come, the welcoming of those with strange magic, the weird, the queer, the diverse. Those traditionalists were afraid that they would bring perversion, and extinction to the way of life they'd always known. A sentiment that I…shamefully once shared… Desmos wanted nothing more to prevent this, and though he considered himself a Holy man, he had no qualms about partnering with me, the fallen pixie, turned evil witch.

"He wanted to infiltrate the royal family, to be king *himself* and return to what he considered greater values."

"And you helped him do it," the Violet Sprite growled through his teeth with disgust.

"It's not so simple, my dear, for there is more to the story than you know…more to the story than he knew. Though I found great power in black magic, I suppose you could say I was lonely. And I further, you could say that I missed you. When he explained what he wanted to do, I heard so much of who I was in his ideas. And, for the first time, I realized how truly horrific it sounded. I promised to help him, but it would not be in the way he thought. You see, *I too* had plans."

****

After considering word counts, and what not, this was the one part of the chapter I decided to trim. First of all, it gives way *too much away about the ending. I decided surprise was better, so I'll fill you in on the details you need to continue reading for now. Basically, the Celtic Witch only pursued dark witchcraft in order to change her son's sexuality, but that didn't work, and cost her everything she held dear. When Desmos asked her help, she used her power of foresight to see if there was a happy ending possible. There was, but it would be risky. Now, you're pretty much up to speed. Back to what matters.*

****

The Violet Sprite stared down his mother as he tried to consume every word she'd said. The story was indeed fantastical; perhaps too much so, even for practitioners of magic such as they. Still, there was something in her eyes that made him wonder; something he hadn't seen for some time, but something he'd never forgotten, try hard as he might…It was love. A love that only a mother could give. It made his heart beat fast and his soul quiver, for though he'd never admitted it to himself, it was an affection he deeply missed. Still, he knew he must proceed with caution and was sure to remain strong.

"It sounds as though your plans backfired greatly," he scoffed. "But those dangers are of your doing. Why should I risk life, limb, and firm arse to undo your mistake?"

"Because the king didn't damn his own soul *just* for the power. He plans to use it to trap the prince in the Underworld forever."

"*What*? Why, that barbarian can't do such a thing! A spell like that is forbidden."

"That matters not to him. He only cares about punishing his stepson. And once the prince is gone, with no one to challenge him, who *knows* what he intends to do."

The Violet Sprite huffed with fury as his eyes went wild with likened distraught. "Very well," he finally agreed. "I don't trust you completely...but, for the good of my friends, I'll stand with you. We must warn the lovers."

"I only hope we're not too late."

****

Louis fell atop Eric, his postcoital breath a near heaving. The sweat on his muscular build smeared against his scribe's pale, thin core. Their lips grazed against one another, exchanging hot, sweet breath, as Louis' eyes took in the features that were responsible for creating his beloved Eric's face: the sculpted nose, the sharp cheekbones, small pink lips, and his blue-brown eyes that were somehow both boyish, yet carried all the wisdom in the realm.

He ran his fingers up Eric's thin, toned legs that remained wrapped around his body, feeling every hair along the way until they came to his smooth, small hips. They continued their journey upward until they gently caressed either side of his face. Louis' lips trembled as he lightly massaged Eric's cheeks with his thumbs.

"Are you all right?" Eric asked.

"I've never been better." Louis smiled.

He filled Eric's curls with his fingertips, and the two came together for a passionate, beautiful kiss. Though they'd only just finished their love making, both felt their bodies fill once more with uncontrollable passion.

Their lips parted from the wet kiss long enough for Eric to ask with a chuckle, "Do you want to go again?"

Louis returned the light laugh with sensual breath. "Yes," he admitted. "Only this time, it's your turn."

The two rolled around one another, readying to assume their next positions, but before anything further could take place, there came a banging on Louis' door.

"Oh, for the love of the gods," Louis whined.

"Perhaps they'll go away," suggested Eric.

The boys remained silent, but there soon came another series of thuds.

"Oh, very well!" cried a frustrated Louis, as he rose from the bed and threw a royal robe around his body. He trudged to the door with irritation, and looked back upon his beautiful, naked scribe. "You should probably hide all that," he jested.

Eric grinned cunningly. "You sure?" he asked as he stretched his chest forward, his hands behind his head.

Louis shook his head with a playful roll of his eyes. "At least hide yourself until whoever it is has gone."

Eric chuckled and threw the blankets over his head. Louis watched, beaming as his scribe struggled to arrange the blankets. When he was still, the prince recomposed himself and opened the door with his normal regality.

The blank face of Nicholas once again glared at the prince, only this time, Louis was not frightened but annoyed. "What is it, *now*?" he asked with vexation.

Nicholas wrinkled his nose. "A robe in the middle of the day?" the guard asked.

"Yes," scoffed Louis. "Don't you know I just got back from a voyage? I'm *exhausted*."

The guard attempted to peer past the prince, who readjusted himself domineeringly against the door frame to block his view.

"What can I do for you?" Louis ordered to know.

"The king…" said Nicholas, returning his attention to the prince. "He wishes to see you."

"Wishes or commands?" Louis asked. "If he's asking, I'll be returning to my sleep."

"I think you know this is an order."

Louis inhaled vexingly through his nose. "I'll need a moment to ready."

Before the guard could order further, the prince slammed the door in his face. He turned back to the bed. Eric pulled the sheets from him with a disappointed smirk.

"I'm sorry, my love," said Louis as he sank to sit with his scribe.

"You'll just have to make it up to me," Eric teased with suggestive brows.

"Oh, do I take orders from the scribe now, too?"

"Tonight, you will."

****

The Violet Sprite and his mother used their respective forms of travel to get themselves to the palace in a hurry. As the sprite soared above the kingdom, he spotted his mother, waiting in the shadows near the entrance to the undercroft. He quickly changed direction and landed with a slide.

"What are you doing here?" he asked. "I thought we had to get in the palace to stop a madman."

"We do, but after what happened between Desmos and I, the whole castle will be on high alert. I won't have the privileges I once did, not even if I wore a disguise. He would know. We'll have to break in through the underground and use as little magic as possible."

"What happens if we get caught?"

"We'll cross that bridge when we get there. Now, come on!" She led the way past the large, metal bars that were meant to keep the rabble locked out of the palace.

"This is one time I wish I didn't have my iconic arse," remarked the sprite as he tried to follow the witch through. "Can't I just shrink down to get inside?"

"*No magic*! Only in case of emergency."

They managed to get through into the cellar.

"Where to now?" The Violet Sprite asked.

"I'm sure Desmos is going to execute his plan as soon as possible. We must find Eric though. He wouldn't dare do it in front of an army of three of us. He knows he's not skilled enough to wipe out more than one being at a time. And fenced against our power, *he doesn't stand a chance*."

With that, the unlikely duo began their way through the undercroft, sneaking up into the palace through a trick door that only service people knew about.

"Where should we check first?" asked the sprite.

"If I know Desmos, he'll have Louis alone as soon as possible."

"The prince's room," the sprite suggested.

"Why not his scribe's chambers?"

"When you're as steamed for each other as those two are, you don't spend extra time at work."

"All right. I trust you."

****

Nicholas led Louis down the many flights of stairs and across to the king's chambers.

"He'll see you right away," Nicholas stated without so much as a knock.

It was peculiar to Louis that Nicholas did not bother to check. His stepfather was not one to welcome visitors in without query. The emotionless guard pulled the door open, and the prince ventured into the chamber.

He found his stepfather facing out his window. He did not acknowledge Louis' entrance, or the guard who'd brought him in without permission.

Nicholas pushed past the prince and made way for the still-motionless king. He whispered something to Desmos, and the king whispered something back. Louis felt his gut grow tight, as he waited. Nicholas turned from the king and trudged by Louis without a glance in his lifeless eyes. Louis looked back to his stepfather, who remained unturned from the window.

Nicholas sealed the door behind him. Adrenaline filled Louis' body, but he swallowed his fear. "What is it that you want?" he called. "Is this because of the ship? Because I called you a liar?"

King Desmos stood silent for a moment more before he finally answered the frustrated Louis. "So naïve of you to think it only one thing after all the years we've been forced together. Since I took the throne, you've undermined me, you've argued with my policy, you've questioned my authority. I've had to put up with your *incessant* mouth, your challenges, your *disgusting* way of life. And *I*, Ti'Louien...I'm tired of it. I'm tired of having to fight you to inflict any real change in my own kingdom. And I'm *tired* of *you*."

The king's voice had never sounded so malevolent to Louis before. In each word, he carried a chilling disdain, each syllable a blood curdling gruffness. Suddenly, it was no longer only the passion he missed in Eric's arms but the safety.

****

Eric emerged from a bath that he'd drawn for himself. After the time he spent in the Divine Lady's kingdom, he took advantage of any time he could spend in unsalted waters. As he began to dress himself, the door to the chamber flew open. He jolted and spun around to see the Violet Sprite entering with a strange, hooded figure.

"*What's going on?*" he exclaimed.

The Violet Sprite eyed the still shirtless Eric for less than a moment. "I can't believe I'm saying this but finish getting dressed!" he ordered. "This is an emergency."

"An *emergency*? Wha—what? I thought you went back home. And *who's this*?"

The Violet Sprite was speechless for the first time in his life. The combination of urgency and questions flabbergasted him. He knew not whether to explain or command, and he hadn't the *faintest* idea how he was going to expound his mother.

"Oh, why must scribes be so nosy?" cried the Celtic Witch. "We're in a hurry!" She threw her hood down, revealing her to be the infamous sorceress.

Eric's eyes went wide, and his mouth hung open. "You—you're the—"

"The Celtic Witch. Yes. I've also been masquerading as the queen for several weeks. Oh, and I'm also the fairy's mother, we'll explain it all later. Now get your tight little arse in gear! *Louis*, not to mention the rest of this blasted kingdom, are in great danger. Now come on!"

The Celtic Witch flew through the door with a furious pace.

"Huh, she made that easier than I expected," noted the sprite.

"Louis' in trouble?" exclaimed Eric as he tossed on his shirt and soared past the sprite, who soon followed after.

They rushed down the halls with the greatest speed they could muster, and still it was not enough. Eric's long curls were blown back by the breeze his racing feet created. They took the winding stone stairs as though they were grass. After what seemed an eternity, they were finally on the floor of the king's chambers.

"Come along," ordered Eric as he slid onto the landing. However, he was not prepared for what lay in wait for him, for he stopped just short of meeting the end of a vicious blade.

The sprite and the witch were too caught off guard as they halted behind the scribe to see the threatening sword pointed directly at Eric's neck. Holding it at hazard was Nicholas with stern and overpowering in his stance.

"The king knew you'd show up here," the guard explained lifelessly. "He gave me very specific orders."

"I'm sure I can guess what they are," Eric challenged bravely.

"Surrender, and I'll make it easier for you. I'll only stab you in the heart."

"That's easy?" Eric scoffed.

"Don't surrender, and I'll cut out your tongue, then off with your hands, and, finally, your head."

"At least you're leaving me my bits."

With impressive precision, Eric pulled a torch from the wall and began to joust with the guard.

"That's right," cheered the Violet Sprite. "You show that brute what a sensual boy from the country can do!"

The applauding would not last long, however, for the inexperienced Eric quickly had the weapon knocked from his hands. The guard kicked him to his knees and once again pointed the blade at his throat.

"This would be a good time to use magic, right?" the sprite frantically whispered to the witch.

"I suppose so," she replied hastily.

She waved her hands over the flames of Eric's now dropped torch. The pyre grew, catching the attention of both hero and villain. With a curl of her fingers, the flames rushed up Nicholas' sword and melted it completely. When the flame dissipated, the guard eyed the hooded woman.

"Whatever power you may possess, I assure you parlor tricks are no match for the king and his court."

The witch cackled passionately. "You may think your king great," she commenced with wicked glee. "But no one's power will ever match that of *the Celtic Witch*!" She threw back her hood to reveal a face turned skeletal and haunted.

For the first time since King Desmos brought him back from the Underworld, Nicholas showed great emotion, and that emotion was terror. The witch waved her hand and the guard fell to the ground, his eyes shut, but his lips still opened with stun.

"You didn't kill him, did you?" asked Eric.

"And what if I did?" asked the witch, her face returning to its proper form. Her traveling partners glared at her with disapproval. "Oh, he's only asleep. I know you wouldn't let me have any *real* fun!"

Eric commenced running once more, the sprite and the witch following his lead.

"I thought you would have been more skilled in a joust," acknowledged the sprite.

"Why?" replied an irritated Eric.

"What were you doing all those months at sea?"

"Writing."

"Oh my gods," groaned the witch.

"Well, it's gotten you this far, I suppose," continued

the fairy. "I'm sure it will come in handy once more."

****

King Desmos now stood facing Louis, casting upon him the iciest glare the prince had ever faced. Still, he was determined to hold strong.

"You know, Ti'Louien," the king spoke, as he took slow, calculated steps toward his stepson, "it wasn't easy for me. You've no idea the deals I had to strike, the sacrifices I made, the loss I experienced to get ahead in life. And yet, no matter how hard I worked, how loyally I complied, there was something that stood in my way."

The king inched closer and closer, threateningly. Try as he may, Louis could not keep his bottom lip from trembling. "*Me*," he managed in an attempt to hide his fear further.

King Desmos' lips formed an evil sneer. "*You.*"

On the other side of the door, the trio determined to rescue the prince arrived. Eric pushed on the black, metal door handle, only to find it locked. "Open this door!" he exclaimed, as he used all his force to beat upon it.

Louis spun around with both shock and desperation. "Eric!" he called. "Eric, please help!"

With the prince distracted, the king used the chance to strike, reaching into his robe.

In the hall, the Celtic Witch pushed past the scribe, as she ordered him to "Move!" She waved her hand, producing a spell that sparked and flashed against the sealed entry. However, it was of no use, the spell rebounded, knocking the heroes to the ground.

As their attempt turned to defeat, on the other side of the door, the king produced a poisoned spindle. The prince rushed to the door and attempted to open the door with wild desperation. The king's pacing did not change, for he strode proudly toward Louis.

"The bastard must've known I would come back," realized the witch. "Used my own book against me."

"Well, he's not expecting *me*," the sprite proclaimed, as he pushed his way through. He waved his wand in an attempt to destroy the door. Still, it was not enough. He groaned with frustration. "No one spell is enough to counteract *his*!" exclaimed a furious sprite, as Louis' pounding continued from the other side.

An epiphany came to the Celtic Witch. "Perhaps not *one* spell, but *two* together."

The Violet Sprite shot his mother an enlightened look. They both stood back. She raised her hand, and he, his wand. Without a moment to spare, they blasted the door with their respective flumes of magic. The knob began to wilt and waiver beneath their great, combined powers. It dissolved, dripped, and dissipated into a puddle at their feet after only a moment. Eric pushed his way to the door and threw it open. However, in the haste of the moment, neither Eric, nor the sprite, nor the witch had noticed the sudden absence of Louis' knocking.

"It's all right," exclaimed Eric as he barged through the doorway. "I'm here!"

His call of heroism and reassurance turned to that of distraught and horror, for just mere steps in front of him lay Louis, face down upon the cobblestone. Eric's entire being, from his lips to his fingertips, shivered as he took in the sight. The body drew no breath. Eric's eyes wildly searched the boy up and down and found a stream of blood pouring down from a puncture on the prince's neck.

"No." Eric quivered. "No!" he screamed, throwing himself at the lifeless Louis. Before he could even land upon the body of his prince, however, a swirl of black smoke surrounded it. When it cleared, there was no longer a Louis over which to grieve or even land on, for that matter.

The disappearance caused Eric to shake more. The blood drained from his face as his vision clouded. He could not catch his own breath, and he nearly passed out. The only thing that kept him conscious was the *mortal need* to save Louis...if there was still a chance.

"W—" he shivered, "where is he?" He flashed his bloodshot gaze to the king, whose towering shadow did not scare him at a time such as this.

"I have no duty to answer you, scribe," the king said in a deep rumble.

Eric shot to his feet. "You'll regret not answering me when I break your neck!"

"With what?" sneered the king. "*Your jousting words*? That's the trouble with perverted heathens such as you: You think all you need do to make your mark on the world is use pretty words and to 'live and let live.' Well, you idiot—'live' is to be a stretch for you, for you soon will be reunited with your Deplorable Prince forever, in whatever hell awaits monsters such as you."

The king drew his sword and charged the trio. Shock trapped Eric's body in place, whilst his heart begged him to run. Less than an inch before doom met his belly, a disorienting cloud of violet engulfed him. When it cleared, he was no longer surrounded by the dangerous walls of King Desmos' chamber but by the dark, wet partitions of a deep alley.

"Where—where is he?" Eric cried.

"Technically, scribe, the question is 'Where are *we*?'" corrected the Celtic Witch.

Eric spun to see his cohorts with him. "What happened to my Louis?" Eric demanded to know. "Is he *dead*?"

"Not exactly," the witch tried to explain.

"What does that mean? I don't want any foolishness. I've had enough of the consequences your sorcery has brought!"

"Eric," the Violet Sprite attempted to reason. "It's more complicated than that."

"I don't care. The witchcraft you both practice, both light and dark, has done nothing but tear us apart. No riddles, no lies! Tell me if my Louis is alive. And if he's not, I'll see to it that you're both *damned* to hell."

The Violet Sprite wore a stunned guiltiness on his face. For a rare moment, he was completely without words. The Celtic Witch, on the other hand, could not resist wearing a wicked smirk.

"What's so amusing to you, *witch*?" Eric demanded.

"It's just ironic, is all. Because, *hell*, is not very far from where we must go…"

Chapter Sixteen

"The Secret City of Outcasts"
Published in The Scribe's Collection *as "The
Crusade of the Secret City of the Outcasts."*

*There's definitely a real trend going on with these
chapters. I'm sure you know by now where this is
headed, so I'll save you one rant and basically just tell
you the hero/villain roles are flipped, and there's
somehow another gag-worthy heteromance. Anyway, I
don't want to take too long, because there's a really
unique twist on magic in this entry that I'm going to want
to rave about.*

****

The king's sword still hung where it should have
stabbed the scribe. He clenched his teeth, as he watched
it linger in the air still filled with traces of the sprite's
magic.

With a slow, painful walk, Nicholas came around
the corner.

"*Where were you?*" King Desmos growled, his eyes
still focused on the spot from where his three enemies
had vanished.

"I was incapacitated, sire," Nicholas said.

"Such fancy wordsmanship from one so *dull.*"

"It was the Celtic Witch, my king. She lurked in
these halls with the scribe and some other magical
perversion. She was by far the most terrifying thing I've

ever seen in my life."

For a moment, King Desmos was distracted from his trouble, for the guard should not have been able to feel fear, or *anything* for that matter, not after the time he spent in the Underworld. As his frustration began to boil over, he told himself that it was not his spell that had failed, it was the powerful evil of the witch that had destroyed their Holy meaning. He was determined even more so to destroy the scribe, his stepson, and anyone who supported their way of existence.

"You're right," the king suddenly agreed. He simmered his temper and calmed his tone. "After all, you are my strongest soldier, aren't you? Who else but one so blasphemous could best you?"

"Yes, Your Highness," the guard agreed.

"We must be vigilant," Desmos continued with false ally-ship. "And we must warn the others. If she's planning what I believe her to be, the uprising could end us all."

"The uprising, your grace?"

"The uprising of the outcasts, the undesirables with the most *perverted* desires in their black hearts. They've been waiting for someone as evil as her, underground in the shadows of their own secret city. With her help, who knows what wicked disaster they could release on Belle Terre."

"We must not let this happen," acknowledged Nicholas. "We must *stop them* at any cost!"

The king's wicked stretched his lips thin. "I'm glad you see it my way."

****

Eric did not wish to follow the Violet Sprite and the Celtic Witch farther into the shadows, but his choices were limited, and his love in grave danger, or worse. He knew without the help of the magical duo, he would have *no* chance of saving Louis from where he was now.

"Are we almost there?" Eric asked.

"Keep quiet!" ordered the witch.

"I'm sorry," Eric bantered back. "But when one tells you that your lover is trapped in the Underworld, possibly forever, it's quite *impossible* to keep quiet!"

"Enough bickering," ordered the Violet Sprite ordered. "We're nearly there."

The scribe and the witch both begrudgingly silenced themselves and continued to follow the sprite farther into the darkness, until at last, they came to a dead end.

"Just promise me neither of you will draw attention," the sprite said, as he turned to face his traveling companions. "This is the place."

"Draw attention?" began a flustered Eric. "Draw attention to *what*? There's nothing here. What games are you playing."

" 'Nothing' is only as it appears," the sprite explained cryptically. Slowly, he lifted his foot over the piles of hay below, then dropped it rhythmically three times.

Eric locked a curious side glance with the witch.

"There's nothing sadder than your child losing it before you," she whispered.

Eric's impatience was only growing, but before he could voice its prominence, the ground beneath the silage squeaked. The Violet Sprite took a step backward and the fodder began to fall, as the ground folded upward. Eric jolted slightly, as he tried to make sense of the confusing sight, for in the center of the cobbled terrain was a trap door that one would never spot with the naked eye, and the one who opened it was none other than Yvonne.

"Oh, am I glad to see you," Yvonne sighed. "I was worried when we all ran from the docks. Wait…where's Prince Louis?"

The Violet Sprite sighed. "That's why we're here."

Yvonne need not ask any further questions to know something truly terrible had happened. "Come in and come quick."

Yvonne led them through the strange and winding underground below the village. Only lit by torches, every few feet, the farther the group traveled into the hideaway, the more nervous Eric became. He was anxious to be out of the surroundings and determined to find a way to save Louis. To him, this journey seemed to become more and more a side quest. He listened as the sprite explained the entire story of their failed conquest to Yvonne, and wondered if there was still indeed a happy ending to be had, or if the love story he shared with his prince was but a tragedy, one that could never be resolved.

"The poor prince," Yvonne shivered as the tale came to an end.

"Can we get to him?" asked a desperate Eric.

"I can get us there," Yvonne nodded gracefully. "But the Underworld is a dangerous, unpredictable place. One can lose both mind *and* soul there. But for Louis, his body too is at risk, and thus his very eternity. It won't be easy to get there, and we *can't* go alone, which is why we're here."

With a carefully calculated stretch of the arm, Yvonne reached into the darkness that still lay ahead. As the enchanter's fingertips lingered in the air, ripples like those caused by a stone cast into a pond filled the emptiness with beautiful bioluminescence. The waves grew and grew, before, finally, the smallest ripple began to illuminate at its center. The glimmer of brightness spun and sparked as it exploded into a glorious portal that gave the heroes a glimpse into a colorfully inhabited world.

"What is all that?" Eric asked, as he watched herds of grinning misfits waltzed through a life he'd never before seen.

"*This* is our home," explained Yvonne. "Welcome to the Secret City of Outcasts."

Yvonne guided them through the portal through the joyfully crowded city streets.

Now, in the warmth of the enchanted hide, Eric could not help but finally feel hope, for there was something special about this place—something different and truly magical. Perhaps, just perhaps, Louis could be saved here. However, victory would not prove to be easy, for unbeknownst to the newly inducted outcasts, something evil was close on their trail.

****

Yvonne led the heroes farther and farther into the city until, at last, they came to a large, vibrant caravan. As the heroes approached, Zest popped his head out from the rear flaps.

"Oh, it's the scribe," proclaimed Zest.

"What scribe?" called Glacé, as he too peeked his head out.

"The one we helped the prince rescue."

"Then where's the prince?"

"He must be the one under the robe."

"That's enough you too," Yvonne ordered.

The twins complied with their silence.

"Oh, fabulous, it's frick and frack," groaned the Violet Sprite. "It's incredible how boys as cute as they can be so irritating."

The Celtic Witch did not respond to her son's suggestion. The sprite wondered if it was part of her effort to keep her profile low, or if she was still resistant to his urges, despite her desire for amends. There was no time to ask such a question, however, for their matters were pressing.

"Prepare my cauldron and fetch my herbs from the altar," Yvonne asked of the twins. "I'll explain everything to you in a moment. For now, we must be quick!"

The twins immediately retracted into the caravan, as Yvonne led the group to follow. When Eric pulled himself up off the last step, he came to a halt, floored by what lay in front of him.

The caravan's insides were many times the size of its outside. His stunned stillness blocked the way of his companions.

"As much as I enjoy glancing at that thin arse of yours," began the sprite. "I'd like to get *mine* through the door."

Eric, still with his dazed dropped jaw, shuffled to the side, allowing the sprite and the witch to enter. Their jaws too dropped as they saw the large, eccentric room that lay before them. The walls were lined with shelves of books. Peculiar plants hung from the ceiling. The plank wood floors were covered by a large, deep purple rug that had mauve symbols sewn into it. the most mesmerizing detail of all was the large black cauldron that sat at the center of it all, but it was not fearsome, or strange as those portrayed in fairy stories.

The twins scurried in and out of the room, carrying various vials and bottles filled with herbs, liquids, and sand.

"We couldn't find the Saffron," Glacé informed Yvonne.

"But we thought the Sumac would do," added Zest.

"Thank you, boys," Yvonne said with grace. "That will be all. Now, go stand guard. The spell we're casting is unpredictable. I can't be disturbed."

The twins agreed and sprinted from the room, as Yvonne rounded the cauldron.

"Before we begin, I must warn you of the risk we take by casting such a spell. This spell is—"

"Yvonne!" cried Glacé, as he threw back the caravan's curtain. "Soldiers!"

"From the palace," Zest added, peeking in from behind his twin.

"In *our* city?" Yvonne exclaimed.

"How did they get in?" asked Glacé.

"Yes, how did they get in?" Zest asked as well.

"Desmos," the Celtic Witch muttered with anger below her breath. "It's Desmos," she repeated for the curious stares she received.

"The king?" questioned Yvonne. "It can't be. How—how did he get in? How did he *find* us?"

"Magic," explained the witch, as she removed her cloak. "Magic of the darkest sorts."

There was no time for explanation or even shock over the witch's reveal.

"We have to go," Yvonne proclaimed.

"What?" asked Eric. "We *can't*. Not until we finish the spell."

"Oh, don't you worry about that, young scribe.

We'll take the spell with us. Boys!"

Zest made hastily darted from the wagon, proclaiming "I'll drive!"

"And I'll fight," Glacé said.

Yvonne's face grew concerned. "Be careful. These men are very dangerous."

Glacé gave a nod, before drawing his sword. He raced from the wagon to join the battle outside, which was growing more and more audible.

Eric's mind was still set only on his prince. "What do you mean we'll take the spell with us?" he asked impatiently.

"There's a reason my apothecary is in a caravan," Yvonne explained. "I need you to think of a safe place."

Eric was growing both frightened and ever more impatient. "What?"

"Just do it."

He thought for a moment, his mind racing so greatly it was hard to decipher *anything* at all. "Louis' my safe place," he said finally.

"Oh my gods," groaned the witch.

"That's lovely," Yvonne said, "but not what I mean. It has to be an actual *place*. One where you will *always* feel at home. Now, close your eyes."

Desperate, Eric did as he was told. When he listened to his instinct, *really, truly* listened, the answer was so simple: the place where he'd always feel at home was not that of the palaces and balls he'd begun to attend. *It was the home he'd grown up in*. The place he'd returned to after his time at sea, the place where he'd love to take Louis to live, far away from the trials and horrors of royalty.

"I've got it," Eric firmly stated.

"*Wonderful.*" Yvonne grinned. "Now hold on to something, everyone."

As the sounds of battle grew louder and louder around the transport, the heroes grabbed onto anything that they could to keep safe, the wagon began to buckle. The sound of swords clinking, and the blood-curdling screams of warriors shook their safety. The caravan began to slowly float upward, surprising the newcomers.

The Violet Sprite and his mother peered out at the battle over which they now flew. Horrific massacre was at the end of each sword. The outcasts battled the king's nights valiantly, but those knights did not have to fight fair, and fight fair they did not.

Overseeing it all was King Desmos, who watched the bloody slaughter of the outcasts with a wickedly gleeful grin. Amidst the battle, the heroes spotted Glacé, whose skills with a sword were undeniably among the strongest. He defended the caravan intrepidly, allowing it to soar to tremendous heights; heights that caught the displeased leer of the king.

Nicholas stood loyally by the king's side. With eyes still barred on the caravan, he whispered something to the knight, something threatening. Before Nicholas could act, however, Glacé had defeated a good many of the army that challenged him, and made a heroic run for the king. With sword drawn, he leaped high toward the ruler. He came down, his blade less than an inch from its goal, and it seemed that the king's reign may be at its end. The witch watched, hoping the boy would be successful. If he wasn't, she knew, in the wake of the battle, she'd have to make a decision that could tear her son from her forever.

Both she and the sprite watched intently, hopeful,

and certain that the young outcast would prove victorious. However, Glacé's launched attack became hovering stillness. With a wave of his hand, the king had cast a spell that froze Glacé.

"No!" cried the sprite, calling the attention of Eric and Yvonne, who joined their viewing.

From within his robes, King Desmos produced the Book of Tellers. He flipped through the pages, until his found that for which he was looking. A quick, undecipherable reading commenced, and suddenly, without restrain, the frozen Glacé turned the sword upon himself. With a violent, involuntary flick of his wrist, the young warrior ran himself through at the heart.

"Glacé!" cried Yvonne.

Zest remained ignorant of the loss of his brother. Yvonne did not have the heart to tell him while he steered the vessel, and it was far too important that they reach safety, thus he could not stop.

"I can't—I can't believe it," shivered the sprite.

"These things happen in war," his mother expressed coldly.

"He was our *friend*, not a casualty of war."

"He won't be the last," the witch continued. "Both sides will have to make trying choices. It's the only certainty if one wishes to win."

The sprite stared at the witch for a moment, curiosity in his glance. He did not care for her cryptic nature and sought to put an end to it immediately. "What are you planning?" he asked.

She gave a cunning grin, her eyes tilted to the side. She knew the jig was up, but she also knew she could not tell him everything. Not yet, not while the king had power enough to destroy her. "Someday soon, you'll understand what one must do to be on the winning side," she said simply.

The figure of the Celtic Witch disintegrated into black smoke, smoldered, and floated through the wind.

The sprite's emotions raged within him, as the caravan picked up speed. Suddenly, it launched into an enchanting portal of ripples that took them far from the Secret City. Now short an ally, the Violet Sprite shook with anger, having been betrayed by his mother once again.

****

I haven't truthfully decided how I feel about this chapter. On one hand, it's relatively quick, on the other, it's the literary definition of "shit hit the fan." That being said, I tried not to play with it too much, because it's incredibly important in the case of the moral of the story. Speaking of which, you're trudging along, and we're getting to that, so instead of getting too wordy here, I'm just going to say continue and discuss your *thoughts on it at your next big, gay book club meeting.*

Chapter Seventeen

"Journey to the Underworld"
Published in The Scribe's Collection *as "Hercules' Journey to the Underworld."*

There's this not very famous fairy tale story that— and I wish I was making this up—tells a story that involves Jesus and monkeys. It's rarely republished for obvious reasons, and it's likely never to find life as a classic in any way, but it is somewhat of a precursor to what this chapter became, only with Hercules. It actually wasn't as uncanny as the Jesus story, but it definitely lost a lot in translation.

****

On the orders of her son, Ruth had gone back to her home when the crew had returned from the sea, for he did not want her mixed up in the disaster that seemed imminent when Nicholas dragged them from the dock. Of course, nothing he imagined then could compare to the horrors that had come to pass of which Ruth was unaware.

It was now sunset. Ruth had spent the whole of her day sitting around the fire pit. Every hour, minute, and now, second, she didn't hear from her son, caused her heart to break more and more. Was he alive, or had the king had him killed? Were he and his love exploring the palace blissfully hand in hand, or were they separated by the bars of dungeon cells? She told herself that if she heard not soon, she'd storm the palace and find out herself.

As she prepared herself for her tirade, a gust of wind from the sea beyond her home swooped down upon her, dousing her fire, and raging her laundry line. Within the gale, magical ripples formed, and through them came the caravan.

"Well, hi there, Ruth," called Zest from the seat upfront.

The shock of it all knocked Ruth back into her seat. She wondered if her worries had caused her mind to go mad. But then, from the back came her Eric. Adrenaline coursed through her and shot her to her feet.

"Eric!" Ruth cried as she ran to greet her son with wide open arms. "My dear, I've been so worried."

In the warm, tight embrace of his mother, Eric was still chilled from all that had transpired that day. His face was stone, his stomach in knots, and his heart aching. Not only was Louis still trapped in some hellish purgatory, but now they had lost a friend, the Violet Sprite had lost a mother, and the weight of battles to come weighed heavily upon his heart.

"My boy," Ruth said inquisitively, as she pulled her head from his chest. "My boy, what is it?"

"Oh, Mother," he responded with a quivering voice. "Mother, so much has happened. And I fear our world is coming to an end."

****

For the next hour, Eric told his mother of all that had occurred since that morning, whilst Yvonne and the sprite took the unpleasant task of telling Zest that he no longer possessed a brother. When all parties finally came back together, they silently sat huddled in Ruth's hovel.

Words were not easy to come by, but Eric could not sit in respectful silence for long. He was eager to get to the Underworld and save his prince.

"Well, we can sit here and pretend to sulk in the day's horrors, *or* we can do something about it and begin our journey to the Underworld," he stated.

With each glance that landed upon the scribe came a different look: Yvonne's was gentle yet knowledgeable, the sprite's awkward, Ruth's concerned, and Zest's outright spiteful.

Yvonne drew a breath. "It will be a complicated task."

"I *know*," said Eric, "but is it not best? Louis is still down there. We can't put it off any further. Besides, isn't rescuing him the perfect way to undermine the king and his army?"

As the room returned to silence, Eric looked around at the eyes upon him. He could not miss the anger in Zest's.

Eric realized that the now twinless twin had every right to be upset, but he could not risk letting Louis spend any more time down below. Thus, he thought of a solution that he was certain would benefit *both* parties.

"It is a world of purgatory," acknowledged Eric. "That means Glacé could very likely still be down there. If we can bring back Louis, we can bring him back as well."

"That's not how it works," explained the sprite. "Louis is not meant to be there. He's not even dead. He was cursed to the realm, body and soul. Thus, bringing him back here is only restoring the balance of what should be. *Glacé*, however, Glacé is gone. And to bring him back with us would have repercussions of *unthinkable* horrors."

Silence returned. Eric felt as though he were the court jester, instead of the royal scribe. Still, he was not willing to give up. He was going to the Underworld *tonight* if he had to cast the spell himself.

"I'm sorry," said Eric. "But I can't just sulk. What happened today has been horrific for all of us. But it's even more so for Louis. We don't stand a *chance* against the king if we all just sit here. We *need* Louis if we're going to win this war."

"And I needed my brother," added Zest. "I depended on him for everything...even to finish my sentences. Now he's gone all because of you and the prince. We should never have gotten involved. And I refuse to get into this any *deeper*."

Zest moved toward the structure's door and sought to exit.

"Where are you going?" asked Yvonne.

"I'm going home," Zest answered. "Or to whatever's left of it. I won't have any further part in this plan. Not after what it did to my brother."

"But we *need* you," cried Yvonne.

"What good is a swordsperson in the realm of the dead anyway? I'm leaving."

With that, Zest was gone. The Violet Sprite looked around at what remained of their once valiant and strong crew. So many had left their family of misfits in one way or another:

The captain had traded a life of running for a new one where no man could hurt him, Glacé had been murdered, Evers heartbroken, and his mother left to preserve herself. Even the brave Prince Louis' fate was uncertain. The king had done what he set out to do:

destroy the band who dared to love and live, no matter how strange or how unique they were in their ways.

The sprite wondered how many more eccentrics would suffer at the hands of King Desmos. Deep down, he knew that this battle was only the beginning of the war. With the king so powerful and the heroes so defeated, it seemed hope may very well be lost for the Kingdom of Belle Terre, and all who dared to be distinctive within it.

However, that's when he *truly* knew that Eric was right. They *had* to take the greatest risk of their collective existences and *save* Louis from the realm of the dead. Not just for the sake of the lovers, but for the sake of *all*.

"We have to go," he stated, finally breaking the most horrible silence they'd experienced yet. The others looked at him with puzzlement, unsure of what he meant. "To the Underworld…" he explained. "*Tonight*."

"Are—are you sure?" asked Eric, fearful of getting his hopes up, but encouraged, nonetheless.

"Yes," the sprite stated firmly. "I've never been more sure of anything in my life. Louis needs our help. And he'd do it for us. He's challenged the king when no one else was brave enough to do so. He's the rightful heir to the throne. I know, if he were here, he'd stop at *nothing* to put an end to this coming war. We *must* have him by our side if we wish to survive."

"What about Zest?" Ruth asked.

"What about my traitor mother?" replied the sprite. "I'm sure she thought there was no chance of winning and went right back to the king to beg forgiveness. We can't speak for those not brave enough or strong enough to fight evil. All we can do is find the courage in ourselves to face it. We're going to need everyone we can get, and I can think of no better leader than Prince Louis."

Eric's small lips formed a touched smile, as he fought to hold back tears.

"All right," agreed Yvonne. "Then let's begin our quest."

****

It took Yvonne the better part of an hour to mix the potion properly. It was a spell never before attempted by an herbal based practitioner such as Yvonne. In fact, it was one about which only theories existed. The unpredictability of its nature caused Eric worry, but he knew the risk was necessary.

He paced with his mother, as Yvonne worked within. By midnight, he could feel all patience leaving his being.

"When will Yvonne be done?" he asked.

"My dear, these things take time. Magic is not easy," replied Ruth.

"We've wasted so much time, already, Mother. How much longer—"

Before Eric could finish his complaining, Yvonne appeared from the back of the caravan with a grin. "It's ready!"

Together, Eric and his mother rushed to the caravan and climbed inside. Within the large cauldron brewed a most peculiar mixture. It smelled of contradiction; each of the herbs tumbled over one another to create a smell that Eric would only describe as "Well-meaning skunk."

"I know it isn't the greatest of all scents," Yvonne acknowledged. "But herbal magic is quite different than that of gods and fairies."

"I like it," blunted the sprite.

"How does this work?" Eric asked Yvonne.

Yvonne sighed. "That's the tricky part I've been warning you about. This potion will allow us to cross into the Underworld, but returning, that'll be hard. This is a realm beyond anything we've ever experienced; one that was not created for the living to come and go from. Opening a portal home will take magic greater than anything I've ever seen."

The concern among the group was great. Traveling to the realm of the Ankou without a way home was more terrifying a task than most could imagine, but, for Eric, there was nothing more horrific than a life without Louis.

"I'll find a way home," the scribe declared. "I know with Louis by my side, we'll be able to think of something."

"What's this '*I'll* find a way' nonsense?" Ruth asked. "*We* all will, *together*."

"After hearing the risks, I can't ask you all to come…just in case I'm wrong."

"Oh, we're not doing that *shite*," complained the Violet Sprite. "Not after Zest's dramatic exit. You should at least be smart enough to know that it's bad manners to overshadow another's spectacle. We're all going to save Louis."

Yvonne agreed. "The king wants people like us to be apart. He's already succeeded in taking away Louis, the witch, Glacé and now Zest. Those of us who remain must be brave enough to fight as one, or those who came before us left in vain."

"To be fair, Zest *did*," suggested the sprite.

"Stop it, I'm having a moment," Yvonne quipped.

Eric looked upon his friends with touched eyes. "All right, if you're sure, let's go get my prince back."

Yvonne explained that they would each have to take a swig of the potion. They would then join hands, until the group formed a circle. Concentrated on their destination, a portal would open to allow them passage into the beyond. They'd have to walk close, as they made their way through the unknown, or risk permanent separation. But confident in the bond they shared within this makeshift family, *they knew they had a chance*.

After each took a sip of the foul-tasting concoction, Eric took his mother's hand in his right and Yvonne's in his left. Yvonne latched on to the sprite, who closed the circle with Ruth's remaining grasp. They all concentrated on their goal. With the realm being unclear to them, it would take extra effort to get there. Moments upon moments passed, each member of the group eagerly awaiting their transport.

The tension mounted for all, and within the Violet Sprite, he felt something stirring. It boiled and bubbled until, finally, he released a loud hiccup.

"Oh, sorry all," he shouted. "I think that tonic gave me a bit of a buzz."

"Quiet!" ordered Yvonne.

They all returned to their concentration. A breeze from outside began to rock the planks of the caravan, slowly at first, then gradually growing. The caravan itself began to move in the bluster, causing the group to shift and stumble.

"Stay mused," ordered Yvonne.

The group did their best not to budge, as they kept their eyes firmly shut and their hands locked. Soon, the very wood of the transport began to shake and shudder. One by one, the walls broke and snapped, until all that was left was the floor beneath the heroes.

"Yvonne?" cried Eric, fighting to keep his eyes shut.

"The portal," Yvonne answered through concentration. "It's opening beneath. Stay firm everyone and prepare for what comes next.

The earth beneath them began to quake, the floorboards now too cracking beneath them. Still the group remained strong. Through the darkness of their closed eyes came the flashes of light, and the sound of thunder. The breaking of wood and the growing unsteadiness of the world beneath them served as the last threat to their faith. Yet, in their determination and through their hope in love, they weathered the storm, until finally they felt the wheels of the caravan lurch forward, the wagon being pulled toward the now fully opened portal.

"Brace yourselves!" Yvonne commanded. "This is it!"

The wheels bumped and rolled forward until they came to an unsteady stop on the portal's edge. The storm reached its crescendo and the wheels finally gave out sending the cart and the heroes plummeting into the realm of the afterlife.

Part Four

Chapter Eighteen

"In the Realm of the Ankou"
Published in The Scribe's Collection *under the same name.*

Welcome to the fourth and final part of the book! Before we follow our heroes into the Underworld, I'd like to give you the heads up that this is not going to be another multichapter adventure, a la Part Three. Semi-spoiler alert: The Underworld is more of a setup for the final battle that's coming. I won't go that *much further into detail, but needless to say, it goes quicker than the merman arc. As far as translation goes, it actually made a relatively good story, despite, you know, the censorship.*

****

What remained of the caravan was destroyed when it hit the hard, brimstone rocks at the bottom of the portal. The heroes were spread across the floor, all unconscious from their journey, but preserved in life thanks to the spell. Eric was the first to wake. The darkest form of darkness blocked him from seeing his surroundings for a moment. His memory was foggy from both the potion and the fall. But as his eyes adjusted and his sight returned, so did his memory. He looked around, searching for his companions, until he found his mother. His body was sore from the fall, thus he crawled to her.

"Mother," he said shaking Ruth awake.

"Eric?" Ruth called back, as her eyes flew open. She rolled on her side and hugged her son. "Where—where are we?"

"I think…we're in the Underworld," Eric shuttered, finally able to slowly stand.

"We are," said Yvonne, approaching with the Violet Sprite. "You smell that?"

The heroes all inhaled the stale, dusty scent around them.

"It's bitter, and rotten," acknowledged Eric.

"Sulfur," explained the sprite. "The land of the dead's foul calling card. We must get moving. We don't want to stay in one place for too long, and the longer we stay here, the harder it will be to get out."

"All right, then let's go," Eric agreed.

The group ventured through the caverns in which they found themselves. The dark was treacherous and winding, but it eventually brought them out of the cave, and led to a valley and at the foot of a macabrely built kingdom; a city filled with strange curvy houses and dead, black trees. At the heart of it all stood a tall, black fortress, not unlike the location of Louis' own home.

"The kingdom of the Underworld," proclaimed Yvonne.

"The Kingdom of the Ankou," the sprite confirmed. "Fairy legend always said it was built like no other. Seeing it for myself, I take it that means 'built with no taste.' "

"Well, whether you agree with the architecture or not, we better get a move on," said Eric, taking the lead in front of the group.

"Stay close everyone," Yvonne suggested. "The last thing we want is to get separated here."

"Or kidnapped by a demon," added the sprite.

****

The valley was a much longer trek than any of them had imagined. The grass was not grass, but long, overgrown asphodel. The farther they traveled into the field, the higher it became. Once they reached the meadow's middle, it towered over the entire group. Still, Eric cut through it proudly with each determined step, swiping the blades swiftly with his forearms. Ruth followed closely behind, as did Yvonne. By the time it came for the Violet Sprite to pass, however, the growths often swung back with a forceful hit to the face.

"How much longer 'till we're there?" the sprite asked indignantly.

"Don't worry," Eric said, unable to withhold a slight chuckle.

"Do you think that face of yours can survive?" teased Yvonne.

"That's right," bickered the sprite. "Make fun of me because I have a sense of style and a wonderful a—"

Suddenly, the sprite was silent. Yvonne and Ruth stopped immediately and turned around.

"What is it?" Eric asked, noticing he was alone and pacing back to meet the group.

"*The sprite*," said Yvonne. "He was right behind me and now he's gone."

"Impossible," said Eric. "Perhaps he fell behind. His footwear was not meant for such terrain."

"No, he was in the middle of complimenting himself and then he stopped," Ruth stated with fluster. "He would never do something like that."

"I'm sure you're both over reacting," Eric reassured as he made his way farther back through the field.

"Where are you, sprite?" he called. But there was no answer. Eric was concerned but tried to remain calm. He cut back farther through the growths, calling for his magical friend, still there was nothing. Ruth and Yvonne followed, as Eric became more and more vexed along the way.

He swiped the blades madly as he plowed through, until finally, he was face to face with a set of horrible, familiar eyes and a pale, unearthly face.

"…We meet again…" said the horrible creature from the tower. "…Only now, you're in *my* world, and you shall do as I say…"

****

The undead monster escorted the group through the city with such command, that none of them dared to run. The leering eyes of souls who dwelled in the realm until their day of absolution followed the heroes with a curious glow as the living heroes passed through.

"Why are they staring at us?" Eric whispered to his earthy companions.

"They're the dead, who belong here, I suppose," said Ruth, who'd read about afterlives in her studies of magic. "To them, *we're the spirits*."

Their glares indeed unsettled Eric, but they were nothing compared to the chills that rushed down his spine as the group was led into the dark, deathly courtyard of the palace.

"…We're here…" growled the creature.

Eric looked up at the twisted spires, the lurking gargoyles, and the rotting structure. Around the fortress was a moat littered with algae and mold, the smell of decay wafting up from the warm, stagnant waters. The drawbridge rocked and creaked beneath the weight of the group as they crossed into the palace.

The insides were every bit as dreadful as the outsides. The halls were dark, deep, and smelled of lingering death.

"I don't think I like it here very much," Yvonne whispered to the group.

"...It matters not what you like..." answered the creature. "...You will face the king..."

The heroes each shot terrified eyes at one another. They'd known their mission would be one of peril, but never did they imagine that they would become prisoners of death itself.

Though they'd quite literally walked through the valley of death, and were eyed by souls it had taken, being led into its throne room was a whole other kind of terror. A long rug made of the blackest leather led the way down to a towering, onyx throne. Torches on either side were mounted upon the wall with peculiar green pyre coming from them.

The creature led the heroes down the gothic hall, until they were at the foot of the throne's dais.

"...Wait here..." the creature ordered.

"You know I'm going to escape again," stated Eric to the shock of all.

"*Eric*," scolded Ruth.

"No, I will! We've all survived his evil before. And this time, I'm more determined than ever. I've got better places to be and more important things to do than be party to your punishment, so you can either let me go now, or I'll leave the moment you turn your back in the slightest. What's it going to be, *demon*?"

"There's no need for escape," came an old, raspy voice that was somehow a whisper that echoed.

The heroes jolted and looked around.

"Who is it?" Eric ordered to know. "Who's there?"

A rush of cold air swooshed through the windows and banked around the room. It circled the heroes with a tight, icy grip before it gusted toward the throne. Manifestation began. A large figure many times taller than that of any earthly man, woman, or other began to form upon the seat. As it became more prominent, it became clear that the towering, bony figure was *not alone*. Something small and impish was at its side upon one of the throne's macabrely carved armrests. As both figures became discernable, the misfits prepared themselves for whatever horror it was that awaited them.

After a moment, though, Eric squinted his eyes for a closer look at the smaller of the two apparitions. "That…That looks like—"

Before he could finish, he found his suspicion confirmed, for upon the right armrest sat the Violet Sprite. "The most lust worthy fairy this side of Orion's Belt?" chuckled their old friend, now fully appeared. "It is indeed."

Before the group could even consider celebrating the joyous return of their magical friend, the accompanying figure completed its own manifestation, as the last, violent gusts whirled around each other. The skeletal figure was wrapped in a cloak made from the black feathers of ravens. The collar reached all the way to the bottoms of his eyes. His brow line and above were covered by a dark, wide brimmed hat. In his right hand, he held a brightly lit lantern; the most illumination the heroes had seen since crossing into the Underworld. There was no question as to the identity of the deity: It was the god of death himself, the Ankou.

Ruth and Yvonne both trembled in his presence, as Eric took a brave breath and stood proudly at the feet of the reaper.

"I'm not afraid of you," Eric proclaimed. "I've faced your demon assailant before and escaped its tower trap. I can defeat you too. *I will,* for you hold captive the most precious person who's ever roamed the Earth, and there's nothing you can do to keep me from bringing him home. The legends of your malevolence are great in my realm. But greater than that is my love, and it shall be your downfall."

The power of Eric's speech reverberated off the walls and impressed his frightened companions. For a moment, there followed an immense and fearful silence. The intensity was finally broken when the Violet Sprite turned to the Ankou.

"Didn't I tell you he was cute?" the fairy asked the idol of death.

"And he clearly thinks the world and beyond of you," replied the Ankou in his whispery rasp.

"Oh, no. That's his prince. It's a whole other story."

"You've talked so much, it's hard to believe there could be more—"

"*Pardon me!*" barked an impatient Eric with flabbergast. "What's going on here?"

"Oh, right," the Violet Sprite looked to the scribe. "Eric, meet the Ankou. Ankou, dear, meet Eric the scribe. He's good."

"I don't understand!" continued Eric. "I thought—I thought that *demon* kidnapped you for its vengeful schemes, for sacrifice to this, this *monstrous* seeker of death and destruction!"

The Ankou looked upon the sprite and the sprite

upon the Ankou. Suddenly, the two outbursted with laughter.

"We're sorry—we're sorry," the sprite managed through his chortling. "It's just...oh, there's no need for that. You, you take it Ani. I'm slightly delirious. We haven't slept in days."

"Well," began the Ankou, his voice far calmer than the heroes expected, after lifetimes of legends, "my guard to which you refer is not a demon. Those creatures are reserved for a far worse afterlife than this one. And *one* was kidnapped. Not really. You see, we've had far too many comings and goings from this realm recently; comings and goings that should not be. When your party came into my realm, I sensed the great power of the Violet Sprite immediately."

"*Great power*," the sprite gleamed to his group. "You hear that?"

"I wondered if it were he disturbing the balance of life and death," continued the Ankou. "So I thought to investigate. He made it *clear* that it was not of his doing and it was that of the untrue king from your land."

"He's done *terrible* things," Eric bravely mustered.

"So I hear," agreed the Ankou. "The Underworld is not a place of punishment, but a place of waiting. Souls were not meant to come here for an eternity, only to visit as they prepare to move on. However, the unnatural magic the king practices seeks to send one here body and soul. Exposure to our realm for too long contorts the mind with trauma and depressions, until the mind forgets all that came before, and the soul breaks."

The weight of meaning in the Ankou's words was not lost on Eric. "Your excellency, the king is planning something much worse. He's trapped my love down here, body and soul with no intention of bringing him back to the mortal world."

"So I've been told," replied the Ankou, as he gestured to the sprite. "It seems your king holds many intolerances; prejudice passed on from generation to generation. So like mankind… In a thousand years' time, the generations will behave no differently. They will try to destroy those they don't understand, and punish them for their differences, when all they ever dared do was exist. I have experienced this for an eternity and more. Fairy stories and legends alike have always described me as a great, malevolent evil. One who gets pleasure from ferrying souls to my realm. However, all I've ever done was perform my purpose and give souls a home while they awaited judgment. I don't control my ghoulish features, not the land I inhabit. This is how I've always been, and how I always shall be."

The entire group drank in the words of the Ankou. All had been raised on the frightful stories of the deathly deity and had always assumed them to be true. But, to stand before him now, and to hear his tales of woe, made the misfits realize that they had far more in common with death than they'd ever had with those the world deemed "ordinary." Perhaps that's what made them great. Perhaps that's what made Eric's love for Louis the most passionate romance the kingdom had ever known. Perhaps that's what made Ruth a worthy mother whilst in a business for which many had condemned her. Perhaps that's what made Yvonne's heart so true and warm. Perhaps that's what the sprite so beloved beyond his powers. And, perhaps, it was *all* of these things together that would defeat King Desmos.

"Your excellency," Eric cooed genuinely. "I'm

sorry the world has treated you in such a way. I promise to write an ode to you and your true nature when I return home. And I promise we will defeat the king. But we can't leave without my love. He's the true heir to the throne and we must see that he rules. It's the only way to save our people from the war the king has waged."

"Yes, I know of the war. I could sense it. A great many souls, beautiful souls, will find their lives cut short and themselves in my realm should the king win. He must not. But you need not make excuses. Your lover must be special indeed for you to come to my world."

Eric breathed a sigh of relief. Though the Ankou had sympathized with them, the scribe worried technicality would keep his beloved Louis trapped.

"There is a caveat, however," the Ankou explained. "The king's magic is maniacal indeed. And it seems they used an unholy sort of curse."

"Unholy—*what do you mean*?" asked Eric.

The Ankou and the sprite exchanged a glance.

"You see, my boy," the Violet Sprite began, "the poisonous needle was imbued with a spell. It's trapped Louis here with a blood lock, meaning Louis *can't* return to our world."

Eric wrinkled his brows with angry confusion and parted his lips, revealing his front teeth as he clenched his bewildered jaw. "Can't return? That—that makes no sense. He doesn't belong here, the Ankou just said that. He can return us to our realm."

"I cannot," admitted the Ankou. "The spell is of a devilish sort, and my power is that of nature. To break the laws of my purpose would have catastrophic consequences for all realms."

"Rich thing," a now infuriated Eric barked. "You

speak to us about challenging the expectations people have set for us, but you won't challenge your own nature."

"It is complicated, young Eric. It is too late for me to change the ways of the universe…but perhaps, it is not too late for you."

"What do you mean?"

"Find your prince. By now, he won't remember you. However, with a love as strong as yours, I know you can make him remember again. And maybe, just maybe, you'll find a way to cheat death itself and start life anew, the way it should be."

It was a hefty task the Ankou had laid upon the shoulders of the humble scribe. Despite escaping prisons, besting sea beasts, and returning home against the odds, this seemed the most impossible of undertakings yet. Eric could not fathom how he was going to get Louis to *remember* him, let alone how he was going to open an impossible portal. Still, for his prince, it was worth it.

"Where is he?" Eric asked.

"My guard will take you to him," the Ankou replied, motioning to the creature.

"Can we trust it?" asked Eric.

"Yes," explained the Ankou. "When you encountered him last, he was under the control of an evil spell. Manipulated to be something he's not. Now that he is free, he will lead you well."

The group looked to the creature, and Eric gave it a nod. It would be hard to break their fear of the guard, but then, the same could be said for their own existences in their world.

"I wish you the best of luck," said the Ankou. "For

your sakes, as well as those of your world."

Eric nodded thankfully to the deity, before he and his travel partners turned their sights to their former enemy-turned-guide. The creature motioned for the heroes to join him.

"May the gods keep you," wished the Ankou as he watched the band of unlikely heroes venture toward their next great challenge.

****

Eric, the Violet Sprite, Ruth, and Yvonne followed their guide closely. They walked down narrow, winding streets; through gnarled neighborhoods and jagged towns for what felt like hours, until, finally, the creature led them to the doors of a bar and brothel.

Sounds of belligerence and pleasure emanated from the tall, blood red building. Eric looked up at the edifice, completely confused and slightly offended.

"Why are we here?" he asked.

"…This is where he is…" answered the creature.

The pub was dirty, loud, and falling apart. "This is…where he lives?" Eric asked.

"…And works. He is in the tavern in the back. You'll have to face many temptations on the way, but remember your muse, and you may just succeed…"

With that, the creature vanished.

Eric looked back to the brothel. His gut filled with unease, his eyes with sadness. Ruth walked to her son's side and placed a hand on his shoulder.

"It'll be all right," she reassured. "We'll get him back."

"But what's he gone through in there, Mother?" Eric asked with breathy fear. "What have they made him do? Who has taken advantage of him?"

"It's probably nothing worse than what I've experienced all my life. You have to be strong, and brave to do such work. I am, and so is Louis."

"But what if he—what if he was with someone else?"

Ruth took a deep breath. "He was doing what he had to do to survive, my dear. Life is tough and the afterlife doesn't look much easier. Survival is the most basic instinct we all have. But, you know, whether he was with the company of another or not, it does not affect how he feels about *you*. Nothing could change the love you two share. And nothing ever will."

Eric glanced at his mother in a way he never had before. He'd grown up with her work around him. It was routine and nearly dull. He never considered that his mother's work was not born out of some lifelong dream, such as his, or that it was about something beyond payment for pleasure. The truth was that Belle Terre was not the kingdom it pretended to be. It was one that benefited the royals, members of the court, or other nobility, not those such as Eric's mother. For the first time, he saw his mother as a full-fledged person; one who struggled with the harsh realities that lie beyond the world of fiction and one that had not been gifted with a love such as the one Eric and Louis shared. He could not imagine the endless sacrifices his mother had to make, or the agreements she made to give her son a good life. He pulled her into a tight embrace. The tug caused Ruth a brief startle before she too embraced her son.

"*Thank you,*" Eric said.

"For what?" asked Ruth.

"For everything. For giving me a good life. For loving me as I am. For making Louis part of our little family. And for coming to save him with me." He gave his mother a boyish grin as the embrace broke apart.

"Where else would I be?" Ruth replied, as she gave him a loving, playful punch to the shoulder.

"He'll still be my Louis," Eric announced, reassuring himself with a new respect warming his heart.

"Nothing will change that. Now, let's go get him."

****

Me again, hello. What follows next is kind of interesting. It took some time to track down the next section. It was kind of bizarre. Finding the beginning and end was not hard at all, but the middle was difficult. I worked with two of my contacts, who helped me try to track it down to no success. I then turned to Professor Sherman.

Surely the person who loved this story enough to turn me *on to it could and would* want *to help. I had texted her with the problem and we again agreed to meet for coffee. When we met up, I explained the trouble I was having. She said I reminded her of a screenwriter she once knew who was working on his first indie film. He had written a great outline, a solid first draft mostly, but could not crack the third act. Hearing the story, I was sure she was about to give some great advice about how she helped him figure it out, which obviously meant she had the answer* I'd *been searching for.*

Imagine my surprise when she said: "I'm going to tell you the same thing I told him: If you want to be a real writer, you're on your own."

I sat in stunned disbelief. "But I'm not *a writer," I explained. "I'm an adapter. Sure, I filled in little blanks here and there, but I at least had context and stuff to work from. Here, I have* nothing.*"*

"An adapter," she said as her paper cup filled with steaming coffee lingered below her chin. "What do you think screenwriting mostly is?"

"Again, those writers have context."

"Oh, come on. You can't tell me you'd be comfortable only cramming novels into three act structure your whole career. You're too creative for that. Think outside the box. Make it your own. What would Spielberg do?"

"Make a genius film that runs over schedule and budget and still makes a trillion dollars."

"I'm serious," she smirked, shaking her head.

I thought deeply for a while. Then, I thought some more. "Tell the story," I said finally. "Any creative person would just tell the story. *"*

"Right."

"But what if I don't do it justice?" I asked.

"I'm going to tell you a secret, one that separates the influential from the forgotten: Write it from the heart. That's the only way to *write. In the end, the publishers, the producers, the studios, they're going to make the changes they want. But if you don't write using the very* best *of your abilities to begin with, you'll never have true success. Risk fuels the business, and when it pays off, it can very well change it."*

There was a logic to everything she said, but there was still a healthy amount of fear in me. The key word being healthy. *Regardless of if I was ready or not, I had to finish the story.*

Professor Sherman stood up, threw her purse over her shoulder, and took what remained of her coffee. She began toward the coffee shop door, before turning back over her shoulder. "Oh, one small suggestion."

I turned back, still at the table thinking over everything she'd said. "Yes?"

"Remember how Eric was always looking for his perfect composition? It's never really paid off in the text we have. I always thought it should have been in this chapter."

With that, she left. I reached into my satchel and quickly pulled out my laptop. I opened the screen and chugged a hearty sip of my coffee. I had a lot of work to do.

****

The tavern was far more feral than the heroes imagined. As the misfits entered, they were immediately struck with obnoxious sounds, as the whiff of poorly aged booze assaulted their nostrils. The bar sat in the middle of the room. Around it were a heap of ghouls and ghosts, enjoying green, bubbling beverages in their tankards. The ground floor seemed to stretch back forever, while three floors of mysterious rooms towered above. The doors to said rooms opened and shut as heaving sounds of private pleasure came from within them and cascaded down to the haunting howls of fun below.

"How are we *ever* going to find the prince in this place?" asked Yvonne.

"*We'll find him*," Eric stated surely. His determination would not waver, knowing his love was in this very building somewhere. "We'll split up. Mother and I will search downstairs. Yvonne, you and the sprite will search above."

The sprite looked up as a door flew open. A particular chiseled soul came panting out of it and landed against the railing. Though his skin was ghastly green, he was clearly quite the catch during his lifetime. A succubus followed him, and placed her gnarled finger around his broad shoulders, pulling him back into the room, the door shutting itself behind them.

"I guess I could do that," accepted the sprite.

"We'll reconvene in an hour in this very spot," Eric ordered. "Leave no stone unturned, no crevice of this place unexplored. Search everywhere twice and then twice more."

"This is going to be fun," the sprite elbowed Yvonne playfully.

The parties separated and began their respective hunts. The sprite and Yvonne were quick to reach the second floor, before further splitting up to search more rooms at once.

"Is it wrong that I still hope they don't find him up there?" asked Eric.

"Not in the least," Ruth reassured. "Now, let's get moving. How hard can it be to find one who's living still among all these…" She stopped as a drunken spirit with a glass filled with spirit passed through her. "I won't even pretend I have a follow up for that…How should we start?"

Eric thought as he looked over the sea of people. Every inch was crowded with the dead, with no sign of life at all. That's when he realized how they would do it. "Well, if he *is* here, he'll have stood out to *someone*. So let's ask them all. *Everyone* until we have our answer."

With boiling and exact determination, the two also parted their party and weeded through the departed crowd.

Asking the dead if they'd seen Louis, however, proved a greater task than Eric had realized, for getting the attention of the chilly patrons was a task itself. "Excuse me," he called at least a couple of hundred times as he passed through the crowd. Not one acknowledged his questioning. Once he reached the other end of the bar with no success, his path crossed with Ruth's who too had not found the answer.

"This is never going to work," sighed Eric. "Not like this."

"Don't give up, my dear," Ruth comforted.

"I'm *not*. If I have to start a brawl with the dead, I'll *make them* help me."

It was then that Eric's salvation came in the form of a familiar voice.

"Need some help?"

For a moment, Eric could not believe his ears. Still, he knew the call could belong to no other; no other in the Underworld anyway, and indeed, he was right. As he turned, Eric was greeted by the now ghostly face of Glacé.

As he was still a new arrival in the Underworld, Glacé's complexion had not yet changed to that of the green, ghoulish sort. Instead, his milky skin now glowed with a shimmering light.

"You—*you're here!*" exclaimed Eric.

"Well, you did see me die, didn't you?"

"Glacé, I don't have words sufficient enough to make up for what happened."

Glacé sighed. "You know what's funny? When you're alive, you fear death more than anything. But once you're here in the Underworld, awaiting passage to your eternity…you realize *life* is just the beginning."

The thought was nothing short of shocking. In life, Eric had always accepted Glacé and Zest as immature and nonsensical. He realized now how he'd underestimated the twins. When he made it back home, he would carry the Glacé's words of wisdom with him and hoped to share them with the remaining pair.

"It also doesn't hurt that I don't look like *these* rotting banshees yet," continued Glacé as he grabbed a nearby spirit, who quickly moved from his grasp.

Eric could not help but laugh, for even in the afterlife, Glacé's spirits were the same.

"But, enough of that," continued the ghostly ally. "We had a quest before I died, and neither of you looks dead yet, so I assume you're still looking for Louis."

"We were told he was here." The frustrated Eric sighed. "But we've had no such luck finding him. And *no one* has been of any help here."

"Don't take it personally. These sad souls, they're the ones that never found their reason for moving on. The ones who are still awaiting a better afterlife but have not let go of their Earthly purpose. They may be stuck here forever if they don't let go, rotting away at the soul."

"What about you?" asked a disturbed Ruth.

Glacé grinned. "I stayed around to help. So let's get to it."

"You think we can find him?" Eric asked hopefully.

"No need to find him," Glacé explained in the nonchalant way he so often shared with his brother. "I already know where he is."

"You—you *do?*" asked Eric.

"Sure, I do!"

"Glacé, I cannot thank you enough."

"Don't thank me just yet," said Glacé, taking a tone far more serious. "Knowing where he is, and knowing *who* he is down here are completely different tasks.

"I was warned of this," Eric sighed. "He doesn't know who he is, does he?"

"I'm afraid so."

"Then, it might be too late." Dread filled every ounce of Eric's being.

"*Glacé*?" called an approaching Yvonne.

"Is that really you?" asked the Violet Sprite. "You're *glowing*. I mean that both literally and figuratively."

"This is no time for jokes," Eric remarked. "Glacé knows where Louis is, and he's already lost his memory to the Underworld."

"No," cried Yvonne.

"It would appear this battle is far from over."

"Well, we're not going to win by standing around, being all wish washy," added the Sprite. "Where is he?"

"Come with me," Glacé motioned.

****

The heroes followed Glacé through several small, twisted halls until they came to a smaller bar at the back of the establishment. A minstrel roamed through the crowd, strumming an erotically paced song upon his gittern. There were a few souls clustered around the bar, a few mingling as they drank. Their dressing was much like that of the misfits. Colorful, different, not of rich stature, but beautifully their own all the same. Eric noticed the ghost of a man dancing with another. It was, at first, romantic and one that he'd *dreamed* of sharing with his own lover. Before long, however, their dance became more of a private act. Eric averted his eyes, and it was just as well. There was no time to linger on such distraction.

"All right, this is interesting sure," Eric said to

Glacé. "But where is Louis? If he's back here and forgotten who he is, I don't like the prospects of how he may be treated."

"So uptight," teased Glacé, "but there's no need to worry. He's right over there." He motioned toward the crowded bar.

Eric moved closer to the bar as three men waltzed away together, hand in hand, *at last*, revealing Louis. He worked behind the bar, standing out among the crowd for his lack of spectral glow. Still in the clothes he wore when the king banished him, they were now stained with beer, and liquor. His hair looked frail and had fallen from its usual well-kept style. Beyond the vanities and heartbreak Eric felt for his lost prince, there was something that hurt him even worse: In Louis' eyes was all the sadness in the world; the same sort Eric had seen all those years before, when he first laid eyes upon the man he'd loved for most of his life. It filled his heart with even more determination: He was going to *make* Louis remember the prince he was, and bring him home to his kingdom, if it meant trading his own soul to the Ankou.

Eric made his way to the bar. At first Louis was too busy emptying tankards of beer to notice the scribe. When he turned back from his task, he spotted Eric immediately. For a moment, Eric's heart fluttered. It had only been a few hours since he'd seen those eyes, yet without them, it seemed as though it had been years. He found himself wordless, unable to speak in the presence of the love of his life, despite the intimacy they had already shared. His mouth hung open slightly as he gasped for air with a slow, tremble. His blue-brown eyes were focused on Louis' hazel.

"What can I get you?" Louis asked plainly, breaking

Eric's absorption.

"I'm—I'm sorry," Eric replied, shaking himself free of hypnotization.

"It's all right, I suppose. What would you like to drink?"

"Nothing, thank you."

Louis gave Eric a questioning gaze. "Very well, then," Louis responded as he turned to continue his work at the other end of the bar.

"Wait!" called Eric, stopping Louis before he could take more than a step.

"Yes?" Louis asked, with a near annoyance in his voice.

"You don't—you really don't recognize me, do you?"

Louis sighed as he shook his head. "Look, a lot of people come in and out of here. It's impossible to remember everyone."

"I don't stand out to you? Not even as another of the living?"

"Living? What are you talking about?"

"You—you're in the Underworld. Don't you know that?"

"I don't understand what you mean, and I've got far too much to do."

Eric's eyes drooped sadly. Louis continued his walk down to the other end of the bar, leaving Eric alone in his sadness. The scribe turned and paced back to his allies with a defeated stomp.

"What is it?" asked Ruth.

"It's worse than we thought."

"What do you mean?" asked Yvonne.

"Not only doesn't he remember me, he has no idea

where he is, or what's happening."

"He's losing himself further," said the sprite. "Time is running out. It'll be *impossible* to get him back soon."

"That's not acceptable," Eric stated without question. "I *have* to find a way."

Eric paced as he thought in anxious silence. He turned and turned, his heels clicking along the floorboards, until he noticed the sly grin on the Violet Sprite's face.

"You have an idea," Eric acknowledged.

"I suppose you could say I had the idea *months* ago," the sprite said with a hint of wisdom. "You can't tell me that the great scribe of Belle Terre doesn't see the poetic irony here?"

"What do you mean?"

"For so long, you've wondered and worried if you'd *ever* write your best work. Now is the time to do so."

"My best work?" asked a flustered Eric. "You're not suggesting I *write* now, *here*, when I'm in the middle of a crisis such as this."

"Why not? After all, you're beautiful, kind, and intelligent, yet it's your words that set you apart from all others. It's your words that the prince fought for, and your words that won you a place in the palace."

"It was magic. We both know that...*your* magic. The magical quill and parchment you gave me made my words sufficient enough before the court for them to accept Louis' proposal. It had nothing to do with my gifts as a scribe, not really."

The sprite giggled impishly. "Oh, dear boy," he said in a sweet, artful manner. "You don't *really* think I used such a powerful spell on something as simple as human love, do you? Magic, no matter how potent, cannot compete with the power of the heart, for when hearts that were made for another finally meet, something far greater than a fairy tale is born."

"Are you telling me that the night I first came to you, the weeks I worked tirelessly, hunched over the supposed enchanted parchment, with a cramping hand thanks to your fraudulent magical quill were all a *lie*?"

"*No*, of course not—*well*," the sprite stopped his denial to recount the details. "Yes, yes. You're right, I suppose. But allow me to explain: It's true that neither parchment nor quill carried any sort of enchantment. There was a risk that the effort would not reap the reward. But you see, that was the point. I certainly could have used magic to manipulate nature and make your wishes so, but it would not have been right, nor would it have been true. You had to put the work in yourself and express your love in its purest form. It was not supernatural magic that brought you and Louis together; It was the purity of your efforts and the strength of your determination. You see, no spell could have created a love as great as the one you share with the prince. *That is the most powerful magic of all.*"

A whirl of emotions spun out from Eric's heart. He felt no anger toward the sprite for his confession. In fact, it made him feel even more certain that Louis was worth fighting for, a strengthening he did not think possible. Still, in this strange world, one that had already threatened their union, Eric worried that, this time, his gifts as a scribe would not be enough without the safety of enchantment.

He thought in anxious silence for a beat, and then another. Ambition and uncertainty weighed heavily on his mind while fear pulsated his heart.

"But what if…what if, *this time*, it doesn't work?" Eric asked with the worries of a child. "What if I *can't* create something powerful enough…something *perfect* enough to bring him back? What if I fail him?"

The sprite smiled knowingly. "When it comes to passion and love, we could search the world over and not find another pairing as perfect as the two of you. Your story has not been without struggle, it's true. It has not been without opposition, no doubt. However, despite every challenge, every loss, and every battle, your love has only grown stronger. If there's any romance that can beat this darkest of darkness, *it's yours*. You don't *need* an enchanted quill, nor magical parchment. You don't even need *unmagical* ones. What you need is to write from your heart and speak the words aloud for your prince to hear."

Eric flashed the sprite a fleeting grin. Nerves filled his belly, as he turned toward his prince, whilst twiddling his fingers. He looked back upon his group, seeking courage before he took his daring steps back to the bar. Each member of the misfit brigade gave Eric an encouraging glance. Though he felt the support of his loved ones, they could only help him so much. He'd have to do the next part on his own. He turned back around and drew a deep breath. His eyes remained fixated on his beloved prince; the beloved prince who no longer knew him. But that mattered not. If there was even a shred of possibility that this plan would work, *Eric was going to see it through*.

He paced to the bar with all the gallant bravery a scribe could muster. It was true that while other young men his age brandished a sword, he brandished a pen. While they dreamed of knighthood and quests, he dreamed of composing fairy stories and romances. And, despite the manly stories he'd heard while growing up in the Kingdom of Belle Terre, it was *his* abilities, *his* dreams that were all that could save the day.

"Excuse me," Eric called to Louis.

The prince was busy slinging two tankards of ale to a pair of handsy ghouls when he turned to see Eric. "Oh, it's you," he said without much enthusiasm, after handing the beers off. "Did you decide what you want?"

"I've decided what I want. *I've always known.* I've known since the first time I saw you all those years ago. It's ironic that, after all we've been through, I should be in the same position. But I suppose it doesn't really matter what we've been through or how long I've known you; I'll always want the very same thing."

"You're truly a mad one, aren't you?"

"I'm not in the least. Believe it or not, you wanted the same thing too. And I know that, deep down, you still do."

"And what is that?" Louis sighed.

"I want you to know me…and to love me."

Eric's voice was breathy, yet full. Cool, yet passionate. Strange, yet like home. Still, Louis had dealt with enough rabble in this place and knew they were only in search of one thing.

"You're *truly mad*," he replied.

"Louis, if there's anything I'm mad about, *it's you*."

"What did you call me?" Louis asked, unable to hide his peaked curiosity.

"Why, Louis, of course," repeated a confused Eric.

"No one calls me that," Louis explained, dropping his eyes, unable to hide his interested grin. "They all just call me Ti'Louien."

"You've never liked that name though," flirted Eric. "It always seemed so pretentious."

"Can I tell you a secret? Back in *our* kingdom, people always called you by your birthname as well, amongst other things. But they never got to know you as they should have. And the more I got to know *Louis*, the more I realized something incredible…"

"And what was that?" Louis asked, now completely unable to hide his fascination with the thin, curly-haired young man, whose blue, brown eyes created a lively shade of green that he'd not before seen in the Underworld.

"I realized that, powerful as it was, the love I felt for you at first sight was *nothing* compared to the love I've felt ever since I've gotten to know you."

Louis blushed with undeniable rosiness, while his heart filled with a warmth that only those in the land of the living could experience. "Well…" Louis managed. "Isn't that just, a lovely story? But stories such as those, they don't happen. Not really, do they?"

Eric looked into the hazel eyes of the lover who remembered him not. He knew it was pointless to reminisce about things that only one of them could recollect. "I suppose you've believed that for a long time. Before we met in our land, you'd had such a trying life. When we fell in love, you treated me as though I were a daring knight, instead of a scrawny scribe; a hero who'd saved you from that life in which you so suffered. But what you didn't know was that *you* saved me just as much…just as you have many times since. And now…I'm going to save you."

Eric closed his eyes and took a deep breath. He searched his mind for the most beautiful words he knew but soon realized that no amount of articulation, elegant wording, or poetic rhythm was sufficient to describe the pure, prevailing love he shared with the prince. For the first time in his life, he decided not to write from the head, but instead from the heart. Perhaps it would not be his most well-worded work, perhaps it would not even be one that any other enjoyed, but, if he truly spoke the way he felt about his prince, it would indeed be his best work. His eyelids rolled open. He exhaled and, with all the love in his being, he began:

"When our eyes first met, I felt I knew you.

Though you were far away, it was that very day that I said "farewell" to my heart.

I sailed away, to be my best,

To win you was my greatest quest.

Yet from the day we met,

I found your lonely heart accepted me.

Without you, my life would have no bearing.

I knew it was only you with whom life would be worth sharing.

You and your lonely heart that too longed for me.

Unseen, yet outspoken,

It was you who had awoken,

The secret parts of me.

Fear you inspired,

Lust you acquired,

And, always, more of you I longed to see,

You and your lonely heart,

The one that rescued me.

Yet, now, here we are,

At death's blimey bar,

Strangers again,

Just as back then,

Back before you and your lonely heart found me.
This time, however, we'll end up together,
Now and forever.
You've fought for me dearly,
Truly and clearly.
Oh, why must we fight anymore?
Ambitious it may be,
Without you, I can't be me.
The fighting is done,
No more tears shall run.
From this day and forever,
We'll battle together,
Hand in hand, side by side.
They've never torn us apart,
No matter how they've tried.
I stand here,
Waiting for you,
And though I seem the hero,
I implore:
Please, my love, the one I adore,
Save me once more!
No matter how far I must go,
I'll find a way to make you know that it's you,
It's always been you from the start,
You, who can rescue my lonely heart."

Eric exhaled, his eyes intense and filled with the passion only true love could express. His jaw quivered, as he stared with hopefulness at the prince. Louis stared back, an array of confusion, intrigue, and amazement on his face. The young man's confession left him stunned and flattered. Suddenly, a ray of light burst force from within him and spread through the room with a warm, lively breeze that had never before graced the likes of the

Underworld.

Its power was so great that it knocked Louis to his knees. He clutched his chest and kept his head down as he recovered from the enchantment. Eric dropped to his knees as well and reached for Louis' shoulder to comfort him.

"Louis?" he asked frantically. "*Louis*?"

Louis' eyes finally came up to meet Eric's. The glimmer within them was not like before the scribe's recital. Instead, it was familiar and filled with what Eric knew to be undeniable love. The scribe grinned greatly. He knew, without a doubt, that his Louis was back.

"Oh, how I've missed you so," Eric cried breathily, as he embraced his beloved prince.

"It's you, my scribe," Louis teared up, tightly returning the clasp.

"My prince."

"It was your *best* work."

"I don't know," admitted Eric as they both fell back to their knees. "Somehow, I feel like my best work was never meant to be my words, but the love we've created together. Now, let's go home."

****

Well, there you have it folks: My attempt at blindly finishing a previously unfinished chapter. Did I do a good job? That's for you to decide. Is it blasphemous to replace another writer's work with my own ideas and theories? Maybe. But I like to think I did what was necessary. If we get sued because of it, it's the publisher's problem, I guess. What follows may seem a little disconnected, or maybe that's just me. It's all retrieved text from the original text. But I didn't want to go down the rabbit hole of changing things to fit my contribution. This is, after all, supposed to give voice to a previously silenced author. I hope this section only added *to that.*

****

For the lovers, their reunion felt miraculous. Eric and Louis walked hand in hand, as they ventured with the rest of their traveling companions beyond the village of the Underworld. They climbed the hill above the valley and meadows through which they had passed when they first entered. At its peak, they looked down upon the town below. Though the heroes once found it mysteriously spooky, they felt as though they had a better understanding of the realm, and therefore, saw the dutiful beauty that the Ankou did within it.

"We did it," Eric sighed with relief.

"Now comes the tricky part," Yvonne reminded. "Getting home."

"I have to admit," chimed Ruth. "It does seem a little impossible."

"No," Eric corrected. "No, it's not impossible. Look at all we've done. We can get home. And we can win the war."

"We *will* win the war," Louis amended. "Not just out of the spite I feel for my stepfather, though that is reason enough, but for *everyone* he's hurt, mistreated and destroyed."

"I like the sound of that," Glacé smiled.

"You're coming with us, of course," Louis continued.

"I'm afraid that won't be possible," came a disembodied voice.

In a swirl of black smoke and with a gust of heavy wind, the Ankou appeared.

257

"Oh, please tell me we weren't wrong the whole time and this wasn't some sort of trick," sighed the Violet Sprite.

"Not in the least," the Ankou replied.

"Right, of course. I knew that," the sprite chuckled nervously.

"Something is different in my realm, though," continued the Ankou. "Magic that has never before been here has spread throughout the land. Magic that I believe came from your love."

The Ankou nodded to the couple, who in turn looked at one another.

"What does that mean?" asked Eric.

"It means that your love is strong enough to create a force of nature of its own. I sense that it is strong enough to get you home if you harness it for a portal."

"You mean, it's that *simple*?" Louis approached.

"Nothing is simple," replied the Ankou. "But you've already faced challenges greater than most, and your love has continued to grow stronger through it all. Carry that power with you into battle, and I sense the balance will be restored to the realms."

"Sir," asked Eric sheepishly. "Is there any way you will allow our friend to return with us? He's a great warrior, and his brother misses him."

"I cannot condone such unnatural practice. But I *can* offer hope." The Ankou turned his attention to Glacé, without whom, the heroes never would have succeeded. "Your bravery on Earth was great dear boy, and your unselfish ways in this world unmatched. It is time for you to move on to your eternal reward in the next life."

"You mean," began Glacé, "you mean Heaven?"

"Yes, dear boy. It is time to go."

"But what about my brother? Will he be all right?"

"In time he will, and from your place with the Greater Lord, you will be able to see and help him once more."

Glacé smiled greatly. "I guess it's time to go." He began to follow the Ankou, before turning back to his friends. "I know I'll have a better vantage point, but do you think you guys could keep an extra eye on Zest for me?"

"It would be an honor," Louis nodded.

"In that case, I'm out of here." Glacé waved goodbye, as the Ankou nodded.

A white light surrounded him. It was warm, beautiful, and bright. It grew and expanded until it reached its crescendo. Then, it vanished, and so had their friend. The misfits could not help but feel solemn initially, but found comfort in knowing that their ally was in a better place.

"All right," said Yvonne, taking on a serious tone. "Let's get started."

Yvonne and the sprite felt the magical energy all around them. With their combined powers, they felt confident enough that they would be able to open a portal. Without a vessel, however, they would each have to hold tight to one another to keep from being separated in the magical vortex. They formed a circle with hands clasped tightly the way only the makeshift family could. Yvonne and the sprite began the incantation of sense. Slowly, the warm breeze that had come with the release of Eric and Louis' magic swirled around them. It grew greater and felt more beautiful, forming a stunning vortex of magic.

Suddenly, the warmth Eric felt from the spell was

gone and replaced by a cold foreboding aura. He opened his eyes to find that the group now stood in the very spot from where they had departed. But something was different, and *far* from as it should have been. His jaw dropped when he turned to see what now lay around them in the land he once knew so well.

"Look," he called to his group's attention with urgency.

The misfits opened their eyes and too turned to see the destruction that their land had become. Eric's childhood home was desecrated, the trees burned and destroyed. Beyond, the cries of women, children, and others echoed as the frightening clanging of swords traveled in the wind. The sky above the distant palace was blood red, as embers rose into the atmosphere. The war had come, and it was time for the heroes to face the battle of their lives.

Chapter Nineteen

"The Battle of Misfits and Royals"
Published in The Scribe's Collection *as "The Battle of Outlaws and Nobles."*

Sigh. Do I even have to say it? At this point, I don't think so. But, just in case it's not mind-numbingly obvious, this was again *another story where the misfits were turned into villains, and the hero was "the good king." I* am *going into some detail here, because this chapter had an annoying little troupe in adaptation where there was* one *royal who was a villain alongside the heroes...The Queen. Go figure. But I don't want to give too much away. After all, if this were a script, we'd call this the "Break into Act Three," which essentially means we're almost to the end. So I'll restrain myself as best I can.*

****

Though it had been only a few hours since the heroes left for the Underworld, it had been many days in the land of the living. At that time, the Kingdom of Belle Terre had fallen deep into the despair and bloodshed of war.

The Violet Sprite used enchantment to create disguises for each of the misfits. As they walked through the dark streets of the once thriving village, Louis did not recognize his own land. Ravaged by war, and painted with death, he shivered at the sight of his once great land.

"He's a monster," Louis shivered angrily beneath his cloak. "Worse than any we've faced before. And he'll pay for what he's done to my people."

As the heroes continued to sneak down the cobblestoned streets, they found the book cart turned to ash, the village artist's paintings destroyed, even Max Day's Sausage & Buns was once again ruined, only this time, with intention.

"I don't understand," said Yvonne. "How can the king see nearly all his subjects as the enemy?"

"Fear of himself," acknowledged the sprite. "Those with the most secrets will hunt and destroy all in attempt to preserve themselves."

Louis stopped. A chill that one only experiences while being watched by prying eyes rushed down his spine. He peered through the ember red fog that surrounded them, trying to find the lurking culprit. Suddenly, he no longer felt the leer upon the group. It was as though the stranger left out of fear of being caught. "It's not safe to be out in the open," Louis declared. "We should find a place to hide."

"But *where*?" asked Yvonne. "All of our safe places are gone."

"I believe I can help with that," came a familiar voice from beyond the blood painted mist.

The heroes immediately recognized the voice as that of Evers. They spun in the direction of his call and found him standing tattered and without pride.

"Evers!" called Eric. "What happened to you?"

"What happened to me is what happened to *much* of this land, Desmos." Evers spit as the name tumbled from his lips.

"He will pay for this," Louis declared with angered

pride, as he stepped toward the fallen guard. "But we need your help. We need a place to hide and to plan. Are there many others left?"

Evers shook his head with solemness. "Those who did not join the king in fear of punishment ran, many of whom were killed. Those of us who survived found refuge in an unthought of place."

"Take us there," Louis proclaimed. "Take us there, and we will do everything in our power to defeat the king."

Evers nodded. "I shall, but you must prepare yourselves. What lies in our fortress will test you."

"We've been to hell and back," explained Louis. "Whatever it is, I know we can face it."

****

The closer Evers led the group to their destination, the more Louis dreaded it. He had an inkling of where they were headed, a place not of joyous memory. Indeed, his suspicions were correct, as they stood at the bridge that led to the fortressed asylum Desmos had sent his mother.

"This is where the brave have been hiding?" asked Louis.

"Indeed," Evers responded, knowingly.

"Why here?"

"Because this is the one place King Desmos won't dare to topple. Not yet."

"Why's that? It's of no use to him anymore. My mother's gone," sighed Louis. "She's under his wing and control."

"That's only as it appears," said Evers.

The Violet Sprite stepped forward. "He's right. You see, there's something I've been keeping from you. I wasn't sure for the longest time, and I feared, if I was right, the truth may be far worse than the illusion."

"Oh, enough of the cryptic nonsense!" shouted Louis. "Someone tell me what's going on!"

"I think it's easier to show you," Evers explained as he motioned for the heroes to follow him across the bridge.

The halls were still filled with the stale stench Louis remembered. He shivered with both sadness and fury. His stomach was in knots, and his mind ill at ease. Eric took his hand gently at first, then squeezed it with a caring grip that brought Louis back from memories. After climbing the treacherous, uneven, circular staircase, the group finally came to the floor where the refugees resided. Sad and worried eyes met the misfits immediately. They were clothed like that of Evers, many of them the friends the group had known before they traveled to the Underworld, and *none of them* in as well a state they were back then.

At the end of the hall stood Zest. Tattered but still brandishing his sword as he leaned against a pillar. His eyes were distant and still filled with anger as they had been before he left the group. He noticed the heroes coming down the aisle formed of broken souls. Through his anger, he could not hold back his interest in their return. However, it was the figure beyond him that caught the attention of Louis. It was not long after that it also captured the sight of the others, for there standing high above them all was Queen Krystal.

"*Mother*?" called Louis, his shock echoing down the hall.

Queen Krystal spun around quickly. "Louis!" she returned as she rushed to him. "My boy, I was so worried

I was never going to see you again."

"Nor I you," Louis returned. "In fact, after everything with Desmos—I wasn't sure that you *wanted* to see me again. I thought you were too far gone."

"There's much to explain, my son, but before I do, please know that I never meant for *you* to be caught in the crossfire."

"Caught in the crossfire? Much to…?" Louis mumbled his confusion. "Mother, what's going on here?"

Queen Krystal took a deep breath and released it with an equally heavy sigh. "My dear, the last few years… I've been deceiving you. In fact, I've deceived everyone."

"What do you mean?"

"You see, many years ago, a powerful sorceress came to me. It was not long after your father's leaving, and a young man had visited with her to make a deal. A peasant in the neighboring Kingdom of Flowery, who wanted more power than his kingdom could offer him. And with that power, he was determined to bring about changes that were disturbing and dark. That peasant was Desmos, and the sorceress was the Celtic Witch."

"We know about their deal," said Louis.

"You don't know the whole story, though," said the Violet Sprite.

Louis looked upon the sprite with confusion, and the sprite looked back to the queen, who nodded and continued:

"The witch saw many paths for the future, all of which were filled with great darkness should the peasant succeed in his quest. Though he'd promised her his soul, and glory brought upon her name if she helped him, the witch had locked herself away with her own regret for some time. The hatred and wickedness that Desmos spoke reminded her of her *own* ways from years before ways, ways that brought her the loss of her son."

"Hello, this is where I enter the story," called a humiliated sprite.

Queen Krystal smirked sympathetically at the sprite. "It was through Desmos' dealing that the witch found a way to finally make things right. Desmos would have executed his vileness with or without her. *With* her, though, his defeat would be possible. She came to me, and we devised a plan. We switched places, so that she could operate within the kingdom in accordance with the deal she made with the king, whilst having the ability to undermine him."

"Mother, are you saying that all *this*, your exile, the mockery that's been made of me, the way Eric and I have lost one another…was all *planned*?" Louis asked with shocked disgust.

Queen Krystal sighed. "No, my dear, not all. We never planned for the king to get the Book of Tellers, we never planned for your trip to the Underworld. And, of course, we never planned for this war. But it doesn't mean we can't defeat him now! We must, for the greater good—"

"The *greater good*? Mother, I *suffered* for years. I almost lost Eric forever more than once. We've lost friends and family. Our kingdom has fallen into tyranny. *How* is there any greater good here? The witch tricked you, don't you see? She tricked the Violet Sprite too. Everything these last years was a lie."

"I wish it didn't have to be this way," Queen Krystal attempted to comfort.

"Much good it did!" shouted Louis. "Now, the witch has double-crossed us all, and Desmos is in power."

The prince stormed off from the group before another word could be uttered by any. Eric watched him go for a moment, before turning his eyes to the queen, then back to his lover, then to the queen again.

"You're the real Queen Krystal?" asked Eric.

She nodded.

"This isn't how I thought we would meet. In fact, I thought we had already."

"I know all about you dear boy. You've been the one light in Louis' life since I left."

"And he in mine. I'll talk to him. It won't be easy, but he'll do the right thing."

"Thank you. I know he cares for his land and his people; despite the way they've treated him. And I know he'll do what's right for the cause—"

"*That* right there, that may be something you rethink."

"I beg your pardon?" The queen asked, royal indignation in her voice at the scribe's challenge.

"Louis loves me dearly, that I know. But you're the person who means the most in the world to him. I know you did what you had to do. You did it for him, you did it for everyone. But that doesn't change the fact that Louis spent years of his life alone; years that he needed a mother. There had to be another way. And if there wasn't, it doesn't mean it was any easier."

"If I had taken him with me, our family would have lost *all* ties to the throne and the war would have come sooner and greater."

"And that's probably true. But, right now, Louis needs his mother, nonetheless. Not 'the cause,' but his mother."

****

Eric found Louis alone in an empty, narrow corridor. "There you are," he called gently.

Louis turned to face his lover with tears in his eyes. He quickly wiped them away with his sleeve as he sniffled. "Sorry. I shouldn't have stormed off without you."

"Don't be sorry," Eric cooed, taking his prince's hands in his own. "You needed your time alone. And that's as it should be sometimes. What was thrust on your shoulders is far more than any should ever have to endure. But I think I have something that can help." Eric looked to the corner from which he just rounded.

Queen Krystal came around with cautionary approach. "May I please speak with you, my darling?"

"About what, Mother?" Louis asked snidely. "How you *abandoned* me when I needed you most? How you never even gave me a hint that you were all right when I came to visit you."

"My dear boy, when the witch made her predictions, I was given certain instruction. I didn't want to ruin your future. But now, if I could, I would have done it *all* so differently. What I mean is, the only reason I did any of this in the first place was for you."

"For me? What of the cause?"

"Louis—I'm calling you Louis—you *are* the cause."

"*Me*?"

"Of course, it's you. Do you think I would strike a deal with a witch and lock myself away for anything else? My crown and nobility mean *nothing* without you by my side...After your father, it was you who kept me going, you who reminded me of what I had to do, *you* who *reminded* me how to love. Desmos knows nothing of love. Thus, he was a threat to you...you who will always be my world. I *had* to do what I did to protect you from his evil."

Louis' jaw hung open. His tears continued to build, but this time, it was out of pure, raw love.

"I've made such a mess of things listening to that witch," the queen sighed, herself beginning to weep.

"You did what you thought was right," leveled Louis, wiping his newly fallen tears. "For me, for all of us." He took a breath as he thought over the tasks that still lay ahead. "And, no matter how we got here, we'll fight together. And together we'll win."

Queen Krystal could not help giving a grin. She'd once been as sure as Louis, but with the state of her son, kingdom, and the deal she'd struck, she was lost in uncertainty. "You really amaze me, you know that?" she said to her son. "Despite it all, you still believe we can win?"

"I've faced so many trials and creatures since this love began. All of them, determined to destroy those I love. If there's one thing I know for certain, it's that the hatred of man and monster alike is of no match for the love we all share."

Queen Krystal's grin grew, as her son's proclamation began to return hope to her heart. "Well, I say it's time to rally the troops.
****

Not long after Eric and Queen Krystal went after Louis, Yvonne led the Violet Sprite and Ruth over to Zest.

"How are you?" Yvonne asked.

"I'm alive, if that's what you mean," replied Zest with an animosity in his voice. "I see you all made it back from the Underworld."

Yvonne nodded, unsure of how to reply to Zest's anger.

"We saw your brother," Ruth stated, taking the lead, the others filled with surprised uncertainty at her brazen statement.

"Are you sure you want to—" the Violet Sprite attempted to intervene.

"I know what I'm doing," she replied with confidence, turning back to Zest. "He helped us quite a lot, you know. And he looked good. He was *glowing*—literally. Anyway, without him, we never would have rescued Louis and, truthfully, I don't think we ever would have gotten out."

"Glacé?" asked Zest. "He did all that?"

"Yes. Yes, all that and *more*. He was a real hero."

Zest stood thoughtfully silent for a moment. "Well, you brought the prince back. I don't see my other half anywhere."

"It didn't work like that, Zest," Yvonne explained. "Louis was never really dead. But, Glacé, he was—well—"

"Really dead. Because of the battle you all started. Wonderful." Zest turned from the group, his arms folded, and his eyes filled with dagger-like sharpness.

"That's enough of that!" ordered Ruth. "Do you not understand what your brother did? I won't let you ruin his legacy, or *any* of those brave enough to fight a tyrant like the king. Your brother is one of the *bravest* people I've ever met. And I've met them all: soldiers, navy men, and confused court jester. *None* of them hold a candle to

Glacé. You don't have to agree with the cause. The fact that we must fight this war to begin with is wicked. But it's here, it's happening, and we must *all* play our part in whatever way we can. The gods gifted you with the talent of the sword. Use it. Use it for the artists who can no longer use their art to make a point, use it for all the children who were ripped from their mothers because they were different, use it for all the lovers who can't be together, use it for those who are no longer there to use it themselves."

Zest's eyes were now firmly fixated on Ruth, his heart gripped by her passionate sermon. His stone-cold face melted away and was replaced by that of epiphany. He stood silent for a moment, unable to form words of his own in the face of ones so powerful. Finally, his eyes fell to the floor, a flabbergast slowly parting his lips. "Yes," he exhaled. "Yes, I'll fight for Glacé. I'll fight for all of us. How—how can I not?"

Ruth nodded calmly.

"There's just one thing," he continued. He inhaled, his expression thoughtful and filled with fear that none in the army of misfits had ever seen him don. "Glacé and I, we fought in so many battles, but we always fought them together. I've never fought *anything* without him. How am I supposed to fight the biggest battle of my life without my family?"

Ruth smiled sweetly, placed a hand upon his cheek, and without a second thought, said: "You *will* have a family with you. *This* family. I'm not perfect, but I'm a pretty good mother, if I do say so myself. So what do you say, shall I be your mother now, and the rest of them your siblings?"

Melancholy rolled down Zest's cheeks. Ruth

brought his head to her shoulder, as she embraced him with all the motherly love in the realm.

Queen Krystal and Louis came back into the hall hand in hand, with Eric too linked to the line via Louis.

"What's going on here?" Eric smiled.

"Oh, just a bit of healing," Ruth winked. "My dear, I think we'll have to rebuild the hovel with an extra-large loft to accommodate your new brother. He'll need a place to sleep and hide when I'm busy with business."

Eric gave Ruth and Zest and beaming nod. "That sounds wonderful."

"Perhaps we talk about an in-law wing in the palace," Louis added. "But, *first*, we take back the kingdom. And we take it back together."

Queen Krystal stepped forward. "Gather all the troops. The battle to save Belle Terre is about to begin."

Chapter Twenty

"The Fallen Prince"
Published in The Scribe's Collection *under the same name.*

Yeah, same name, but holy God, is it different. It became this weird twist that was like "Cinderella" meets "The Frog Prince." If it's all right with you, I'd like to not talk about it and would rather just dive into the chapter.

****

The heroes devised their plan within an hour. Each had a voice, each had a veto, each had a role. It was not the grand plan of battle that the likes of Zest and the sprite hoped for, not at first anyway. They decided their first approach would be that of diplomacy. If such an attempt failed, they would resort to further battle, though the group was confident they would be able to best the king, for together they were more than muscle and anger, but wit and cunning.

They headed out across the bridge, dressed for battle, thanks to the sprite's magic. Louis, Eric and Krystal led the way, followed by Zest, Ruth, Yvonne, the sprite, and Evers. Behind them came three more lines of the refugees that Queen Krystal had taken in. Down into the burnt-out valley they went, and across the massacres that were formerly battlefields. The sprite's magic provided protection enough to get them to the palace.

They waited behind Louis at the foot of the drawbridge, as the prince looked up at his home. Though structurally the same, the palace seemed dark, and unwelcoming.

"Are you all right?" Eric asked.

"I will be when that bastard is off my throne," replied Louis with intensity.

With that, he bravely strutted forward across the bridge, the rest of the army closely in tow. When they arrived at the grand doors, they found two guards dressed in blood red armor, their faces covered, and strange markings of three black stripes across their chests.

"What are those?" Eric asked quietly, as they approached.

"A mark of the darkest sorcery," explained the Violet Sprite. "Symbols that demons in hell will often leave. It seems that the king has taken to his new power full heartedly."

When the heroes were visible to the guards through the mist, they drew their swords.

"Let us pass," ordered Louis.

"If it isn't the Deplorable Prince," growled one of the faceless guards.

"You know, you're not as pleasant as the guards that used to be at this post," Louis replied with snide sarcasm. "But you're right...I am the prince. And this is my palace. So I'm going to tell you one last time... *Let us pass.*"

The guards charged the misfits.

"We warned them," called Louis.

Yvonne's eyes closed, as the other misfits jumped out of the way. Suddenly, two powerful stalks broke out from beneath the path, their green the only lively horticulture in the entirety of the kingdom, now. The first wrapped around the arms of the guard to the right, the other around the left guard's waist. With a violent pull, each vine threw the guards from the path of the heroes.

"Will they be all right?" Eric asked.

"Does it matter?" added the sprite.

"They'll be fine," explained Yvonne. "Once they land a few kingdoms away from here."

Louis led the charge into the palace. The sight with which he was greeted was even more unrecognizable than the outside of his home. Most of the familiar members of the court were nowhere to be seen, their robes filled with ominous new faces. Those who did remain from time's gone by looked to be in a much darker way than Louis remembered.

All eyes, new and old, immediately went to the misfits.

"It's the Deplorable Prince!" called a face unknown to Louis.

"And as the Deplorable Prince, I command you all to back down!" responded Louis. "Take me to my stepfather at once. To disobey *is* treason!"

The whole palace stood and stared at the prince, not one moved a muscle.

"Did you not understand me?" Louis continued. "*Take me to the false king.* Your prince commands it!"

"Perhaps they don't listen, because you are no longer the prince," came the disembodied voice of King Desmos. The crowd soon parted down the middle to allow the king passage. He walked taller than he once did, and his robes were even more regal. In his hands, he carried a dark spell book. Indeed, he looked like a great and powerful sorcerer.

Louis took in the sight of his stepfather, at first surprised by his change, but soon disgusted. "What do you mean? This kingdom is mine by blood, and I'm ready to lay claim to my throne. Thanks for keeping it warm for me."

King Desmos chuckled wickedly to himself.

"What's so funny, Desmos? You've already lost. Even *you* aren't above the law, and I'd say you've broken quite a few of them."

"*No one* is above the law," the king grumbled. "But in the time you were gone...*I made a few new ones.* Specifically, when it comes to succession. You see, after the freaks and perverts in the hidden realms of the city decided to come up and invade our kingdom—"

"*Invade*?" shouted Eric. "You destroyed the very cloister you forced them to hide in. Where else were they supposed to go?"

"Oh, the mouthy scribe, and his only defense: *words*. Words won't save you this time. *This is war*. To protect my loyal, wholesome citizens, I began to lay down laws that would rid our land of those without values; those who are ungodly."

"Ungodly," Yvonne stepped forward. "You call my people ungodly, yet it's *you* who carries an unholy book of damnation."

"My motives are pure and punish those who deserve it. Those not unlike our former prince. Very impressive that you escaped the Underworld. I expect nothing less from a marauder such as you. I'll soon remedy that, *permanently*."

"Enough games, you demon. You and I both know you can't remove me from succession without just cause. Being 'deplorable' isn't that, otherwise we'd both be out of a job."

"When one's very existence is perverted and vile and goes against the new laws of decency, removal from succession is of *very* just cause."

Louis realized that Desmos had exposed the secret nature of his relationship with Eric to what remained of the kingdom. He passed the laws just before doing so, and thus his succession truly no longer existed. "Then it is to be war, indeed."

"You need an army to go to war, but all you have is a small, pathetic cult of freaks and witches. Do you think because you broke dear Mummy out of her asylum you'll be able to rally warriors? Don't be daft. If she wanted to stop me, she should have done it before we were *all* double crossed by that witch."

"She's not returned to you?" the sprite blurted out before he could control himself.

Desmos shot the fairy a disgusted and disgruntled look.

"That's why you were afraid to go near Mother's asylum, isn't it?" Louis chuckled. "You're afraid she's planning something behind your back. Regardless of what army she chooses, our strengths *are* equal Desmos. And *we will win.*"

Desmos stepped to meet Louis' stance equally. "You'll have to make it to the battlefield, first," the king grumbled.

Suddenly, he threw open the book and cast a spell. Louis was sure he'd been defeated for a moment, for a swirl of violet fog and light encased him. When it cleared, however, Louis discovered he was now back in the asylum. He turned around quickly to see that the rest of the group was too with him, and the Violet Spite's wand spewed the magic that had brought them back.

"That bastard!" shouted Louis. "War it is then."

"Darling," Eric said, following him. "Please take a deep breath. We'll win this battle. We *always* win these battles."

"That's just the point," Louis spun back around. "We fight fairly and win, but there's *always* another battle. And, what happens when our luck runs out? What happens *then*?"

The room stood in stunned silence. For a moment, Eric did not know what to say. He sighed and walked to his prince with care. Placing both hands upon his shoulders, Eric looked into Louis' eyes. "As such is life," he cooed "That doesn't mean we stop fighting. Because the moment we do…that's the moment we all lose each other."

Louis took in what his scribe had to say. Thoughtfulness and melancholy adorned his face. As he got further lost in the thought, and as Eric looked upon his prince with protection, there came a booming voice from beyond the valley.

Louis and Eric went to the window. The voice was that of Desmos, projecting across the line via a spell. "…And be forewarned, any citizen who fails to comply will face the same fate. Furthermore, any citizen caught *helping* the fugitives will be sentenced to death, immediately! The Deplorable Prince has ruined our kingdom enough! Now, we take back our kingdom *once and for all*! Down with the Deplorable Prince, for he shall be forth known as the Fallen!"

The words echoed in Louis' ears for a moment after. "If I stop fighting, and stop fighting fair I let him win one way or another," he said, his eyes still over the red land below. "And then I'm really no better than him."

Eric ran his hands over his prince's shoulders, and softly kissed the top of his blond hair.

"We have no choice," Louis said surely. "For every dreamer like us, for everyone who wants to fight, but can't, we *have* to win. And we have to win the *right way*."

Eric rested his chin atop Louis' hair, as he leaned him into a backward embrace. Suddenly, something in the distance caught his eye. "Wait—what's that?"

With a gust made of strong, and well-versed power, the red embers that clouded the sky began to part across the land. A hoard of familiar faces now stood before the tower, faces such as those of the Divine Lady and a far more agile Captain Armond. The creature that had guarded the tower, the nobles of neighboring kingdoms with their daughters that had rejected Louis, and members of the court who'd gone missing lined the field proudly. Though all unexpected and surprising in nature, the one who led them all was also the one who brought the most flabbergast, for in command of this makeshift army was none other than the Celtic Witch.

Chapter Twenty-One

"The Final Battle for Belle Terre"
Published in The Scribe's Collection *as "The Brave Knight's Battle," "The Sword and the Prince," and "Spindelshanks the Imp."*

Well, congratulations on making it to the penultimate chapter! This one was among the harder to get together. In fact, the only challenge greater than this one is in Chapter *Twenty-Two, but we'll get there when we get there. Anyway, what made this one such a pain was that it was split up into three stories—three stories that were scattered around in random orders throughout the original. "The Brave Knight's Battle" was, at first, the easiest to translate. It's honestly more of a composite of the first part of this chapter, with the battlefield elements watered down. "The Sword and the Prince" was a little more troubling. It was more of a take on King Arthur,* but *the pages from the original manuscript were largely intact, so it just took a bit of ingenuity to get it back where it belonged. Then, there was "Spindelshanks." And let me just say "UGH!" This was maybe my least favorite adaptation. They took the big, gay climax of the story and turned it into a half-witted take on "Rumpelstiltskin." This was also the segment that took the longest to shuffle back into place. I had to call on basically all my contacts to get pieces of it together. But somehow, for this chapter, that also felt right. Anyway, let's get to the final battle.*

****

"Everyone," Eric called, looking back at the group of misfits. "Come quick! You have to see this."

Everyone from Evers to Zest to Ruth to Yvonne to the sprite rushed to the window with curiosity. They looked down upon the army of friends, former enemies and those undecided below.

"Oh, for the love of the gods, it's my bloody mother," whined the sprite.

"But look at all she's brought in tow with her," added Evers.

"She probably put a spell on them to kill us."

"Don't be so foolish," Ruth said. "She's a mother still, and we should hear her out."

"Besides, if there's a chance she'll fight with us, we need all the help we can get," proclaimed Louis.

"Very well," the sprite agreed with reluctance, as well as a hint of sarcasm. "I suppose we'll hear what she has to say. Which one of you will do the unlucky deed of listening to her squabble?"

The entire group looked upon the sprite.

"Oh, all right, fine, fine," he muttered, as he shrank himself down to his fare-folk size and floated upward. "Make the one who didn't even want her here bring her in just because she popped me out of her lady bits."

He flew down bravely to meet the mother who, as far as he was concerned had double crossed him twice in life. When he landed, and returned to his larger form, he was met by a humble sympathy from the witch. However, *she* was met with the unamused scowl her son wore so well when he felt it just.

"I suppose you're quite angry with me," she said.

"I'm not angry. I *never* get angry."

"You're almost exclusively angry."

"Oh, all that contradicting, and you wonder why."

"I'm not here to fight," replied the witch, shifting to a tone of solemn regret. "I'm not here to fight *you* anyway. I've come—*we've* come to join the battle against the king."

"And how do I know that's the truth this time? You were in cahoots with him, before making amends with me for less time than a climax before you vanished with your cryptic ways to join him again."

"Oh, my darling. You have it so stupidly wrong."

"Thanks for that."

"What I mean is: I didn't run off to join Desmos. My cryptic ways were only for that of safety. When I saw the horrors the king brought upon the misfits, I knew it was time to enact *my* greater plan. After all, that annoying boy he killed could have been *you*, and though he wasn't, he was still a mother's son. I quietly vanished to ensure Desmos did not hear a word of what it was I must do. *He* may now be the most powerful warlock in Belle Terre, but I've gathered the most powerful deities from land, to sea, to what lies beyond. He doesn't stand a chance. Not with Louis and Eric at the command, and not with the world ready to fight."

The Violet Sprite looked over the crowd. Indeed, he could tell his mother was sincere. However, having the goddess of the sea upon the land, a creature ripped from the Underworld mingling with the living, and a witch of questionable magic leading the brigade *did* bring about an important question: "How did you manage this? The forces of land, sea, and the Underworld were meant for the occasional meeting, but never meant to dwell in one world for long. The balance would be greatly disturbed by this."

A thoughtful look filled the eyes of the Celtic Witch, as she dropped her glance to the ground for a moment. She smiled to herself knowingly, but this was not a smile of cunning or of anything to be feared. This smile was *pure*. "Allow me to worry about such things," she finally said.

Normally, such secretive nature would have raised the sprite's suspicions, but now, in his heart of hearts, *he knew to trust her*.

"All right," he agreed. "We'd better get you inside." He glanced down at the horde that lay in front of him. "Oh dear, *all* of you."

****

The Violet Sprite reentered the hall with the eclectic army in tow. "They fight with us," the sprite announced.

"Wonderful," stated Louis. "We must have a solid plan for the battlefield. All ideas are welcome, and I don't want any arguing. Desmos will come prepared and in greater numbers than our own. We mustn't give him even the slightest of opportunities to break us."

"The prince is right," agreed the witch. "As someone who spent many months under his thumb, not to mention other musty places I don't wish to talk about, I can confirm he'll be looking for such falter. And *I*, for one, would like to make sure the only falter he finds is his own going up against the far more fabulous army."

As the others began to pitch their ideas and their specialties, Louis felt his mother's eyes upon him. He turned to see her glancing upon him with a proud, loving grin.

"What is it, Mother?" he asked with the same tone

of curiosity he had as a boy.

"You lead like a true and rightful king," replied Queen Krystal with a passionate tremor in her voice.

"That he does," added Eric, his eyes locked on Louis as though he was all that was good in the world.

"Annoying, isn't it?" the witch jested as she came around to their side of the room. "It's fair rulers like *you* who are going to put witches like *me* out of business. Hello, Krystal," she said as she turned her attention to the queen.

"I had heard talk you'd abandoned us," Queen Krystal said.

"After all the years we've been working on this? Don't be silly, Your Majesty. If there's anyone who is looking forward to your husband's defeat the most, it's the one who was actually married to him. And, I say, you all owe me greatly."

The queen, her son, and her son's scribe shared the first chuckle they had in some time. As they watched and rejoined the execution of their stand, each realized in his own way that they were finally beginning to feel once again and sensation they'd worried was gone forever: *Hope*.

****

The riffraff army led the dawn across the battlefield. Louis and Eric bravely stood at the helm of the horde. The witch and her son used their magic to part the red mist that encased the kingdom to alert the king of their ferocious presence. Finally, they approached the wrecked village of Castro Street.

The king's faceless hoards awaited them. Noticeably absent was the king himself. In his place, was an emotionless Nicholas, seated high upon horseback. It was a treacherous sight for all to see, especially Evers.

"This is your last chance," called Louis. "Surrender now and we shall show you mercy. Fight for the king, your absent ruler, and there shall be nothing left."

Nicholas looked down upon the misfit army. Evers hoped dearly his beloved would surrender, that he would come to his senses, but he knew, deep down that it was not to be so.

The horseman raised his sword and, without feeling, shouted a command: "Destroy them all."

Eric and Louis locked eyes. It was the battle they so hoped to avoid but knew would come to pass.

"Prepare for battle!" ordered Eric.

The mortals drew their swords, while the magical folks charged their power.

"Attack!" Louis cried, and soon, the two parties charged toward one another.

Sword met sword; body met body. The king's army fought with a frightening fierceness. Immediately, they brought injury to many of the nobles that had joined and maimed the denizens that had survived the king's first attacks.

Louis and Eric watched at the witch's side. Try as their army might, they could not harm the king's hoard.

"I don't understand," said Louis.

"I do," said the witch, as she watched Nicholas with concentrated eyes.

The knight did not fight himself, but sat high on his horse, holding out his sword.

"It's the sword," the witch proclaimed. "The king has enchanted it. We have to take it from him."

"How?" asked Eric.

"Don't ask stupid questions," the Celtic Witch

groaned. "We fight magic with *magic*." She spun around, in search of her fellow possessors of enchantment. She signaled, and one by one, the creature, the Divine Lady and Armond, and the Violet Sprite appeared by her side.

"Get the sword!" she ordered. "If we get the sword, we win the battle."

They nodded with understanding. Immediately, each shot off on their mission.

The sprite was the first to approach. He shrunk himself down and attacked Nicholas' eyes vigorously, blinding him with his natural, spritely glow. Armand, now of more lively spryness, was the next to approach.

"This be for all the years of runnin' your bloody king made me do!" he called, as he launched himself into the air with a flip. He nearly grasped the sword before Nicholas quickly pulled it away. "Oh, bugger," screamed Armand as he continued a lengthy tumble into the crowd.

The Divine Lady then began her stand. "Nobody throws him around but me!" she remarked, as she threw a tentacle around Nicholas' neck. She used another to lay her claim to the weapon, just as the creature approached the guard from behind.

It grew its form to tower over the horse and the man upon it. "…This sword destroys the balance. Give it to me!"

Just when it seemed the magical beings were to be victorious, there came a cry that stopped the attack. "That's enough!"

All magical entities immediately ceased their attack and turned their attention to its surprising source. There, before them, stood Evers. He'd been a shell of his former self for weeks, but now stood proud and sure.

"*I'll handle this*," ordered the disgraced guard.

The enchanters exchanged knowing looks with one another. One by one, they released their claims upon Nicholas. Once he was freed, Evers bravely approached.

"Your perverted ways won't make me surrender my weapon," Nicholas grumbled.

"Perverted?" responded Evers. "I've spent a lifetime trying to hide who I am. I hid it from my family, from the rulers, from all. I kept past loves a secret in order to protect my image. But then came you. Though I'd kept secrets my whole life, it was hardest to keep you to myself. And that's because, despite our bickering and differences... *I love you*, Nicholas. I don't want your sword, not really. What I want—is something far more precious."

Nicholas scoffed at the insinuations made by Evers and prepared to release a judgmental remark. But, before he could mutter anything of the sort, Evers used every bit of strength in his body to launch himself aboard the horse. He landed partially in Nicholas' lap and pulled him in by the neck for a heartfelt, passionate kiss, the first of its kind ever performed publicly in the streets of Belle Terre. Louis and Eric found their eyes drawn away from the horrors of battle, amazed by the sight.

The sword began to shake in Nicholas' quivering arm as the beautiful expression of love grew more passionate. Then, a burst of magic soared from the two guards and across the battlefield. Its swooshing sound and warm touch stopped the clanging of swords and soon all eyes were on the display. The stunned silence was twice as loud as the war had been before it was finally broken by the chiming of Nicholas' dropped sword. His hand hovered in the air for a moment, before, finally, he wrapped his arms around Evers, and pulled him into an ever more intense caress. *The spell was broken.*

"Get the sword!" ordered the Celtic Witch.

Eric sprinted and swept up the weapon before any of the hoard could even make a step. The guards' kiss ended, just as he returned to his group.

Nicholas looked into the eyes of Evers, a whirlwind of emotions filling his formerly dulled pupils.

"Evers," Nicholas breathlessly muttered.

Evers grinned boyishly and leaned his nose against that of Nicholas. "My dear love."

"Now's our chance," the witch whispered to Eric and Louis. "Use the sword to declare the battle over."

The lovers looked at one another, and each placed a hand upon the weapon. Together, they raised it above their heads, their eyes following it upward. They needn't speak any words, for the power of their romance and the strength of their desires spoke to the sword. The blade glowed with hues of pink, racing toward the point. Once it reached the end, it exploded with a warm, beautiful magic. It shot to the sky and lit up the air like a firework. The remnants of red from the king's destruction cleared, the enchantment from the sword bringing life back to the world around them.

As the dazzling sparks cascaded down around the king's hoard, they began to drop their weapons. Then came the greatest surprise of the battle. One by one, the forms of the king's army fell into nothing but armor.

"I don't believe this," said Ruth. "They're not real at all; nothing but an illusion."

"You know what this means, don't you?" Louis asked his fellow leaders. "It means the king has no true followers at all. Only those he's cursed or those he's made up. It means, now *the king is alone.*"

****

As the rest of the army waited outside, Louis and Eric led Queen Krystal, the witch, the sprite and Ruth into the palace. They stormed the hall, which was now filled with awakening members of the court, none of whom dared stop the leaders of the victorious army. They ran up the stairs, their various weapons drawn from swords, to wands, to wits. When they reached the corridor outside the throne room, they were certain the king was awaiting them.

"I should probably do this alone," said the prince.

"No chance!" Eric argued. "The last time you faced him alone, you ended up in the Underworld."

"Precisely. He's *powerful*. I can't risk him harming any of you. We may have won the battle, but this is the end of the war. And he'll be merciless."

"And that's *why* we'll face him together," stated Ruth.

"That's right, my dear," Queen Krystal joined. "Never again will I let you battle alone."

"Besides, as powerful as he may be," approached the witch, "he doesn't stand a chance against all of us."

Louis smiled as he laid a touched glance upon his loved ones. "All right," Louis agreed. "Let's get him out of my kingdom."

The king awaited them with anger as he stood in front of the throne. When the heroes marched in, his eyes were on them like daggers. His new spell book was clasped proudly in his hands. Little did he know, Louis too grasped a weapon just as powerful: The sword he'd confiscated from the bewitched Nicholas, and beneath her robes, the witch held the Book of Tellers.

"The abomination lives still," King Desmos

growled. "But not for long."

"It's over Desmos," Louis remarked. "Your army is defeated. And now, I possess the sword you used to command them." He brought the blade out from behind his back.

Desmos looked down upon the prince, disdain, and rage in his glare. Then, there came a low, evil chuckle. "You think I couldn't take that sword back if I wanted? I possess the book I used to create it."

"That's the funny thing about you, Desmos," intervened the witch. "You never think about the consequences of your actions. You only think of your power. But your power would be nothing without me. And I know *far* more about it than you ever will. For example, have you ever thought about what would happen if I just decided to *take* it."

With a flash, the book disappeared from the hands of the king and manifested into those of Eric. The witch revealed the Book of Tellers and gave it to the scribe as well. Desmos came down the stairs with fury.

"You *evil bitch*!" he exclaimed.

"Do it!" ordered the witch.

Eric slammed the books upon the ground, as Louis lifted the sword high, before driving the blade into both of the blasphemous publications. The pure pink magic created by the lovers poured forth around the tomes, and formed a large, black rock, trapping within it both books and the sword.

"Try casting a spell without your precious books," the Celtic Witch grinned with immense, vengeful joy.

Desmos glared at her for a moment before a despicable smile stretched across his lips. "Luckily, I already did."

"Don't be coy *now*, you bastard," ordered Queen Krystal. "What are you talking about?"

"I created a potion, a sort of failsafe, if you will. I may not have my magic, or my army, but I will have the loathsome nature of perverts such as all of you rid from my kingdom once and for all, *even if I have to destroy it.*"

The king quickly removed a vile filled with red liquid from his cloak. He chugged it down before the heroes could either lurch for him or cast a spell to stop him.

Suddenly, a cloud of magic with the thickness, and glimmer of blood surrounded him. It grew taller and taller. When it cleared, the king had been transformed into a beastly dragon. It growled and roared with a monstrous threat as it turned its head upward and released a flume of flame upon the wooded roof. The heroes all looked at one another with unmatched fear. The witch and the sprite both launched into action, casting spells that transported them from the chamber and back to the battlefield.

Their army of magical beings and royals rushed to them.

"What happened?" asked the Divine Lady.

"It's Desmos," began Louis. "He's—"

But before he could finish his explanation, the dragon formed king soared through the top tower of the palace, flames following him forth.

"A dragon," Louis finished with fear.

"Looks about the same to me," replied Armond.

Airborne, the dragon swooped around and released his flaming breath upon the castle's exterior. Soon, the whole of it was ablaze. It was then that the king cascaded toward the army.

"Finally, a fair fight," grinned the Divine Lady. She transformed into a leviathan that traded its fish tail for clawed feet.

Armond drew a sword made from the sharpest of sea materials and followed Morgana toward the monstrous king.

The creature from the Underworld however only looked upon the heroes, and cryptically declared: "…'Tis time…" With a whoosh of green smoke, he was gone.

"Helpful as ever he is," Eric stated with a roll of his eyes. He looked around at the remaining army, as they too drew their weapons. As the only unarmed member, he knew he had to do something, for he could not let his prince fight alone, again. That's when the idea came to him. He turned to the sprite, who was armed with his wand nearby. "I need to write."

The Divine Lady launched herself at the dragon king with her mouth agape. The dragon met her with his clawed foot before she could chomp, however, sending her to the ground with an Earth dragging fall.

"That's my—well, I'm not sure what she is, but ye leave her be!" Armond ordered, launching his sword at the dragon.

The king caught it in his chomps and swallowed the weapon. He swooped down upon the pirate-turned-merman, turned temporarily back to human, and used his powerful wingspan to send him flying out of sight.

Now, it was Louis who approached. With his charge, he brought no magic, no tricks of form. Only his sword and his determination. For the king, it was finally his chance to destroy his stepson once and for all. The dragon opened his mouth and took a hefty breath, his throat already burning as the flames within boiled. He moved them from his belly to his mouth, and, with a powerful roar, released their rage at Louis.

The prince felt the heat on his face as the flames approached. He stopped short in his tracks, skidding across the cobblestone. The fire was imminent, and there was no time to turn back. Indeed, the prince knew that his reign was about to end with his stepfather's poison breath. He closed his eyes as the approaching pyres readied to melt his flesh. But meet his flesh, they did not.

Eric jumped in front of his prince, holding up the greatest weapon of all. It was not enchanted, nor forged by a blacksmith. It was but a simple parchment, which Eric held high in front of him. He too closed his eyes, uncertain that his plan would work, but accepting that the possibility was far greater than the risk. With a burst of magic, the flames were sent back toward the dragon. Louis opened his eyes, to see his brave scribe's action. He could not believe the purity of the power that surrounded them, protecting them from the king's wrath.

As the pyre poured back toward Desmos, the king tried to fly back away, but was not quick enough nor experienced enough with the magic he wielded to avoid their strength. They forced him to the ground. When they cleared, King Desmos was back in his human form, his spell tarnished by his own arrogance.

"You saved me," cried Louis to his lover.

"I figure we're about even now," Eric jested, before kissing the prince's nose.

They turned their eyes back to the king, who lay pathetic and injured on the cobblestone but still alive. The rest of the heroes approached from behind.

"Get behind me," Eric ordered Louis. Once the prince was safely clasped to his arm and out of the king's reach, he led the misfits toward the disgraced king.

"We could kill you, you know," stated Eric to the disgraced Desmos. "But we're not going to do that. See, that would be hateful. And, if there's one thing that defeating you has shown me, it's that no matter how *wicked* one can be, the only way to win any war is not to give in to the same darkness as one's enemy."

"You ridiculous fool." The king coughed. "I will never bow to the perversions of your kind. If you won't kill me, you might as well prepare for more war and bloody skies. No matter what's happened today, your *words* alone can't defeat me."

Eric met his fallen enemy's words with a knowing smile. "Today they did." He held the parchment up and began to read:

Chapter One

"The Long Walk Home."

There once was a young man known as Eric Allard. He was charming of face, thin of body, curly of hair, and modest of means. He had arrived back in the Kingdom of Belle Terre from his long, worldly voyage only the day before this, and yet he still faced many miles on the path along the sea before he would arrive at the home of his mother. The many hours he'd face upon his feet did not weary him, however, for he was happy to be home and finally back in the same kingdom as Prince Ti'Louien."

"What in the name of the Underworld is all this?" scoffed the king.

Louis looked upon his lover with caressing eyes. "It's our story," he gleamed at his scribe. He took his eyes to his stepfather. "You were, quite literally, defeated by our love."

Desmos shook with rage, his fury shooting him to his feet. He wrapped his fingers around Eric's neck.

"Defeated by your love, am I?" Desmos yelled madly. "*I'll* show you defeat, even if I have to kill you with my *bare hands*."

The Earth beneath them began to shiver and shake. Then, an explosion of green and black mist opened a massive hole in the ground. When the mist cleared, there stood the creature with the Ankou, wrapped in his robes.

The king jolted back from the scribe with shock. Louis held Eric as he caught his breath.

"What—what are you doing here?" asked Louis.

"Oh, for the love of the gods," groaned the witch. "They've come for me."

"What do you mean, Mother?" asked the sprite.

"Well, you see, I may have…*made a deal with the Ankou*…if he helped me gather this army, and what an army it is, that…" she sighed, her tone becoming serious, "*I* would pay off the debt for my part played in the imbalance that now exists in the realms of life and death."

"Mother, you can't!"

"…And she *won't*…" the creature intervened.

"What do you mean?" the Celtic Witch asked.

"You see," began the Ankou, "though your plan was risky and a far greater wield of power than any practitioner of magic should ever possess, your longing for redemption is something the gods admire. Thus, we have come to a decision, one that will restore the balance and allow you to continue your journey here on Earth."

"What is it?" the Violet Sprite asked hopefully.

"…The false *king*…" growled the creature.

"No!" shouted Desmos. "No!" He turned and began to run from the representatives of death, but the creature was quicker.

It got on all fours and ran after Desmos. With a tackle, it ceased the king's efforts and dragged him back to the Ankou's feet.

"You have spent *years* trying to destroy those you deem different," the Ankou. "You've hunted and killed and condemned them when they are nothing more than you pretend not to be."

Louis and Eric looked at one another with shock upon hearing the revelation.

"How *dare* you compare me to them," Desmos argued. "I would never engage in the perversions they do."

"Not even during long, mysterious voyages on your beloved ship?" the Ankou asked facetiously. "You forget, I am death. I know all past, present, and future. And try as you might, you cannot lie to me anymore than you can escape me. As punishment for your crimes against the natural balance of all, you shall serve a thousand years as an incubus in my court before you spend three million eternities in a far worse afterlife."

"You can't do this to me!" shouted Desmos. "You don't scare me, and I won't let you take me there before my time."

"Oh, don't you know? Your fate is to be *scared to death*."

Suddenly, the Ankou threw his robes from his body, revealing his rotting, horrific form. Decayed muscle and meat clung desperately to his bones. His eyes rolled loosely in their sockets, and his veins hung freely from his arms. He lurched his terrifying face at Desmos.

The disgraced king *screamed* with a fright that echoed through three neighboring kingdoms. All color left his skin, as is flesh turned wrinkled, and his eyes rolled back in his head. The creature waived its hands, calling back the smoke that had brought them to the land of the living. It swirled with violent gusts that blocked the sun and shook the pavement beneath the heroes.

When it cleared, the creature, the Ankou and Desmos had all vanished. The hole in which they stood was closed, yet the destruction the war brought upon the kingdom remained prevalent and depressing to all.

The warriors stood in silence, surrounded by the devastation. Eric held Louis close in his arms, and Louis held Eric closely in his. There was a breathlessness that surrounded all before, finally, the Violet Sprite asked the question on everyone's mind:

"What do we do now?"

Chapter Twenty-Two

"The Dawn of a New Day"
Published in The Scribe's Collection *under "The Happiest Kingdom of All."*

You've made it to the last chapter. Congratulations are in order, I guess. By the time I made it here research wise, I started to feel both excited and nervous. I didn't know how it would feel to be done with it. I didn't know how I would feel without the daily research that waited for me at the end of my school day, or how I would feel when it was no longer in my hands. I didn't know how I would feel about the ending. *Yeah, I was invested in the story. Surprise, surprise. But this chapter, despite being a pretty lovely wrap-up, ended up being my last challenge. And it had nothing to do with either liking or being disappointed with the ending. But I'm getting ahead of myself. I'll tell you more later. For now, let's get into this little ending.*

****

The war was won, but the kingdom in shambles. It would take decades to rebuild what was lost, even with magic. Louis and Eric overlooked the mess that lay before them. The sight was sad, but there was comfort in knowing they had each other, and they had family. Queen Krystal and Ruth approached their sons with motherly care.

"The Violet Sprite and the Celtic Witch are seeing

our friends off," cooed Ruth.

"I'll be forever grateful to them," Louis replied with halfhearted attention, as he looked upon the destruction of his kingdom.

Queen Krystal and Ruth looked to one another, mother to mother. Then, both stepped forward.

"You know," began Queen Krystal, "our ancestors were not always from Belle Terre."

"They weren't?" Ruth played into the queen's story.

"Indeed. We came from many kingdoms far away after invaders ravaged our home."

"You're saying we have a habit of our homes being destroyed?" Louis sighed.

"No, no," the queen continued. "What I'm saying is that our home can *never* be destroyed. Our home is not just a castle, nor a village. It's our family and our people. We can always rebuild the structures around us, but it's important we do it together, for it's through love and acceptance that those structures become a home."

"I've always found that to be true," agreed Ruth. "Before today, I'd never been in the palace, but I know the hovel I shared with my son was far warmer and filled with love."

Louis looked to Eric and Eric to Louis, the words of their wise mothers rolling through their minds.

"Well, in that case," Eric began, "I think we better get to work."

"Yes," Louis agreed. "But not here. Not on the grounds of so much destruction and horrors."

Queen Krystal gave her son a puzzled, curious grin. "Where then?"

Louis looked into his lover's blue-brown eyes with a knowing bliss. "I have an idea."

****

Eric and Louis raced upon their horses down the miles of path along the sea. The prince shot his scribe a cunning, competitive grin. Eric looked upon Louis with a playful laugh and an attempt to match Louis' keenness but could not, for the very sight of Louis was far too powerful an enchantment for him to even pretend. Louis shook his head with determination, before he and his horse pounded farther down the path, leading the scribe to the land where he grew up; the land where the New Kingdom of Belle Terre was being built.

They rode through the humble, beautiful village where the Violet Sprite and his mother worked *together* along with Yvonne and Zest to build warm, welcoming homes for all citizens. At the end of the village was the new palace of the New Kingdom of Belle Terre. Though still under construction, it already stood as a proud beacon of hope for the people.

The lovers rode through the gates, gates that were always open for the citizens without a drawbridge or barrier to overcome.

Once dismounted, they put their horses away comfortably in the stable and met with their mothers in the courtyard. The four built the structure by hand, without magic or labor, for they were determined that it would be built for the people by their leaders.

"Where should we begin today, Mother Ruth?" Louis asked.

"Why don't the two of you take the guest quarters?" suggested Ruth. "I'd like them done before the Divine Lady and Armand come for their visit."

"Very well," Louis agreed.

"Can I get you anything, Mother Krystal?" asked

Eric.

"I'm all right, dear." Queen Krystal grinned with a nod. "Captain Evers and General Nicholas will be here soon to help."

With that, the lovers climbed the makeshift stairs they installed to begin their work. They still had a long way to go before they were finished, but the family knew that, so long as they did it together, it would be the happiest kingdom of all.

****

So here's the kicker: There is definitely one more scene *in this book. I searched for months. I made calls, sent emails, and spent many sleepless nights trying to locate either the scene or someone who at least knew what was in it. But no matter where I went,* no one *could find it or at least confirm how the story ended. I suppose there's something poetic that the chapter about building a new kingdom is unfinished. I struggled with what I should do. Sure, I filled in the blanks before, but did I really want to* end *the whole thing with my words? After all, that could completely change the meaning of the story. What if it hurt the book's legacy? What if my ending stood out like a sore thumb? What would the real Eric think about it? I wondered why Professor Sherman would set me out on such an impossible task if she knew there was no ending.*

But then—finally—I realized exactly *what she was doing. More on that later. I knew exactly what I had to do.* I wrote the ending. *So if you're a purist and haven't enjoyed my narrations and additions so far, go ahead and stop reading now. But, if you trust me, I invite you to come along into this final daring literary task and read what I do best: Tell the story.*

****

The palace was complete in less than a year, for when the neighboring kingdoms heard of the New Kingdom of Belle Terre, each did their part to pitch in. Queen Krystal wasted no time when it came to passing new laws; laws that allowed all to live peacefully side by side, and ensured peace for as long as the people would have it. With each new declaration came a greater understanding among the citizens. For the first time in many years, Louis felt loved within his own kingdom. But even amongst so much warmth and acceptance, nothing could have prepared him for the law that came on the anniversary of the misfit army's victory.

It was early that morning when Queen Krystal came to the room Louis and Eric now shared openly. She knocked lightly and allowed them a moment to get decent. When it was safe to enter, she came into the room with an anxious grin, one that said she had news she could not wait to share.

"What is it, Mother?" Louis asked, sipping his morning tea in bed as he leaned his body against Eric's shoulder.

"I've come to a decision," she said. "A new declaration I wish to pass."

"We'll bring it up to the court next time it is in session."

"Well, you see my dear, I already have, and the court has already agreed."

"Oh, Mother, what do you mean? You know we make all these decisions *together*."

"Yes, normally we do, but I think, just this once, it was necessary."

"Just tell me what it is. You know I can't abide

surprises."

"Ready yourselves and meet me in the throne room. We'll tell you everything there."

"Throne room? We'll? Who? Oh, Mother—"

"Don't take too long, now," Queen Krystal requested, as she backed out of the room and pulled the doors closed.

Louis shook his head. "What do you think it is?"

The scribe smiled thoughtfully. "Something worth waiting for, I believe."

When they arrived in the foyer that led to the throne room, both prince and scribe were dressed in their best. Evers and Nicholas awaited them at the doors.

"What's going on here?" asked Louis.

"Don't give it away," Evers warned Nicholas.

"But it's so hard not to," replied the General.

"Oh, let's just get to it."

With that, the two men opened the doors to the throne room. What awaited within was all of their friends, from the Divine Lady and Armond, to Yvonne and Zest, to the nobles of neighboring kingdoms, to the Violet Sprite and the Celtic Witch. Upon the dais stood Queen Krystal and Ruth, both proudly awaiting their sons.

The men looked at one another, more confused than ever. Louis' belly filled with nerves, evident within his hazel eyes. Eric looked into them and used his blue-browns to give a teasing glance of comfort. After all, it was a year ago on this very day that the prince led the charge to defeat the Evil King, as legend was now calling him. Why should he be afraid of a room full of friends?

Louis smiled at Eric, and the scribe took his hand. Proudly, before the parties present, they walked into the hall, their hands tightly grasped and on full display. When they reached their mothers, they bowed at the foot of the steps.

"Mother, and Mother Ruth," Louis began, "what is this?"

The women looked at one another with grins and cunning eyes, then back to their sons.

"Well, as you know, my dears," explained Queen Krystal, "today marks the one-year anniversary since you both led us to victory. Together, your love *saved* all of us, and it is that love that we hope you'll lead us with as our kingdom continues to grow."

"Prince Louis and Scribe Eric," Ruth continued, "the people have decided. We see no reason for our new kingdom to be led with the old ways. As such, we believe it's time for a coronation."

Louis and Eric shot a glance at each other.

"Mother…Mother Ruth," began Louis. "I don't…what I mean is, I'm not ready to rule alone. I've so much to learn. I-I'm still learning how to be a prince, really."

"I suppose it's a good thing you won't be ruling alone, then." Queen Krystal smiled.

She shifted her eyes to Eric, as Ruth winked at her son. Now it was Eric's turn to jolt with flabbergast.

"You—you can't be serious? I'm just the scribe," he stuttered.

"Oh, my dear, you are so much more than that," Ruth reassured.

"Eric and Louis," Queen Krystal stated with warm regalness, "will you honor our kingdom by ruling as the very first King and King of the New Kingdom of Belle Terre?"

The lovers looked at one another once again. Their eyes filled with shock then fear then wonder then amazement. Eric's small pink lips stretched into a proud, adoring smile as he watched tears of unabashed cheer build in his lover's eyes. The prince chuckled at Eric, then turned back to his mother, and Eric did the same.

"We graciously accept," proclaimed Louis.

The women, too, became emotional as they looked upon their sons.

"Then..." began Queen Krystal, "let us begin."

When the ceremony was over and the celebrations had finished ringing out throughout the kingdom, Louis and Eric made their way to the grand balcony. The newly crowned kings watched as their guests rode off into the setting sun in the distance. Eric turned his glance to Louis and watched as the prince-turned-king gazed out with a blissful surrealness.

"What do you think is of greater shock?" Eric asked. "The fact that we're two kings, or the fact that we're two kings who aren't married?"

"Oh, I suspect the latter will be solved soon enough," replied Louis with a smirk, as he turned to face Eric. "Provided I say 'yes,' of course."

"Now wait a moment, are you assuming it's *I* who must do the asking?"

"Well..." Louis blushed, "you do have a way with words."

Eric beamed at his fellow king's charm. He looked into the beautiful hazel eyes he'd loved since he was a boy, and caressed Louis' face. With a passion so great and a love so true, they shared a kiss so beautiful, that it is said to have outshone all sunsets and sunrises from that day to this.

And though the Kingdom of Belle Terre, old and new is no more, their legend lives on...
FIN

Postface

I suppose you're wondering why I didn't finish my segment with "And they lived happily ever after." I could have. But there were a number of reasons I didn't. For one, I think it was hard for me to accept that I was actually *done* with their story. Reluctant as I may have been at the start, it obviously grew on me, but more than that—it *spoke* to me. But then, that's exactly what Professor Sherman wanted.

It took me basically until the discovery that the last scene was missing for me to understand *why* she'd given this task to me. She easily could have done it herself. But she gave it to her struggling student, her student who was so desperate to see himself in a screenplay, that, instead of representing himself accurately, he crammed every trick and stereotype he could into his script. Desperate to fit into the mold that he didn't fit in; a mold he shouldn't *want* to fit in. The lesson I learned on this journey is that there is no clear path to success and to your dreams. It's messy and long, and no one really knows the outcome. *You* alone are solely responsible for what you want, no matter how crazy it may seem.

Life is no fairy tale, and I think we often forget our dreams or *give up* the more and more we face rejection in life. We may even think those dreams are crazy, but then again, they're no crazier than a scribe marrying a prince, or a group of misfits besting powerful villains, or two people in love building a life together, no matter what others think. There will always be challenges, there will always be gatekeepers who reject you and tell you 'no.' We hope that we can change their minds. Sometimes we can, and sometimes, it's impossible. But what matters is that, even when others reject us and try to keep us down, we accept *ourselves* and hold on to the ones who love us. It's a lesson I carried with me as I began working on my other book, but that's another story.

Today, and every day since I started this journey, I wake up feeling closer and closer to the success of which I dream. But without this little story, a story that was almost lost forever, I don't think those feelings would have ever been possible for me.

So why didn't I end *The Prince and the Scribe* with "Happily Ever After?" Maybe that's because the *real* happy ending was the one they gave to me. And, maybe, during these days of division and rejection, the answer is clearer than we realize…

Maybe, we just need to get lost in a fairy tale…

A word about the author...

Logan Kelly is an author, journalist, screenwriter, and, with the publication of The Prince & the Scribe, the world's first professional queer troll. This is his second novel, following the LGBTQ+ Historical-Romance, Brighter Stars. He currently works as an entertainment journalist for Collider. For more information on Logan, follow him on Instagram/Threads: @loganjkelly

Thank you for purchasing
this publication of The Wild Rose Press, Inc.

For questions or more information
contact us at
info@thewildrosepress.com.

The Wild Rose Press, Inc.
www.thewildrosepress.com